The
Straight
and
Narrow
Path

BOOKS BY HONOR TRACY

The Straight and Narrow Path

The Deserters

Mind You, I've Said Nothing

Kakemono

The
Straight
and
Narrow
Path

HONOR TRACY

 Random House   New York

To Neville Faulks

The
Straight
and
Narrow
Path

"What we have to do, my dear brethren, is stay on the straight and narrow path between right and wrong."

—FRAGMENT OF IRISH SERMON

ONE

"B UT what on earth am I to write about?" asked Dr. Andrew Butler.

The distinguished scholar was leaning against the public bar of Mrs. Mangan's Hotel in the village of Patrickstown, a small and insignificant place for which you would search the map of Ireland in vain. For the past hour or so he had sat uncomfortably in his bedroom, staring at an oleograph of the Pope and waiting for the Angelus to ring; for it was against his principles to start drinking before six o'clock and Dr. Butler was greatly attached to his principles. At the first sweet chime he had come gladly hurrying down to where Mrs. Mangan, plump and maternal, wary and subtle, stood waiting to dispense information, advice and drink with the grace of a born hostess.

This first drink of the evening in her society was one of the pleasantest things in Andrew's day; but tonight, after welcoming him, she had come out with a surprising request. Mr. Pearl, the English journalist in No. 6, had returned to the hotel in very poor shape. A collection of rascals tolerantly described by Mrs. Mangan as "the boys" had taken him to a fair from which he had returned lying on a gate and reverently borne along by two other drunks. Willing hands had bedded him down; and his last words before he sank into coma were an entreaty that Andrew should write the feature article that he had promised his editor for ten o'clock that night. Mrs. Mangan had passed it on as if it were the most simple and natural thing in the world.

"Sure, what could Mr. Pearl do that you wouldn't do better yourself?" she now inquired.

"But there's nothing in Patrickstown to make a newspaper article. That's the beautiful thing about it: nothing ever happens here."

He glanced out of the window. The little place was drowsing in the gold haze of a June evening. It called itself a town but it was really a village: or rather, like so many Irish villages, it was just a long street. There were in all five water-tight buildings here: the Church, the convent, the priest's house, the parish hall and the National School. Opposite the parish hall at the lower end of the street was a statue to the local patriot and martyr Corney O'Malley: who, while carrying dispatches in the national cause, had unaccountably misdirected his motor-bicycle and dashed his poor brains out against a stone wall. In addition there were a number of shops with cracked or peeling façades, including Bridget Foley's Fashion Arcade and Mary Broderick's hairdressing establishment whose claim to a Parisian standard in cutting and setting was reinforced by a seven-day license. In this latter respect, however, it was only one of thirty-five. Dotted about the countryside were the crumbling mansions of the Protestant gentry: here and there ivy-covered ruins showed their jagged teeth to the sky. Finally there were the cottages where the people lived, washed pink or yellow without, dark and grimy within. Cradled by tawny mountains rising to violet peaks, the village lay in a silence broken only by soft voices greeting

4

each other on the road and by the whispering of the river.

Mrs. Mangan allowed Andrew's remark to pass. The events of that day in Patrickstown, an average one, were briefly as follows. The Guards had raided Tomo Lynch's cabin in search of a missing bicycle and found not only this but a number of silver dishes, for the theft of which another man was at present serving a prison sentence: after consultation, and for the good name of Irish justice, they had agreed to say nothing about it. The young doctor had written out a prescription for Miss Browne of Castle Knock that, in the words of the chemist, would have stretched a dozen: the news of which coming to her ears, she had instantly left her bed and driven to the doctor's gate, where she pulled up and without quitting her gig soundly berated the startled boy in the ringing accents of the ascendancy. Lord Patrickstown had been sighted dancing through his woods with nothing on. Florence, pig of pigs and joy of his owner's heart, had been taken violently ill, poisoned, it was thought, by a rival breeder. Every detail of these occurrences was fully and perfectly known to the proprietress of Mangan's Hotel.

"It's a quiet poor place, all the same," she agreed, with a melancholy shake of her head.

"I shall have to fall back on Some Old Irish Customs," Andrew decided.

He had seen for himself that London editors did not mind how often they played on this string. Another advantage was that it would mean almost no work, as ever since he came to Ireland he had been taking copious notes: this being to him, the Reader in Anthropology at Edinburgh University, as natural as drawing breath. The stresses and strains of a year's field work in the Congo had brought him to the verge of a breakdown; and, on the advice of a London specialist, he was spending three months

5

in a country whose sweetness and nonchalance were sure—his eminent adviser said, lapsing for an instant into the brogue—to restore his peace of mind. He had come provided with fishing-rods, walking-sticks and hobnailed boots; but no sooner was he fairly installed than the resemblance he noted between the local habits of mind and those he had so recently studied in Africa sent him hurrying for pencil and paper. Upstairs in his bedroom now were three fat notebooks filled with his small, beautiful handwriting, the material all clearly arranged under headings and sub-headings.

Mrs. Mangan gave him to understand that it was the notion of a genius.

A third person was present in the bar that evening, a spare little man with a round head too large for his body, and the dimpled hands of a child. What first struck you in him, however, were the eyes, very large, dark grey, thickly lashed and, set wide apart under a pure broad forehead, looking out with an expression of singularly innocent sweetness: the eyes of a poet or a saint. Gravely sipping a glass of stout, he had listened without a word as Mrs. Mangan described the situation of Mr. Pearl and to the conversation that followed: when Andrew announced his theme, a veil seemed to come over the wonderful eyes, as if he were privately communing with himself: this lasted only a moment or so, and then he spoke up.

"It's a good idea you have there," he said, "and a grand piece of writing to be done. And I'll tell you something to make it right for a newspaper. It's Midsummer Eve tonight, and the nuns will be celebrating up at the convent. That'll make an up-to-date little paragraph to round the article off."

"What will the nuns do?"

"That's what I will show you," answered the little man.

"Write the rest of the article now and be done with it. I'll come back for you at sundown and we'll go to the convent together. Then you can add your few words and when the London man rings through, there you are with the completed masterpiece."

He smiled Andrew's thanks aside, finished his stout and, climbing awkwardly down from his stool, trotted out of the bar on his short little legs.

"What an utterly charming person!" Andrew exclaimed. "Do you know, Mrs. Mangan, people can say what they like but nowhere else in the world do you find people of that sort."

"The same as Patsy? I'd believe you," Mrs. Mangan assented.

"That ready sympathy," Andrew went blithely on, "that swift grasp of another man's difficulty, that instant desire to help! Patsy, you say his name is. Who is he?"

Mrs. Mangan picked up Patsy's empty glass and carefully wiped away a few drops from the counter before she answered. All at once her manner had become curiously withdrawn, as if she were seeking to establish now an entire lack of responsibility for what might follow.

"You'd need more than a newspaper article to tell you that," she remarked at length.

"He sounded like an educated man."

"Oh God, he's educated all right."

Andrew sensed a reserve in her feeling for the little stranger and thought he knew the reason for it. "Do you think he won't really come?" he asked, anxiously.

"Ah, he will," she replied. "He'll come back for you if it's the last thing he does." She picked up a cloth and began to polish glasses in the way she always had when she considered that a theme was exhausted.

Andrew was puzzled but he said no more. He already

knew that to each small Irish mystery the solution in gentle oblique fashion eventually comes; and that to insist with the directness of his native land would be taken as a sign not only of poor manners but also of mental incapacity. He therefore went upstairs and fell to work. Across a sheet of paper he wrote the words: "On the Edge of Time, by Esmé Pearl." Under this, in his clean lucid style, he gave an account of certain Irish beliefs and practices that went back into the old pagan Gaelic world. Then he went through it again and again, altering and sharpening and improving until even his fastidious mind was content and he felt that Mr. Pearl need not be ashamed of him. As he wrote the shadows outside were slowly lengthening, until at last all that was left of the sunset was an orange glow on the horizon; and then he left his work and came downstairs, wondering what was the finishing touch that Patsy was going to supply.

The little man had been faithful to his word. He was waiting in the hall and his demeanour was mysterious and important. As they left the hotel he trotted at Andrew's side without a sound and once, when his companion offered to speak, he laid a finger to his lips as if the matters in hand demanded silence.

The convent was at the upper end of the village, standing in grounds that marched with those of Lord Patrickstown. Instead of going on up to it, Patsy turned off through the tall iron gates of the noble lord's demesne, and led the way through a beech wood to the wall that divided the two properties. Here he was to reveal himself in a new and surprising light; for, with the speed and assurance of a cat-burglar, he shinned up a tree and out along a limb onto the top of this wall, signalling to Andrew to follow.

· Seated side by side on the wall, themselves screened by the foliage of the great beech tree's dipping boughs, they had a fine view of the convent, with its mock-Gothic chapel, prison-like buildings and ample beds of hideously clashing flowers. Three bonfires had been lighted on one of the gravel walks, a distance of twenty feet or so between each. A wooden chair with carved arms had been placed on the lawn opposite the middle fire and here was enthroned a massive, resolute lady whom Andrew took to be the Mother Superior. The nuns, giggling like a flock of turkeys, were collected at one end of the path and ran up one after the other, raising their habits to reveal black woollen stockings and now and then a glimpse of black serge bloomers, to leap the fires. In this they were gaily spurred on by the Reverend Mother, whose voice had the deep male resonance of a great bell and might have been envied her by many a rowing coach.

"Ah, come on now, Sister Conception! You can do better than that," she boomed, as a nun with long raking limbs came down among the hot cinders. A paroxysm of giggles swept over the Sisters. "Sister Agnes, you lep like a hare! Show Sister Conception how you lep." A fat little figure went bounding over the flames like a rubber ball. "That's the great girl. Sure, I'm proud of ye! There's none of the Ursulines can lep like that!" This evidently was a convent joke and evoked a new, more violent burst of merriment.

Andrew was shaking with laughter, for reasons of his own. Unable to keep them to himself, he leaned across to Patsy and murmured brokenly: "This is one of the oldest fertility rites in the world!"

Patsy nodded gravely. "And they the Brides of Christ!" he whispered back.

The hilarity pent in Andrew's bosom burst from him in a mighty roar. The effect on the gathering below was instantaneous. The nuns stood frozen in horror, their heads turned towards the spot whence the sacrilegious noise had come. Slowly and majestically the Reverend Mother rose from her chair and, with a sudden explosive bark, sent them hurrying to the shelter of the convent walls: she bringing up the rear with awful deliberation, pausing ever and anon to look back at the branches shaking above the wall, her face working in secret anathemas.

"Yerra, for God's sake! That's done it. Come on away out of this," said Patsy urgently. They scrambled down from their post and ran back through the trees. "Not that way, not that way," he cried, as Andrew made to retrace his steps down the drive. "It's better we shouldn't be seen at all." His equanimity returned only after a long detour through thorny undergrowths, across marshy fields where little pools bubbled up round the ankles with every step, and over crumbling, treacherous walls until they found themselves once more on the main road a mile or two below the town. Then he turned to Andrew with a sweet confiding look on his face.

"Are you pleased with me now?" he asked, shyly.

"Oh, very much so: I'm greatly in your debt," Andrew said, looking down at him with affection.

He thought the evening's adventure one of the nicest things that had come his way in Ireland. There was a completeness about it all that deeply satisfied him. Not only had he an effective last paragraph for Mr. Pearl's article but also the material, to be used at some future time, for a pungently entertaining footnote. He had enjoyed the belly-laugh on the wall, the indignant retreat of the reverend ladies and the delicious panic of his own and Patsy's flight. He loved the chancy way it had all come about: he warmed to the strange little gnome who had been its contriver.

A burly figure loomed out of the falling darkness, grumbling to itself and twirling a cane. It was Canon Peart, the parish priest, setting out on his evening patrol of hedges and ditches in search of loving couples. So far this week he had bagged only four, of which one had proved to be an English pair on their honeymoon: the male had keenly resented the Canon's admonitory cut across his buttocks and had expressed himself with a complete unawareness of who was who and what was what that rankled in the priest's dignified bosom. He was now rehearsing aloud what he meant to say in the event of a similar mishap occurring tonight.

"If you'll forgive me, I had better hurry home," Andrew began, turning to Patsy again when the Canon had passed. Then he broke off in astonishment, for no one was there. Not even a rustling in the hedge came to show by what route the little fellow had taken his departure: it was as if Patsy were swallowed up by the night, and his disappearance seemed to Andrew to have almost a Celtic magic in it, something strange and wild and touched with poetry, something proper to Midsummer Eve. He would have liked now to go roaming through the dusky lanes in search of new, still more fantastic adventures; but, mindful as ever of his duty, he returned instead to the hotel where, having finished the article, he sat waiting for the telephone to ring.

When at last the editor came through, his flat English voice seemed to belong to another world.

"Plastered again, I suppose," it said wearily, when Andrew had explained in nicely chosen euphemisms the non-appearance of Mr. Pearl.

"No, no, a slight chill, nothing serious. But he had the article all ready and he asked me to read it for him."

"Okay. But this is the third chill in seventeen days. What's your name?"

"Andrew Butler."

"Okay, Mr. Butler. I'll put you on to the stenographer

and you just fire away. Then if there are any queries I'll ring you back, if I may. Right?"

"Right," said Andrew. He dictated the article, amazed at the smooth competence of the shorthand writer who read it back without a mistake, commas and all, and hung up, feeling pleasantly efficient himself. Half an hour later, however, the telephone rang again with a London call for Mr. Butler.

"Look here," said the voice again. "Pearl never wrote that article."

"Why not?" Andrew parried.

"He couldn't have. It's written in English," the voice explained.

"Ah."

"We can't put an article of that sort in a series by Esmé Pearl. He's very well known, you see. Did you write it?"

"Yes."

"Thought so. Who are you?"

Andrew told him.

"Well, Mr. Butler, here's what we'll do, if you agree. We'll put in a note to say that the 'Inside Ireland' series is interrupted by the indisposition of the author. Then we'll feature your article under your name. Can we mention Edinburgh?"

"I'd rather you didn't."

"Righty-ho. Andrew Butler, anthropologist, eh? And we'll pay you thirty guineas."

"*Thirty guineas!*" cried Andrew, who was accustomed to the frugal ways of learned periodicals.

"Well, fifty, then. And we're much obliged. That article is hot stuff. If you have any more ideas like that, let us know. I'm Warner, the features editor. Okay? Then pip-pip."

"Pip-pip," said Andrew.

He ate a belated supper of rashers and eggs, soda bread and jam, sweet cake, strong tea and stout, musing as he did so on the structure of contemporary society and planning a list of books to be acquired with the *Daily Packet*'s cheque; and at last retired to a well-earned night's repose.

TWO

HUBERT Vere Lingfield de Bolleyn, Viscount Patrickstown, sat in his enormous shabby drawing-room, fretting over a communication which had just been delivered by hand.

The room was furnished simply and severely in a manner that spoke of centuries of leadership in the family that lived here. Above the great fireplace, spread fanwise with the points turning out, were a number of rusty swords of different ages. To one side of it in a glass-topped case were a collection of medals won by his lordship's ancestors on every field of battle since medals first were struck. Portraits of these men were also here, some stern, some raffish, all with the air of men accustomed to obedience. Tattered flags hung from the walls: guns lay idly in a rack: fishing-rods had turned one corner of the room into a wilderness. All these things remained, quietly accusing him, because the little lord had no idea where else they might go: he himself had broken with the family tradition once and for all.

The ancient line was indeed drawing to a close "not with a bang but a whimper." The last Lord Patrickstown, for it was all too clear that no more could be expected, was a freak thrown up as if in mockery of what had gone before. He was small and soft and round, where his forebears were straight and hard: he shrank back where they had pressed on: reflected and questioned where they had laid down the law. His one boldness was in the matter of dress. To wear, as he did this morning, a suit of lilac-coloured spun silk in the heart of Irish countryside argued some toughness of mind and indifference to accepted opinion, particularly when it went with a huge amethyst ring on the third finger of the left hand. His face was round and solemn, with a babyishness unaffected by the small wrinkles and crowsfeet of early middle age: the prominent imaginative eyes held the look of one who has been deeply hurt himself, yet still had no intention of hurting others. Feeble, erratic and dissipated as he was, he had never done harm to a soul in his life.

"Too frightful," he murmured now, in his fluting voice. "Too frightful for any words!"

The letter was from the Mother Superior of the convent and ran as follows:

DEAR LORD PATRICKSTOWN,—In view of your conduct last night, I have directed the nuns to make no further use of the facilities extinded by you. I have also instructed the workmen to remove the installations put in to safeguard their privacy while in your grounds. No doubt you will wish to bear the expinse.

Yours truly,
TERESA HOOLEY
Mother Superior,
Convent of the Immaculate Conception,
Patrickstown.

"But it wasn't last night! It was yesterday morning," his lordship groaned, clutching his curly head.

It was in fact at about eleven o'clock on the previous day that he had yielded once more to impulse and, throwing off all his clothes, had gone bounding away through the fern like a startled deer. This recurring and irresistible temptation was the source of real grief to him. He would punish himself severely after such a bout, he would go without marmalade for breakfast and recite whole rounds of the rosary while kneeling on the splintery wooden floor of his bedroom. Once he had gone so far as to get hold of a monastic discipline and lay it unmercifully about his chubby shoulders; but he found, for some reason, the sensation so intensely enjoyable as to be inappropriate for a penance. Quietened by his mortifications, soothed and comforted by prayer, he would manage for some little while to live in perfect decorum. Then suddenly the desire would overwhelm him again, and he was off in another wild rush. He could not explain it, unless it was that an evil spirit possessed him, a wild surging pagan spirit, disgraceful to himself and unsuited to his position.

The Reverend Mother's letter could only mean, he thought, that one or more of the nuns had glimpsed him at it the day before. It would have been only too possible, thanks to an arrangement he had with the convent. All the Protestant years of his life he had lived next door to the Sisters and been hardly aware of their existence except for the gentle chiming of their chapel bell. But no sooner had his reception into the Church taken place than the Reverend Mother approached him with a suggestion.

There were no trees in the convent garden, she wrote, and hence no shade where the nuns might sit on sunny days. Would it be asking too much of his lordship, then, if they might occasionally spend an hour or two in that part of his grounds which was next to their own and with those lovely beeches?

Lord Patrickstown agreed at once and undertook to see that his outside men kept away from that side of the house when the nuns were enjoying this privilege. Reverend Mother replied, thanking him for his generosity, assuring him of her prayers and enclosing an estimate for the making of a door in the existing wall which, she opined, was an extremely reasonable one.

The door was finished and paid for, and the shrouded figures of nuns began stealing in and out of the ancient demesne. Shortly afterwards men appeared again and started to work on a tall wooden fence enclosing the beech wood for a depth of some fifty yards.

"I'm sorry did I forget to tell you," the Reverend Mother wrote in response to his startled query, "our Order is enclosed and it wouldn't be right at all for the nuns to be wandering at large in that kind of way. But have no fear the contractor will sting you. I'll see to that myself."

The fence was completed and the bill came in, closely followed by a further communication from the Mother Superior.

"I've been thinking now," she wrote in her engaging, colloquial style, "wouldn't it be a grand thing altogether for the sisters to get a sight of the river now and again! There'd be little enough to do but take down one side of the fince again and extind the other straight down to the river bank itself, the way it would make a little corridor. There's no need at all for you to worry with the arrangements. The blessing of Almighty God be on you, and we'll all ask extra favours from Blessed St. Martin on your behalf. There's no end to be got out of him."

Lord Patrickstown, as a devout Catholic of recent date, could only sit back with folded hands while slice after slice of his valuable land disappeared into the maw of Holy Church. The Protestant gentry were holding their sides in ecstasy and eagerly awaiting the day when he should have to move out of the Hall. Unsatisfactory as the position had been in many ways, however, it was better than this new and terrible development. All his childhood friends had left him at the time of his renunciation of former errors: he must, he simply had got to, keep in with his new associates.

Wearily he took paper and pen and began to write.

"My dear Reverend Mother," he began, "your letter has caused me the deepest distress. But there seems to be some little mistake . . ."

Apologies, explanations, entreaties flowed from him in a troubled stream as he sat there under the cold eyes of the family portraits.

Down at Mangan's Hotel, the affair of Andrew's article was burgeoning into more unhappiness.

"I thought you were a gentleman," Mr. Paul was saying. He was pink-eyed and of a greenish pallor, and he kept blinking his sandy lashes as if either the light or the contemplation of Andrew's perfidy were too much for him to bear.

"I do assure you, my dear fellow . . ."

"I am not your dear fellow. I thought you were a gentleman. Trusted you. If you had been a journalist, it would have been different."

"But Pearl . . ."

"Mr. Pearl," the other corrected him tartly. "It's my livelihood. What's it to you? You've got your university and all. Why pull a fast one?"

"Do let me explain . . ."

"You've written whole books," Mr. Pearl informed him.

"I'm just a poor bloody hack. But you have to come worming in. Reminds me of thingummy's vineyard."

His green face puckered.

"It wasn't my fault . . ."

"Go ahead and finish the series for all I care!"

"The editor spotted . . ."

"Course I haven't had your advantages. Never went to Repton or places like that. Worked my way up. Can't write. You deliberately wrote the thing well, so they could *see*. I don't know what you call it but I call it dirty."

A spasm of pain crossed his face.

"I can't reely tell you off with a head like this," he said, more kindly. "Well, what about a hair of the bow-wow? Can't make me feel any worse."

Andrew ordered two large hairs of the bow-wow.

THREE

A FEW days later Canon Peart was sitting in his garden in the green shade of a mulberry tree. On a table beside him was good Irish whisky in a fine decanter. He was smoking one of the excellent cigars regularly sent him by a pious lady in Mullingar. Outside the cool patch thrown by the spreading boughs the sun beat down, enveloping the scene in a bland yellow warmth. The air was full of the humming of bees and the gay agitation of butterfly wings. Yet the look on the Canon's great purple face was anything but contented.

The weather in Ireland that year could only be described as freakish. Easter Sunday had been a pearl among days, with a limpid cloudless sky such as only the older people remembered seeing before. The Canon had preached on it at Second Mass, linking it with the Resurrection and claiming it as a sign of Divine approbation for a community that was obedient, respectful and willing in regard to his dues. But the elements had not been prepared to let it go at that. One splendid day, one marvellous week, followed another; and now at Midsummer the people had given up remarking on it and asking if it would hold and were simply revelling in conditions more appropriate to the shores of the Mediterranean.

The consequences were not at all to the Canon's liking. Under the kindly influence of the sun a dangerous spirit was stirring among his flock. It was not by accident that he made so mean a score during his nightly forays through the lanes. The young people were nesting further afield, in haystacks, beds of rushes, behind scented gorse bushes up on the hills, beyond his reach; and, as the Canon ruefully told himself, he could not be everywhere at once. And now the inevitable had happened, and little Bridget MacCarthy was with child. It was a terrible shame on himself and the parish, but that was not the worst of it. The routine the Canon followed in cases of this sort was admirably simple. He would seek out the young man responsible, threaten him with hell fire, everlasting torment and the loss of his earthly job and then, having reduced him to a jelly, go on briskly to discuss the details of the wedding. But when Bridget stood before him in his study, she had absolutely refused to say who the father was. Little Biddy MacCarthy! whom he had baptized and prepared for her first communion, whose progress as a Child of Mary he had so carefully watched: this same Biddy had stood there, with her sweet blue eyes not humbly and properly bent on the floor but bravely meeting his own, with even a spark of infernal amusement in their depths, and had gone so far as to say, "Well, now, Canon, I couldn't be telling you that!"

All his roarings had been to no avail. Could it be, the Canon wondered, that she was a Communist? The Canon had next to no idea what Communism was but he was ever on the alert for a whiff of it. And the terrible thing was that he had got no satisfaction out of the family either. The parents agreed that she was a bold thing all right and it was an awkward way for a girl to behave; but his suggestion that they now do the seemly thing and turn her away had fallen on deaf ears. To be sure, when he put it to them they eagerly cried that wasn't he right, wasn't it the only thing to be done? but the days passed and she was still at home, milking the cow and singing about the place as if she hadn't a care in the world. Foiled, the Canon had played with the idea of reading her off the altar, of disgracing her once and for all by a furious public denunciation; but, reflecting that if this too had no result the defeat would be stinging and final, had determined to bide his time.

A ripe mulberry fell with a plop on his skull, matching its colour exactly. He brushed it irritably away and took a pull at the whisky.

Bridget was not the only, or even the greatest, care in the good man's mind this beautiful summer day. His financial position was also causing him grave concern. Earlier in the year he had discarded the old jalopy in which he drove about the parish and had bought an Armstrong Siddeley. The greater speed would bring him the sooner to parishioners in need of him, the greater comfort would lead to a better performance of his duties when he arrived, the people would rejoice to see their Canon decently found. Such was his reasoning; but the purchase had sorely depleted his coffers, and no sooner was it made than he was faced with new and substantial expense.

The priest in the neighboring parish of Maryville had recently appealed to Irish Catholics in Boston (where he had connections) for funds to build a chapel of ease. The response had been so prompt and generous that he had been able not only to run to the chapel but to invest in a Humber Hawk and, of all things, to put in a second bathroom, with shower, at the parochial house. Until he heard that, Canon Peart had been content with the one small

22

bathroom on his ground floor, of which indeed, if the truth is told, he made but a sparing use. But it was a nice state of affairs, he felt, if Maryville was to have two bathrooms and Patrickstown just the one: a state of affairs that reflected both on his own position and on the good name of the parish and ultimately, therefore, must harm the cause of religion.

Accordingly he sent for a plumber from the town and ordered him to transform a store-room on the upper floor. Out of respect for his people, he not only asked for the bath and the shower to be of the latest, most expensive type but also had tiles put down on the floor and halfway up the walls, mentally defying Maryville to go better than that. The work was done and the plumber sent in a bill for three hundred pounds, seventy in excess of his estimate. The Canon raged, but the plumber was courteously, even effusively, intractable. To crown it all, when the Canon turned on the taps in the fine new bath, only a gush of dead earwigs came out. Again the plumber had an answer: his instructions had been to put in a bath, not to make water flow. He had never supposed for an instant that water *would* flow. His experience of Patrickstown was that water flowed only at ground level and in a poor little trickle then, and he had assumed the Canon was familiar with this condition. If his opinion had been asked, he would have given it: but as it was, he had not wished to speak the first.

How to raise the three hundred pounds to pay for this useless bathroom, then, was another of the problems that teased the Canon's mind as he sat under the mulberry tree. All the old dodges had been tried one after the other, the appeals from the altar, the chapel-door collections, the whist drives, the raffles, but the results had been disappointing. First, there was no blinking the fact that the people for some mysterious reason had not been as pleased and proud about either the new motor or the new bath as the Canon expected. They had gone so far as to shun the whist drives, giving the heat of the evenings as their excuse. Such bold conduct was without precedent: it was one more sign of this unruly spirit that Canon Peart noticed among them, a spirit he did not hesitate to qualify as diabolical.

But there was another and a sounder reason for their apparent ungodliness. The weather, glorious at it was, had a poor effect on the livelihood of many people in the village. Patrickstown was famous throughout Ireland for the excellence and abundance of the fishing there and at this time of the year the men and boys could usually expect good wages as ghillies. This season, however, the trout were simply not biting. They lay comfortably in the sun-warmed shallows and never so much as winked at a fly, as if infected by the same wanton mood as everyone else. Mrs. Mangan's Hotel, as a rule packed tight with admirals and majors and brigadiers, stood almost empty. The men lounged about with their hands in their pockets. Cat's-Eye O'Keefe, the poacher, still to be sure brought his weekly tribute to the Canon's kitchen door; but he always used a net.

The Canon understood this and had therefore regretfully decided that it would be unwise at present to double the yearly dues. Nor dared he apply in this instance to the Bishop for a loan, since that crusty old gentleman had set his face against bathing altogether. It was, he said, contrary to the practice of the saints: he defied you to name any respectable saint who had ever indulged in a bath. The Bishop's view that what was good enough for a saint (as regards bathing, at least) was good enough for an Irish Bishop had always been much admired by Canon Peart, who saw it as the fine flower of Christian humility; but now in his present fix it was inconvenient. The plumber was beginning to press for his money and the money had got to be found. But how? He could not sell the motor-car or the people would laugh. He had no one in America. In his distress the poor fellow groaned aloud and fervently clasped his hands.

"Holy Mary, Mother of God," he prayed, "help me get money for this bathroom of mine. If You don't, nobody will. I'm not asking for myself but for the glory and good reputation of Your Blessed Son. And while You're about it, perhaps You could get those taps to work. If it please You to help me in this, be sure I'll do something for You. Mystical Rose, Tower of David, Tower of Ivory, House of Gold."

The Canon was wont to impress on his flock that no humble, sincere petition is ever addressed to Our Lady in vain; and he was now to learn, with delighted amazement, that he had spoken the truth. No sooner had the prayer left his lips than his housekeeper came out of the house to say that Mr. La Trobe, the solicitor, had called on a matter of importance. Canon Peart, who did not immediately suspect that help might come in so incongruous a habit, stirred restlessly in his chair and growled. Mr. La Trobe was a man famed through the countryside for the ingenious and supple workings of his mind, where the Canon, as he would have told you himself, was no intellectual. A few simple ideas, never examined but held with unyielding tenacity, were all that was to be found in his mental armoury and since no one ever dared to challenge either him or them he felt no need of anything more. But La Trobe, outwardly respectful to the point of obsequiousness, had tripped him time and again.

"I'll not see him, then," he said, now. "Haven't we trouble enough?"

"Oh, he's most insistent, Canon," the woman told him.

She was a devoted, yearning creature with silvery hair parted in the middle and a sweet, tremulous smile copied from a priest's housekeeper she had once seen on the films; and she all but drove the Canon mad. "I'd say he brought good news with him. He's as pleased as a dog with two dinners."

"Two dinners for La Trobe is none for the rest of us," said the Canon, with his brutal peasant sense. "Well, send him out, I suppose. And bring another chair and a bottle of stout. I've better things in mind for the whisky."

When Mr. La Trobe appeared, it was indeed clear from the suppressed jubilation of his manner that great things were afoot. Under his arm was a rolled-up copy of the *Daily Packet*, and as soon as he could decently bring his dutiful greetings to an end, he opened it with a flourish.

"Did you ever see the equal of that?" he demanded, in triumph.

"Blonde Bombshell to Cross Atlantic on Raft," read the Canon, his eye caught and held by the illustration. "Is it that one?"

"Ah, not at all, Canon. The other piece there, in the lefthand corner."

"Famous Anthropologist Says, Ireland Is Pagan Still," the Canon proceeded. "Well, if you don't mind!"

"But read the whole thing, Canon."

The Canon read.

Mr. Warner had dealt very justly with Andrew's article. Not a word had been changed, not a comma displaced. All he had done was to divide it into short convenient paragraphs, in case his readers should tire, and give to each of these an explanatory title, in case his readers should miss the point. A shade passed over the Canon's broad face as he read the preamble, headed "Some Quaint Superstitions." It darkened as he came to the passages under

"Power of Curses," which gave some interesting parallels from the Congo. It became positively thunderous as he read the section marked "Witchcraft." But when he reached the last paragraph, labelled "Pagan Fertility Rites!!" the Canon's face turned almost black and he gasped as if someone had dealt him a blow in the solar plexus.

"God bless us, but this is blasphemy!" he roared. "Who did this wickedness, La Trobe?"

"The Englishman staying at Mangan's above. The tall fellow with the Oxford accent."

"And the hair like a fringe of old hay?"

"The very one."

"Then turn him out," barked the Canon. "See that he leaves the town today. I'll have no atheists from England insulting my nuns."

"Wait now, Canon," pleaded Mr. La Trobe. "There's a better way round it than that, with all respect. Look at what the fellow says there again. 'At Patrickstown on Mid-summer Eve I watched the nuns celebrating the day in a manner as charming as it was inappropriate: they were leaping bonfires in the garden of their convent. As readers of *The Golden Bough* will know, this is an ancient fertility rite, practised through the ages in many parts of the world. No doubt the good Sisters were unaware of the significance of their innocent frolic; but it was another example of the way in which pagan observances will persist, and this time in the quarter where you least expect to find them.' Now that's defamatory, Canon."

"Defamatory? It's blasphemous! Obscene! It's against religion!"

"I'm speaking now as your solicitor, Canon," said Mr. La Trobe, softly. "I'm telling you that this paragraph, while hurtful to the Mother Superior and the Sisters, might be

27

taken as reflecting chiefly on yourself as their spiritual director. People could read that article and say, Well now, and what is the parish priest doing all this time? He wouldn't be too busy getting his new bathroom in to attend to the moral welfare of his people, would he? Oh mind you, I'd never say that." Mr. La Trobe went on hastily, as the veins began to swell in the Canon's forehead. "I'm putting to you what evil-minded persons could say. And therefore it seems to me your best course, and your most honourable course, is to bring an action for libel."

He leaned back in his chair and folded his arms while the Canon looked at him with sudden interest, and the first pale flicker of hope.

"Of course I must do the honourable thing," he said, slowly. "Would I get damages?"

"In my opinion, substantial damages, if we built the case up artistically and if it came into Court. But you don't really want that. You wouldn't want these matters made public and discussed all over the country, to the disedification and scandal of souls. We'll have the thing fixed up quietly. There'll have to be a full and adequate apology from the newspaper and the writing fellow, and a reasonable sum for yourself."

"How much?"

"Well, now. It would never do for you to appear mercenary. Shall we say two hundred and fifty?"

The Canon reflected. "Could we not make it three hundred?"

"And why couldn't we? An apology and three hundred pounds. And your costs."

"And my costs, of course," the Canon assented. He had been caught with Mr. La Trobe's costs before. Then a terrible thought struck him. "But suppose they were to fight it?"

28

"Ah, for God's sake, Canon! they never would. These big English papers can't be bothered with actions over here. And the bit of money is nothing to them. And they'll know they haven't a chance against yourself with an Irish jury. They'll just turn the thing over to a Dublin solicitor and tell him get on with it. I'd say it'll be Mickey Behan, he gets no end of that sort of thing. He's a very active religious man, a Knight of Columbanus. I'll have a quiet word with him."

He put his head on one side and smiled at his reverend client. There was at all times a great sweetness in the smile of Mr. La Trobe; and now, as he saw the great fish greedily rising to the bait, it became almost unearthly.

"I'd have to consult His Lordship, of course," the Canon said, drawing a deep breath. But already a new peace was flooding his tired and anxious mind. "Sweet Mother Undefiled, Friend of the needy, Comfort of sinners. I won't forget this in a hurry," he hymned in secret.

"There'll be no trouble there, Canon. His Lordship is great on the authority of priests, as you know yourself. Remember Father Mahoney. That was a cool six hundred and costs. And Canon Walsh. Four-fifty and costs. And Father Lynch. Two hundred and costs. And all at the drop of a hat, if you come to think it over."

"You're a great fellow all the same, La Trobe," said the Canon with unusual warmth. "I'm obliged all right for what you've done here. But what about the writing fellow, now? Couldn't he be made to pay something as well?"

"Ah, he won't have a penny piece. We'll join him in the action, though. He'll have to apologize and confess it was all lies, and he'll never get work again. You'll be satisfied, I imagine, when he's starving. He'll see what it is to libel an Irish priest. Now Canon, you get on to His Lordship and settle that end of it: and will I be drafting the letter to the newspaper?"

"You will," said the Canon, happily.

He drained his glass, rose to his feet and wished his solicitor a very good evening. Then he went into the house and exchanged his worn cassock, dusty with the cigar ash of months, for a dignified coat of broadcloth that reached to his knees. He clapped on a glossy black hat and went to the garage where the Armstrong Siddeley waited, gleaming in cold perfection. Of late he had been inclined to avoid the stare of its polished headlights when he opened the door, fancying they held an expression both quizzical and ironic. Now he affectionately slapped the hood, as he might have caressed the flank of a well-loved horse. As he darted out through his wrought-iron gates two village boys sprang out of his path and respectfully swept off their caps. The Canon gave them a condescending nod. Soon everything would fall into its proper place once more, he felt sure of it.

"Queen of Heaven most Blessed, Stay of the righteous, Bountiful Giver of Gifts," he murmured, lightly stepping on the gas.

FOUR

THROUGH working in remote parts of the world among people of a mentality quite different from his own, Andrew had come to sense very quickly any change in local atmospheres. It had been necessary for him to acquire this perceptive alertness. He had to know, for example, when native bearers were planning to go on strike and to leave him alone and helpless, miles from his base, or when a tribe, well disposed to begin with, had suddenly come to the conclusion that he was responsible for bad weather or failing crops, and were thinking of poisoning his food.

Thus, when the attitude of the villagers towards himself inexplicably and, as it were, overnight veered round, he felt it at once. Up to now he had rather plumed himself on his successful relations with them. They apparently had taken him to their hearts, they buttered him up and told him incredible stories in the hope he would gravely write it all down. Wherever he went he was sure of welcoming smiles and first-class entertainment. They found him, of course, a wonderful joke. He was a new sort of Englishman to them, who knew only the jolly fishing-and-shooting-and-riding type that was not so different from their own gentry. His very appearance tickled them, with the tall bony figure, the unkempt reddish hair that looked like a wig, the large solemn blue eyes in which, nevertheless, there was often a wicked gleam that they failed to notice. His pronounced Cambridge accent sent them into fits of laugher, as did his habit of speaking the truth and of coming out directly with whatever lay on his mind with none of the devious circumlocutions so dear to themselves. A decent poor fellow enough, was the local verdict, not precisely astray in his wits but simple to the point of being a danger to himself and others.

Now everyone in the place seemed anxious to avoid him. The little groups of men that stood endlessly chatting on the road melted away at his approach, Mr. Lynch at the Post Office pushed the stamps across in a peculiar manner without meeting his eye or jerking his head towards the licensed end of the counter, as his amiable practice had usually been. At the same time Andrew knew that he was being closely watched. There were eyes everywhere, eyes peeping from windows and hedges, eyes boring into his back, eyes in the street that dropped hastily when he looked into them. Yet he was conscious of no hostility or malevolence in the air. Rather, there seemed to be nervous excitement mixed with a kind of furtive glee, as it might be in a school where everyone, save the intended victim, knew that the Head was about to administer a beating.

Andrew bore it patiently for a day or two, and then consulted Mrs. Mangan.

"Something is up. What is it?" he asked, with that terrible bluntness of his that to the local people came almost as a blow in the face.

Mrs. Mangan was more or less completely apprised of the facts of the case. All she now lacked was the knowledge of what exactly had passed between the Canon and the Bishop, and even this she expected to piece together as soon as she had an opportunity of consulting the Canon's housekeeper. Subsequent communications by telephone between the two reverend gentlemen, and between the Canon and his solicitor, had already reached her by the good offices of Mr. Lynch. She was holding the money in the fertile crop of bets that always sprang up when by good fortune something happened to disturb the calm of the little place. For a moment now she paused, wondering how much to tell him, who so soon was to know it all.

"I wonder now, would it be something to do with the article you wrote?"

"The article!" exclaimed Andrew. "What on earth was there in the article?"

"Mind, there hasn't been a word said to me," Mrs. Mangan cautiously proceeded, "but what if they thought it was a hurtful thing to be comparing us with the black heathen of Africa?"

"It wasn't a question of comparing you to the heathen, as you call them," Andrew said. "It was just that I noticed, or thought I noticed, a striking similarity in two modes of thought. I'm afraid that I considered the matter purely from a scientific point of view. The last thing I wished to do was to offend your susceptibilities."

"Sure, a great scholar like yourself would have his own way of thinking," Mrs. Mangan agreed warmly.

"Has everyone in the village read the article then?"

"Oh save us, they have. They had it by heart an hour after the papers came in."

"And is that all the trouble? The references to the Congo?"

Mrs. Mangan hesitated. "It was a pity all the same," she

33

said at last, "that when you were writing about the nuns and that, you had to be mentioning Patrickstown."

"And why shouldn't I mention Patrickstown?"

"It was naming us, d'you see," Mrs. Mangan went patiently on, as if to a child. "It was telling them all in England where it was that the Irish nuns did pagan things."

"But all very harmless, surely? And in any case, the nuns did do that, you know. It was perfectly true."

"The truth of it wouldn't interest them here," Mrs. Mangan said, with pity in her voice. "But naming the place would upset them no end."

Andrew felt his poor brain commencing to swim.

"Mrs. Mangan," he said, softly and urgently, "forgive my persistence, but I do want to try and get this straight. First, do you accept my assurance that the nuns were in fact jumping the fires?"

"I do, of course. Sure, everyone knows they jump the fires on Midsummer Eve."

"Do you yourself see anything wrong in their doing so?"

"I do not! I used jump the fires myself when I was a pupil there."

"Did you yourself, when you read my article, feel that what I said was injurious to the nuns?"

"Yerra, Mr. Butler, not at all! I thought it was a grand article altogether."

"Then why should the people here think otherwise?"

"The people?" Mrs. Mangan looked at him in perplexity. "Who said anything about the people?"

Andrew took out a pocket handkerchief and wiped his forehead. "Isn't that what we are talking about?" he inquired. "Didn't you tell me that my mention of Patrickstown had annoyed them?"

"I did not! I said no such thing! And thanks be to God, they have more sense than to worry with that!"

34

Andrew shifted uneasily on his stool. He crossed his legs and uncrossed them again. Then he leant forward, with one elbow on the bar, and covered his eyes with his hand.

"Mrs. Mangan," he resumed, almost in a whisper, "your actual words, as I recall them, were: 'The truth of it wouldn't interest them here. But naming the place would upset them no end.' "

"And wasn't I right?" Mrs. Mangan wished to know.

Andrew looked up at her in something like terror.

"It isn't the people," she explained. "The people could be inclined to feel vexed with a stranger making money out of writing about the place and themselves getting nothing from it. But they wouldn't mind it, really. I wasn't meaning them."

"Then whom, my dear lady, did you mean by 'They'?"

"Ah well now," she said vaguely, and picked up her significant cloth. "Stay with us in Ireland a bit, Mr. Butler," she said then, with the ghost of a smile, "and maybe you'll find that out for yourself." And she began to polish the glasses as if through some oversight they had not been polished in the last twelve months.

That night Andrew lay awake for a long time, puzzling over the mysterious events of the day and the cryptic utterances of Mrs. Mangan. Certainly, it appeared that he had made a blunder; and his blunder had upset Them. But who, he asked again and again of the darkness before his eyes, were They? There was always a They in human affairs. With children it was the grown-ups, with employees the boss, in wartime it was the enemy, in peace the Government. Behind the simple collective pronoun there crouched a shadowy presence, sometimes inimical, often frustrative, always powerful and to be heeded. In this case, it surely could not be the nuns? Could it possibly, he wondered, be the Irish Republican Army? And if so, was perhaps his life in danger? Would a little band of shaggy men come down out of the mountains, slay him and take to their heels again? and were the villagers expecting this?

He hardly thought so. His friend Mrs. Mangan would surely have warned him. And there was dear little Patsy in it as well. Patsy was Irish and knew his own country and yet he had suggested and arranged the whole affair. To be sure, he had displayed real fright when Andrew's sudden laugh had betrayed their presence on the wall. And his disappearance on the road was strange, to say no more. Yes, there was an element of mystery in Patsy's behaviour too; and in Patsy, it might be, lay the key to the riddle. Andrew decided to seek him out first thing in the morning; and with that at last he dozed off.

He was awakened next morning at six o'clock, as he invariably was, by the ringing of the Angelus. As a rule he was inclined to resent this early bell as much as he welcomed its evening sister, seeing in it a symbol of the arrogance of Rome. Not only her own must be roused from their sleep but all others, Protestants, free-thinkers, atheists, Jews, who happened to be within earshot. All right, all right, he would sometimes impatiently mutter, so the angel of the Lord declared unto Mary—and what of it? Today he cheerfully rose at once and began to dress. He felt that he had things to do and he could not lie abed. It was the first time he had felt like this since his breakdown, of which one of the after-effects had been a deadly morning lassitude and sense of futility that made every tiny chore call for a large and painful effort. Now he briskly shaved and, humming a tune, went out into the fresh sunlight.

As he walked along by the side of the river, his thoughts took another turn. The loveliness of Ireland drove everything else from his mind. The countryside breathed out a tranquil sweetness that he thought he had never experienced before, seeming as if it spoke to him of peace and reassurance. The hills were bathed in the wonderful light, soft and yet brilliant as nowhere else in the world. The river hurried past, chuckling to itself, throwing wavy lines on the trunks of trees, foaming crisply about the rocks in its bed: gay yellow iris beflagged its edges: the wings of dragon-fly burned blue and gold over its rippling surface. As yet the leaves had not lost their young radiance. Far above in the milky sky the larks were trilling away in splendid heart. Count on me, the land seemed to be saying; can anything ever be wrong in a place like this? And Andrew, moving slowly over the springy turf like a man in a dream, surrendered himself wholly to the morning's enchantment.

A hideous outcry arose all at once, a confused outpouring of anguish, fury and desire. MacCarthy's donkey in the meadow above felt that he had been silent too long and now was putting things right. Slowly and reluctantly Andrew retraced his steps and returned to the hotel for breakfast.

On the table beside his plate was a long envelope, marked Urgent, Personal, By Hand, and addressed to Mr. Andreas Buttler. He opened it, idly scanned the contents, exclaimed aloud and began to read them again, attentively and with a look on his face that varied between consternation and amusement. There were two letters inside, of which the first one ran:

DEAR SIR:
Canon Ignatius Peart *v.* Packet Newspapers Ltd. and Yourself
Acting on behalf of Canon Ignatius Peart, Parish Priest, Patrickstown, I enclose the copy of a letter to Messrs. Packet Newspapers Ltd. from which you will see that he

has instructed me to commence proceedings against them for libel.

As my Client intends to join you in the Action, please will you be good enough to name your Solicitors, who will receive the Writ on your behalf.

Yours faithfully

JAMES PATRICK LA TROBE

Solicitor.

It was in the second letter, however, that Mr. La Trobe, a man with a distinct feeling for style, had really let himself go:

DEAR SIRS:

The Very Reverend Canon Ignatius Peart *v.*
Yourselves and Another

In the issue of the *Daily Packet* of June 24, published by you and of which a copy is enclosed, there appears an article entitled *Ireland Is Pagan Still* by one Andreas Buttler. The whole trend of this article is tendentious, irreligious, injurious to Ireland's fair name, false and illiterate.

Its last paragraph in particular refers to the Convent of the Immaculate Conception, Patrickstown, and runs as follows:

"At Patrickstown on Midsummer Eve I watched the nuns celebrating the occasion in a manner as charming as it was inappropriate: they were leaping bonfires in the garden of their convent. As readers of *The Golden Bough* will know, this is an ancient fertility rite, practised through the ages in many parts of the world. No doubt the good Sisters were unaware of the significance of their innocent frolic; but it was another example of the way in which pagan observances will persist, and this time in the quarter where you least expect to find them."

The wicked, obscene and defamatory sense of this passage with regard to Reverend Ladies who, by the nature of their Vocation and Rule, are unable to defend themselves needs no underlining. But there is another side to the matter. The Convent of the Immaculate Conception is under the spiritual direction of my Client, the Very Reverend Ignatius Peart, Priest in charge of the Parish. He states that the practices described in the article have never taken place, nor would he permit them; and that the passage complained of reflects on him, generally as a Catholic priest and particularly in respect of his function vis-à-vis the convent: it alleges a grave dereliction of duty, argues a reprehensible laxity of opinion and moral outlook; and it exposes him to hatred, ridicule and contempt.

My Client is the best type of Irish Catholic Priest, humble, zealous and charitable, loved by all in the parish and, indeed, far beyond its confines. He enjoys the absolute confidence of His Lordship the Bishop. In all his long years of toil in the cause of religion, none has ever dared cast aspersions on him before. Accordingly, he has instructed me to commence, without delay, an Action for Defamation.

But while, in the Service of God, he must be stern, he is also merciful. He understands that the publication of this most disgusting libel may perhaps be due to ignorance and thoughtlessness rather than malice and evil intent. If you are willing to make prompt amends sooner than face proceedings in Court, you will find him most reasonable. His terms for a settlement of the matter would be these:

(1) a full ungrudging and meek apology for, and retraction of, the falsehoods contained in the article
such apology and retraction to be made separately by

yourselves and the writer, whom he joins in the action such apology and retraction to contain, in each case, the same number of words as did the offending article itself

such apology and retraction to be displayed, with bold type headlines, in the top left-hand corner of the front page of the issue in which it appears

(2) The payment of a Sum of Three Hundred Pounds, to be devoted to the Charitable Purposes of such Catholic Institution or Charity as my Client shall select and determine; hence, the cheque to be made payable to him

(3) The payment of all legal costs and fees, and extra expenses of every kind, that my Client may incur in the bringing and the settling of this Action.

I am to say that in the event of this Action coming to Court, my Client will seek to recover Damages in the amount of Two Thousand Pounds.

A copy of this letter has been sent to Mr. Andreas Buttler, author of the article under discussion.

Yours faithfully,

JAMES PATRICK LA TROBE.

Solicitor.

Andrew had never had any first-hand experience of the majestic frivolity of the law; and his attitude towards it was rather more that of the man in the street than might have been expected in a person of his intelligence. He believed that lawyers everywhere were a pack of rogues, but that once a cause was delivered into their hands, somehow or other the Right must inevitably triumph. At the same time, the mere thought of becoming involved in its processes filled him with horror. The sight of even the most innocent legal document would induce in him a melancholy frame of mind.

His first reaction, then, to the fantastic communication before him was unqualified and unreasoning alarm. Next, as he examined in detail the proposals of this Mr. La Trobe, he broke into happy laughter. His face clouded over again as he thought of the trouble he had inadvertently brought on the *Daily Packet*. Then, as his brain got to work once more, it became clear to him that the Canon had no case whatever, would simply be laughed out of Court and look a fool for his pains. In this assurance he read it all through once again, relishing the higher lights of insanity and the more grotesque extremes of presumption.

"Two thousand pounds!" he murmured contentedly, as he applied himself with good heart to the rashers and eggs. "I daresay."

And Mrs. Mangan, fearfully observing him through a crack in the door, saw the carefree look on his face and thought he was out of his mind.

As soon as Andrew had finished his meal, he went in search of Mr. Pearl. He found that valiant carouser in bed, with a cup of black tea untasted on the wooden chair beside him. Despite his morning queasiness he greeted Andrew with a friendly smile. Their recent tiff had been quite forgotten in consequence of the *Daily Packet* having since published a letter from a lady reader comparing him, Pearl, to Mark Twain.

"I hate to disturb your early meditations," said Andrew, seating himself on the bed, "but I wish you would look at this."

Pearl read the letters through slowly and painfully, his lips spelling out the words to his dissociated brain, and heaved a sigh.

"Heigh-ho! at it again," he said. "Sorry, old boy, this is

my fault. If I hadn't been feeling so tired that evening, I would have warned you to leave religion alone."

"But there wasn't any religion in it."

"Well, it's what they call religion over here. But don't worry, old man," said Mr. Pearl, kindly, "because you'll never hear another word about it. I've been through five of these things. No trouble at all."

"What happens, then?"

"Oh, they bung it over to the legal boys. Take Counsel's opinion, you know, just for the look of it. Then they shell out and print some tripe or other, and Bob's your uncle. You won't have to find a penny piece."

Andrew could hardly believe his ears. "You surely don't mean to say," he exclaimed, "that your paper would accept these impudent suggestions?"

Mr. Pearl looked hardly less surprised than he did. "Why, of course. What else would they do? You don't imagine Lord Pulvermacher is going to argue every spot of bother that comes along, do you?"

"Who is Lord Pulvermacher?"

"*Who is Lord Pulvermacher?*" echoed Mr. Pearl, now really discomposed. "Baron Pulvermacher, chairman of Packet Newspapers? Where've you been all your life, baby?"

"I may not have heard of Baron Pulvermacher," Andrew said, "nor can I restrain him from printing statements to the effect that everything in his own newspaper is a lie, if such is his conviction. But you may have noticed that I figure as a co-defendant in these proceedings."

"But I'm telling you, old man," said Mr. Pearl, in a gentle patient voice that reminded Andrew of the propri-etress, "that you don't have to worry. That's only a form. All it means is, that the statement is printed twice, once in our name and once in yours. You won't even see it before it goes in. The paper won't even write to you. And they won't think any worse of you, either."

"Indeed! That's very gratifying." Andrew was smiling absently, as if at some private joke.

"That's right, old boy! Give Daddy a little smile," said Mr. Pearl, taking a sip of tea and quickly replacing the cup with a shiver. "These things give one a nasty turn, eh? I fairly shook in my shoes the first time it happened to me. Hardly dared go into the office. Every time the editor sent for me, thought it was the sack. Couldn't eat, couldn't sleep. Then one fine day I opened the paper and there was a little par to say it had all been my boyish fun and the editor was very sorry. No bitterness, no recrimination. And a raise in pay, to soothe my proud spirit."

"Did they raise your salary on the four subsequent occasions?" Andrew inquired, looking interested.

"No, only the first. Then they saw I wasn't going to kick and so there was no need. But it made for nice friendly feelings between self and the editorial," Pearl explained.

"I think it's a lovely arrangement," Andrew said, happily. "The only drawback is . . ."

"Yes?"

"I'm afraid that it won't do!" And with these words he left the room, while Mr. Pearl stared after him with his mouth open.

The information concerning the identity, outlook and habits of Lord Pulvermacher that he had just received, he pushed to the back of his mind to savour at leisure in some future time. It did just flit through his mind that he had been idle to make trips all the way to the Congo when behaviour patterns of a yet more extravagant kind were available for study within a stone's throw of Ludgate Circus. But for the moment he had more urgent matters to see to. The letter to the *Daily Packet* was dated three days earlier than his own. It must by now be in the hands of Lord Pulvermacher's lawyers, who might at that very moment be drawing up the instrument of surrender. He went at once to his room and wrote uncomfortably on his knee as follows:

DEAR SIR:

Canon Peart *v*. Myself.

I have received your letter, the contents of which I note. As this Action will be heard in Dublin and as I am a new-comer to this country, I cannot immediately name my Solicitor, as you require. I will however do so as soon as I can; and in the meantime, I will accept service of the Writ myself. For your information, my Defense will be that the words complained of are true as to fact and fair as to comment.

For the purpose of the Writ and other documents, it would perhaps be as well if you correctly noted my name.

Yours faithfully,

ANDREW BUTLER.

He sealed the envelope with a vigorous thump and took it himself to the Post Office at once. As he approached the door he saw coming out of it the person that in all the world he most wanted to see. This June morning Patsy's seraphic face wore a dreamy smile as if somewhere far away he caught the strains of a celestial choir. A creature of light and joy he seemed, at one with the morning and the blithe sweetness of the summery world. But as Andrew hailed him, his montrous story bubbling on his lips, he started violently and made off in the opposite direction as fast as his little legs could carry him. Andrew stared after him with a faint misgiving already awake in his mind; he utterly depended on this single witness and hardly dared contemplate the possible outcome should Patsy fail him. Slowly he went on into the Post Office and handed his letter over to Mr. Lynch, who stood with it in his hands intently examining the address.

" 'Tis a pity now," he remarked politely, but still careful to avoid Andrew's eye, "that you have to spend the money to register this."

"Why is that, Mr. Lynch?"

"Because, sir, the gentleman 'tis written to," the other gravely informed him, "was in here a moment since!"

FIVE

Lord patrickstown re-
ceived no reply to his letter to the Reverend Mother.
Indeed, she would have been puzzled to answer it, for it
was as confused a document as ever came into her hands.
It confessed on the one hand to hideous offences committed
on the morning of Midsummer Eve, while nowhere being
explicit as to the nature of these. On the other, it denied
all knowledge of the incident of the evening, concerning
which she too had withheld particulars but which had
burned itself so indelibly on her mind. Every time someone
came up the drive he ran hopefully to the window to see
if it was the humpbacked girl that the Convent employed
as a messenger. But she never came and as day followed
day and the men went busily on removing the palisade in
his beech wood, a vague but awful apprehension rose in
his heart.

He knew nothing at all of the events which had given
the village its main topic for discussion at present. He had
cut himself off irremediably from the Protestant grapevine
and had never established contact with the more efficient
Catholic one. The gulf between himself and the people had

if anything been widened by his acceptance of their Faith. They thought it was a queer old way for a gentleman to behave. But he would have been deaf and blind if he had failed to notice that something was afoot; and, believing it directed against himself, he stayed trembling inside his huge dilapidated house and hardly was seen at all.

At last he could bear it no longer and, ordering his horse to be saddled, he rode through the eight or nine miles of winding lane to Castle Knock. Miss Amanda Browne was one of the few landowners in the neighbourhood who still welcomed him, and in fact they were close friends. On the face of it, they were a curiously assorted pair. At seventy-three Miss Browne still rode to hounds, shot, fished and expressed her point of view with a wealth of manly expletive, and at no time had Lord Patrickstown done any of these things. It could not even be seriously argued that art was the common bond, although both were writers. Every five or six years the little lord produced a slim volume of verse, often printed at his own expense and never selling more than two hundred copies. Formerly he had sung of passion and hinted at attachments that might have been seen as unfortunate; but now that he was redeemed, he confined himself to a painstaking description of natural beauties. Miss Browne for her part came out twice yearly at least with a historical novel, full of lace ruffles, cut and thrust, zounds and egad. With all the forceful simplicity of her nature she had turned to literature as soon as she had seen the day looming when, in the absence of a profitable industry, she would have either to take in English paying guests or to sell her place to the Church. Her first attempt had been rejected almost by return of post; but in the acrimonious correspondence to which this affront gave rise she displayed such gifts of style and fancy that the publishers asked to see the manuscripts again. Now she was an established author, whose work paid for horses, grooms, gardeners and beaters and was therefore a source of pride to her. If there was one thing that brought a flush of shame to her cheek and an angry sparkle to her eye, it was to be confused with Miss Joanna Brown of County Wexford, whose sensitive studies in lunacy had been, for a time, the rage of literary London.

Whatever the reason, they were deeply devoted to each other. No one who knew what was good for him ever disparaged the little lord in the presence of Miss Browne; and he for his part did everything he could to help and please her, even down to reading her novels.

As he rode into the outyard he found the chatelaine pent up in one corner by the old turkey cock, at whom she was lunging with a stick with all the neatness of one of her own swordsmen.

"Ah, Bertie! Ride him off for me, will you?" she boomed; and then, as Lord Patrickstown gallantly complied, "That's the great fellow. Ugly old brute! Always puts me in mind of the Canon.

"Sorry, me lad," she added at once, softening her voice till it sounded more or less like an ordinary baritone, "I'm always forgetting. Come into the kitchen. I'm just going to make some toffee."

"Toffee!" said the little chap, his face brightening. "You did say toffee, not coffee?" he asked, timidly. It was an important point, for Amanda's coffee was infamous even by Irish standards. There had been an occasion not long since when, some old cabbage water having inadvertently been served to her guests after dinner, no one had suspected a mistake until the cook burst into the room waving a coffee-pot.

"Toffee it is. Servants all gone to the races, thank God. Have the place to ourselves."

48

They stabled the horse and went into the kitchen together. Amanda tied a pinafore round Bertie's neck and sat him down at the table to peel some nuts; and in her pleasantly business-like company he forgot his sorrows for a moment and went to work with a will, feeling happy, useful and cherished.

"I like 'em whole, don't you? Try not to break 'em," she said. "Now, what do you say? shall be put lemon in it? or stick to vanilla?"

"Lemon! lemon!" Bertie cried.

"Lemon it shall be."

Amanda got down one of the great preserving pans, critically examined its interior and went rummaging in the pantry for lemons, butter and sugar. Strings of military oaths burst from her lips as she came on one atrocity after another. Here a drowned mouse lay peacefully at rest in a bowl of fruit salad. There a hairbrush, grey with age, shared a dish with a piece of cold mutton. The handle of one of her elegant Georgian spoons protruded from a jar of pickled onions, the bowl of it black as night. Some of her discoveries revealed a well-nigh asiatic indifference to smells and dirt as, for example, the bin of pig-food that, lidless beside the range, was fast ripening in its grateful warmth. Others betokened great ingenuity, such as the veritable cat's-cradle of ropes and pulleys by which the pantry-boy spared himself the few seconds' effort of carrying the turf-basket from the turf-shed to the furnace.

"Ah, the sluts! I'd turn the whole bloody pack of them off if it wasn't that I'd get some more just like them!" thundered their mistress. "Now then! I saw you eating those nuts!"

"It was only one," he pleaded, wriggling with delight in the nursery atmosphere.

49

"One too many, my lad. Hurry up there, get a move on. You've still got to grease the tins."

A delicious aroma crept through the kitchen as Miss Browne, muttering witch-like over the pan, stirred the boiling sugar. At last it began to cling stickily to the spoon and to send up little wisps of blue smoke. Bertie insisted at this stage on being given a taste in a saucer of water. Then with a cry of "Ready!" he feverishly tipped his nuts into the mixture and this in its turn, with little whimpers like an eager hound, he poured into the waiting tins. Emotionally exhausted, they sat down to wait for the toffee to cool.

"Did you come over for a glimpse of my beautiful eyes?" Amanda asked, wiping the sweat from her face. "Or for some purpose of your own?"

"Both," said Bertie. "Oh dear, Amanda, I'm in the most awful scrape."

He poured out the story in a voice that faltered now and again, and handed her the Mother Superior's letter. Amanda's face darkened in a familiar way as she took it all in and, as might have been expected, the line she took was entirely her own.

"Things have come to a pretty pass in Ireland," she snorted, "when a gentleman mayn't strip on his own lawn, if he feels so disposed. And never mind the time of day. You should not have answered this note, my boy. I like this infernal impudence! First they come weaseling in, all sunshine and honey. And as soon as they've a toe in the door, whoosh! they're in and you're out. Oh, I know them. I've seen 'em at it. Sending you the bills like that, for God's sake! Oh, and all in the cause of religion and we'll remember you in our prayers. It would never surprise me if this was just another of their tactics. As soon as they've reduced you to pulp—not very difficult—they'll suddenly have at you again and suggest talking peace. On their terms. You'll be lucky to keep the clothes on your back. Arrah, Bertie, I never thought I'd see your father's son come to this!"

"Oh Amanda," said the little lord, piteously, "you make everything sound so beautifully simple!"

"And beautifully simple it is, childeen! Simple daylight robbery!"

Miss Browne's attitude to Holy Church was on the whole a straightforward one. She believed generally everything she had ever heard against it and particularly that it was mounting a fiendish conspiracy against the likes of her in Ireland. She was quite prepared at any moment to sell her life as dearly as she could, while fearing that the attack would come by ruse so wicked and subtle as to be beyond the grasp of honest folk. These powerful convictions induced in her a sort of blindness, or at least a lack of observation, remarkable in so keen-witted a lady. She absolutely failed to notice, for example, that nothing had ever happened to her which might in any way justify them. She further attributed to the Canon the same diabolical cunning as to all of his cloth, whereas time and again he had given convincing proof of being, in matters other than parochial and earthy, as stupid as a bull. The mental conflict of Lord Patrickstown in the years before his conversion, his terrors, his loneliness had equally passed her by; and she had received the news of the disaster with the simple comment, *They've got him!* On the other hand it may be said for this prejudice of hers that she got more real pleasure out of it than from anything in life except a good day with the hounds; and that the sense of being ringed about by unscrupulous foes was a major factor in keeping her, despite her age, so wonderfully spry.

"Of course, you know, there's some haroosh going on about the nuns at present. Very likely they're trying to web you up in it," she proceeded, knitting her brows.

"What sort of haroosh? and how does it affect me?"

"It seems the Canon read something about them in an English newspaper, and bingo! his foxy nose twitched like a divining rod. All I can tell you is," said Amanda, who never allowed an English gentleman to enter the village without fully informing herself of the circumstances, "that this article was written by an English professor, a Dr. Andrew Butler, of the Edinburgh University, who's staying at Mangan's to recuperate after a breakdown caused by overwork in the Congo!"

"I was at King's with an Andrew Butler," Bertie said. He sighed, as he always did at the thought of Cambridge where, for the two years before he was sent down, he had been deliriously happy.

"Would you like me to look into it?"

"Dearest Amanda! If you would."

"Right you are. And I'll ride over in a day or two and tell you. 'Tisn't a case for the telephone!"

"Come to luncheon on Thursday, then," his lordship said, adding with another sigh, "it's my birthday."

"Aha! and how many candles on the little sponge cake?"

Bertie sighed again, still more dolefully. "Forty!" he said, in a tragic whisper. In fact it was forty-two but nowadays it always took him a couple of years to accustom himself to a new age.

"A mere nipper," Miss Browne said briskly. "Now I think we might hit the toffee a crack, don't you? It looks pretty hard."

For a while there was silence, broken only by the sounds of crunching and Bertie's appreciative comments, until at last he said that he ought to be getting home. Amanda put up a generous parcel for him to take away—"nothing like toffee for the nerves"—and went out with him to the stables. As he trotted off down the drive, she raised her voice in a final admonition. It was one of her habits to proclaim openly, and in the tones of the hunting-field, matters that most other people in Ireland would murmur only behind closed doors, among intimate friends and even then with the proviso that they had really said nothing at all.

"And Bertie me lad! Watch your food!" she roared. "Mind they don't poison you! That doctor! he's one of them. He'll have us all under the sod, if it takes him a hundred years!"

Bertie waved his whip at her and proceeded on his way, with sticky hands and face but with a quieter heart than he had known for many days.

 Bᵤₜ amn't I telling you,
Canon," Patsy was urging his reverend client in his gentle
soothing voice, "that it's all a bluff? He hasn't a hope.
He hasn't a witness. And what could he ever do, in a decent
Court, against yourself?"

They were facing each other across the table in Canon
Peart's study, with Andrew's letter lying open between
them.

Patsy spoke to a badly shaken man. The effect of his
own effusion on Andrew was as nothing compared with
that of Andrew's reply on the priest; it was as if someone
had sprung a mine beneath the canonical chair. Something
had happened that was utterly new in his experience. The
parish of Patrickstown extended for some fourteen miles
from east to west and for eleven miles or so from north
to south. Within its boundaries, it was his privilege to
declare what was the truth and what was not. No one but
he had a voice in the matter. He had availed himself of
this privilege in the affair of the nuns and had stated
clearly, unequivocally and, as it were, *ex cathedra*, that the
tale of their leaping bonfires was a fabrication. The posi-

tion had been defined once and for all by him, in the same way as the Holy Father might define a new dogma. And here, as cool as you please, was the English writing fellow, sitting in Mangan's Hotel and giving him the lie!

It was this unsoundness on the theological and doctrinal side that chiefly occupied the Canon's whirling brain. All this talk of witnesses and the Court and evidence and bluff that seemed to interest Mr. La Trobe struck him as beside the point. A challenge had been thrown down which, if not taken up, must surely pave the way for the devil knew what of heresy, schism and anarchy. Yet he was filled with unwonted timorousness as he contemplated the approaching battle, being a man that hit hardest and best when there was no retaliation. He simply was not accustomed to people answering him back, there was the long and the short of it. He felt helpless and afraid, as one moving in a new dimension.

"Well, what d'ye say we do, La Trobe?" he asked now, restlessly twirling with great red fingers the cross that hung round his neck. "What ought we do now?"

"I'd say we should serve the writ. There's nothing like a bit of a writ for recalling fellows to sense," Mr. La Trobe answered readily. "He thinks, you see, you'll let the thing drop after this cheeky note. But once the writ is served and the wheels are set in motion, there's nothing for him but collapse, or a fight to the finish."

The Canon was unable to repress a moan at the thought of the latter alternative.

"But the paper? Won't the paper settle the fellow's hash for him? What does the paper say?" he asked, clutching desperately at this little straw.

"There's been no reply from the paper yet. But there'd be little enough they could do, if the man's determined. As I say I'm convinced it's all a cod and he'll soon be cry-ing for mercy. But he's joined in the action and if he wants to defend it, there's nothing in law that binds him to follow the paper."

"Well, but we haven't actually joined him so far. Can't we drop him out of it?"

Patsy cocked his head to one side in his characteristic way and looked at the Canon very kindly. "Ah wait now, that wouldn't do at all. I'm afraid the implications of that would amuse the parish no end. No, Canon, leave me serve the writ on him. Depend on it, we'll be hearing another tune very shortly."

"Very well, La Trobe, you know your business," the poor Canon said. "But I don't know what His Lordship will say. When he gave leave for this action to start, I'm sure he never meant for me to be dragged into Court!"

"And you won't be, Canon," Patsy told him, comforting as a midwife. "Leave it all in my hands, and you'll be seeing the daylight soon!"

With that he took one of his sudden departures, before the Canon could change his mind.

Left alone, the Canon pursued the dismal train of his thought. As always happened when things went badly for him, he felt bitterly aware of his isolation. There was not a soul in the village in whom he dared confide; he was too far above them all to ask any man for his sympathy. Even Patsy La Trobe heard no more than half what was in his mind, for the Canon did not trust his solicitor from the presbytery to the Church. But whom could a parish priest ever trust? It was all Yes, Canon! and No, Canon! and Be God you're right, Canon! to his face and behind his back complaints and grumbles, slander and ridicule.

Glancing out of the window, his eye fell on the sand pit in the field below his garden, placed there ready for certain embellishments he had in mind as soon as the bathroom was paid for. A number of children had settled on it like flies and were busy making a castle of their own. The Canon charged out of the house and down the path like a wounded bull and, falling on them, dealt out smacks and boxes on the ear with the quick fair distribution that came of long practice. Howling, the little ones ran away and he came slowly back to the house, muttering aloud in irritation but feeling somewhat refreshed by the exercise.

In what seemed to be no time at all, Patsy was back. Three days had passed in fact, but the Canon was already falling into a state, common to litigants, where he seemed perpetually to be listening to the voice of his lawyer. But now it was a Patsy resplendent in black coat and striped trousers, a white carnation in his button-hole and a fat brief-case under his arm, a scrubbed, freshly shaven Patsy, with strong pomade on his hair.

"I won't keep you at all," he assured his client. "If you'll just glance at the papers here, and then sign the instructions to me."

The priest gingerly picked up the long typed document. It set out the tale of his wrongs in still more picturesque detail, claiming that these could only be righted and healed by an award of two thousand pounds. He read it through, his lips moving in the effort of concentration, and put a great sprawling "Ignatius Peart" to a shorter note instructing Mr. James Patrick La Trobe to proceed with the serving of a writ upon Mr. Andrew Butler without delay.

"That's right! Now I'll be away to Dublin and attend to all this," Patsy said, briskly tucking the papers away in his case. He gave a prim little cough as if embarrassed by something; and this in him was always a danger signal, for embarrassment of any kind was foreign to his nature. "I wonder, now, Canon, if you'd make me a little cash payment down? To cover disbursements, I mean."

Canon Peart could never hear a request for money without a thrill of indignation.

"Cash down, La Trobe?" he exclaimed, while a haughty look came over his face. "What in the world can you be wanting with cash? Time enough for that when the business is settled."

"Ah Canon! There'll be certain preliminary expenses. I've got to retain Counsel, you see: and we'll have to have Counsel's opinion."

"And what will you do with a Counsel's opinion, when you already have mine?"

"It's what is always done," Patsy explained. "There's a form to observe in these matters. Mind, you'll get it all back and more. It's an investment—that's the proper way of looking at it."

"And how much am I supposed to invest on this occasion?"

"Well. Shall we say, fifty pounds?"

The Canon all but bounded from his chair. "Why don't we say five hundred, while we're about it? It's no good, La Trobe. It can't be done. The money isn't there and it isn't coming in."

Patsy was all sympathy and understanding. "Why don't you have a chapel door collection, Canon? Sure, if the people know how the Faith has been insulted, they'll be proud to help you. They'll never see their priest put down for want of a beggarly pound or two."

The Canon laughed bitterly. "You think so?" He recalled the last Sunday's second collection, which had amounted to seventeen shillings and fourpence.

"I do, of course. They'd be bound to back you up. Aren't they looking to yourself to get them all into Heaven? *Hors de l'église*, you remember!"

The Canon did not know but was too proud to say so.

He heaved instead a prodigious sigh. "I might let you have ten, but I'm borrowing on the parish fund to do it."

"Twenty!" Patsy cajoled him.

"Ten, I'm telling you."

"Fifteen!"

"Twelve pounds ten, and it's me last word!" The Canon barked, bringing the flat of his hand down on the table.

Patsy yielded with his wonted easy grace. "You can have a receipt for it, Canon!"

"I should bloody well hope I could." He unlocked a tin money-box and, turning his back on the solicitor, slowly and reluctantly counted out the notes from a greasy and wrinkled pile. Then he secured the box once more and hid it away beneath a pile of vestments. He waited with the money in his hand until Patsy had written out the receipt and, with a last mournful look at it, handed it over.

"Well, you can tell that Counsel fellow I expect a favourable opinion after all this."

"And you'll get it, Canon. Depend on us for that."

On the following Sunday the theme of the Canon's sermon was, The Persecuted Church. It was another day of relentless heat and the air inside the sacred building soon became horribly close. Most of the people had but one set of Sunday clothes, and that intended to serve in winter and the cool rainy summers alike. They had walked for miles to Mass in their frieze or serge and now sat there gasping, their faces the colour of boiled lobster and the sweat freely pouring down them. Nevertheless they listened intently, for at the church door were certain installations of which they had immediately divined the purpose.

In almost weeping tones the Canon spoke to them of the sufferings of Catholics in lands under the Communist yoke. For once he did not preach entirely extempore but referred

59

from time to time to a sheaf of notes in his hand. Now he told them of a saintly Bishop imprisoned in Poland: now of some pious nuns tortured in China: now of devoted priests wrongfully accused of black-marketing in Budapest. At one moment by inadvertence he read out a long indignant letter to a Protestant newspaper in Dublin, describing the forced conversions to Catholicism of the Orthodox Serbs during the war. He had reached the end of it before he noticed his error, but made a splendid recovery.

"And there's Tito for you!" he said, passing rapidly on.

"Of course now, my dear brethren," he continued, "we'll be having the laugh of these people at the finish. They won't be dead five minutes before they learn their mistake. The bishops and priests and nuns will all be singing in Heaven and they'll be below, begging and praying for a drop to drink. Of water, my friends. And they won't even be getting that. Because outside the Church, as you know, there is no salvation. I suppose we all remember Delly Gleeze and what happened to *her*.

"But wait till I tell you something," he went on briskly, and a little shiver of apprehension passed over the listening people, "just because we're going to best them finally, 'tisn't to say we can afford to sit back here below. Ah, not at all! And if you think it's all a long way off and nothing to do with us, you'd be wrong. These people are everywhere, in Dublin, in Maryville and here in Patrickstown. Oh God, I could tell you things that would leave you in no doubt of it. You probably noticed a table with a tray on it outside the Church door. I had it put there, and 'twasn't to amuse meself either. There's to be a special collection today, in favour of the Church Persecuted. So lay your money down as you go outside; and if it's the kind of money that doesn't make an awful lot of noise, so much the better and God will reward you presently. You'll get it all back and more:

think of it as being invested in a safe thing, and don't be losing your sleep over it."

With that he turned abruptly back to the altar and proceeded with the consecration of the Mass.

Afterwards, as he sat eating his breakfast, the Canon could not help yielding to a little sinful pride. It had been a fine sermon all right, one of the best for a long time, full of meat and sincerity and with just the little scholarly touches that his people would respect. And they were good enough people, he thought, warming; hadn't they themselves suffered for the Faith in centuries past and wouldn't they do as much today? They'd never leave him fall by the side of the road. He'd likely recoup himself for Patsy's advance by this morning's work, with a handy little sum to spare for the future. But when Father O'hOgain entered the room with the tray in his hands, he knew from the set of the curate's prawn-like eyes that the news was bad.

"Two pounds eleven shillings and fourpence, Canon!" he said, hollowly. "And somebody put down a button."

The two priests stared at each other.

"Satan has got into this parish," said the Canon at last. "Did you see who it was put the button there?"

"I was called away just then," Father O'hOgain told him. "But Lynch was saying, 'tis between Cat's-Eye O'Keefe and Bridget MacCarthy. And Lord Patrickstown put down a whole pound note. So there's only thirty-one shillings and fourpence from all the rest of them."

"Leave the tray, so," the Canon ordered. "And Paddy, you'll find out who gave the button and bring that person to me. What kind of a button was it at all?"

"A trouser button, I'd say," said the curate reluctantly, as if loth to reveal the whole scope and horror of the crime.

"Give it to me."

The Canon examined the button carefully and slipped it into his pocket.

"It's undignified to be bothering with it, and I've a better idea," he said. "Will you announce at Second Mass that the person who did this sacrilegious thing should tell it in confession. My collection tray is not a wastepaper basket."

"I will, Canon."

"And if it's you hears the confession, give them a roasting."

"I will, Canon, all right."

"It wouldn't surprise me a bit if we hadn't been getting a little too soft all round."

When he tried to resume his breakfast, the Canon found that his appetite was gone. Three fried eggs and as many rashers were all he could manage this fine morning. He pushed the plate fretfully away and sat there deep in thought, with a little knob of yolk congealing on the front of his cassock. It was Bridget MacCarthy all right, he decided, who had put the button in the tray. Not content with bringing shame on the parish and herself, she must openly mock him. He had noticed over and over again that people who began by yielding to the lusts of the flesh were apt to sink lower and lower until they ended by insulting the clergy.

Bridget could go on her reckless way to perdition if she must; but what of the rest of the people? There he was, spreading himself to bring home to them the cruel position of Holy Church in the modern world and they answered with thirty shillings. It was less than a halfpenny a skull. And after he had practically guaranteed their own salvation! It did really look as if he were losing his influence with them. He thought nostalgically of how he had built the parish hall, only five short years ago. He had simply and firmly announced the decision one Sunday morning. The better-off members of the community had each been privately informed of the sum he or she was expected to contribute. Not one had jibbed at it. There had been the usual raffles, dances, whist-drives and sales of work, all attended and patronised in the most satisfactory way. In less than two years the hall was built and paid for, and himself charging the people rent for the use of it.

At the memory of past success the Canon's furrowed brow smoothed a little. What had been done before could be done again, and he was not the man to flinch at the very first sign of trouble. There still remained ways to explore and sources to tap. One or two of his aged parishioners looked like departing this life very soon and might be glad to contribute, for the extra send-off he'd give them; although of course he wouldn't put it to them as bluntly as that. And then a sudden, most brilliant notion came to him. He would give the parish the discipline of which it was so sorely in need. The writer fellow should be put down, Bridget MacCarthy driven from her home and peace and order brought once again to Patrickstown. But the iron hand should be encased in a velvet glove. He would make a very great concession and allow a dance to be held in the parish hall. As a rule dances were only held after a long and bitter struggle with himself, and the novelty of one actually suggested by him would be irresistible.

"Isn't that a great idea?" he cried aloud in admiration. He got up and briskly went into his study, where he sat down at the desk with pencil and paper.

The tickets should cost only three and sixpence a head, to make sure of a good attendance; but there should be a nice little profit from the bar in the weather they were having. He'd surely get Paddy MacGuire's band from town for nothing, with Paddy busting himself to get his boy into the priesthood. And having regard to the weather again, he'd make a further concession: he'd allow the dance to start at ten o'clock and go until the dawn, the way the people didn't have the excuse that it was too hot. He'd put Jim Foley in charge of the arrangements and tell him leave nothing undone to make the thing a success. Short of them jitterbugging or dancing cheek-to-cheek, the sky was the limit. The Canon reckoned, busily doodling, that he should clear fifty pounds at least.

He greatly hoped that the affair would not reach the ears of the Bishop. It was His Lordship's dream gradually to do away with dancing, and indeed with pleasure of every sort, all over the diocese. A recent pastoral letter had dealt with the evils and iniquities of modern dances with loving particularity over some ten pages. It wound up by saying that while the matter was absolutely within the discretion of the parish priests, His Lordship "hoped" that, if dancing there must be, it should at least be over by midnight. Trouble in that quarter was highly undesirable at this moment but the Canon, doodling away like mad, saw that he would have to risk it. It was all very well for the Hierarchy to take a lofty and general tone, but what they always forgot were the day-to-day necessities of parish politics. The Bishop had warmly approved the idea of the action against the writing man but had made no proposal whatever concerning the finance of it. Did he think the money would fall from Heaven? And if not, mustn't the Canon be free to do the best for himself and for the cause of religion? It was the old story of the ends justifying the means, a doctrine to which His Lordship had shown himself in the past quite remarkably faithful. If then some snake from the village wrote the usual anonymous letter to the Palace and the Canon found himself on the mat, there would be nothing for it but to explain the position frankly and freely.

All at once the Canon gave a violent start. He stared down at the paper on which he had been drawing with something like horror. While his thoughts flew on, his pencil had kept pace with them; and he now discovered that without being aware of what he was about he had drawn, in great detail, a wickedly rude picture of the Bishop himself. Yes, nothing had been forgotten: the round, unreflecting head, the bulbous nose, shaded carefully to indicate the colour, the peevish pendulous lower lip and a facial expression to put one in mind of an indignant foetus. As the scandalous cartoon lay there accusing him, poor Canon Peart groaned aloud. How was he to quell the rising spirit of insubordination within the parish when he, its overlord, so far forgot himself? And if indeed Satan were abroad, how could he expect to save the people if he too were to fall a victim to those devilish wiles? Clenching his great hand, he dealt himself a blow on the breast.

"Oh my God, I am truly sorry . . ." he intoned, with hanging head.

A burst of childish laughter came sweetly up from the end of his garden. The little ones were at his pit again, scattering the sand all over the place and gaily throwing handfuls of it in each other's eyes. But now, weighed down by his load of sin, the Canon let them be. He finished the act of contrition and went slowly and dejectedly up to his private oratory. Here he fell on his knees and, with a heavy sigh, took out his rosary.

SEVEN

When Andrew took service of the writ, his sensations were all that Mr. La Trobe could possibly have desired. Coming into the hall he was accosted by an individual who, despite the glowing sunshine, was dressed in a dirty mackintosh with a scarf wound tightly about his neck. The individual had further a cast in one eye and a long crooked nose from the end of which there perpetually dangled a drop of water. In a voice thickened by adenoids he had inquired, "Is there annyone be the name of Andrew Butler in this hotel?" whereat Andrew's heart gave a great leap and his entrails seemed to rise like a flock of birds and fly round a little before settling into place again. Mounting to his room with the document in his hands, he had the feeling that his knees were made of water: sitting by the window with it spread open before him, he found that his palms, like the roots of his hair, were damp with sweat: and when he had finished reading it through the room swam in front of his eyes in a crimson haze and his ears were singing like telegraph wires. In a word, his reaction was normal.

This much the solicitor had accurately foreseen; and he

was not to blame if he went astray in his estimation of what would follow. The most lively imagination cannot deal with matters forever beyond its compass. In worldly affairs Andrew had all the timidity and indecision of his kind, but in his own life he was a man of conviction, a word absent from Mr. La Trobe's vocabulary. His position in the present affair was as simple and as clear as the Canon's own: it was just that, even if palsied with terror, he meant to fight to the end for the right to believe in what he saw with his own two eyes. Like Martin Luther, there he stood and could do no other.

The process server had observed the early habits of his kind, and there was time for Andrew, if he looked sharp about it, to catch the midday train to Dublin. The prospect of immediate action brought some relief from mental stress and he flew to the telephone to order a taxi. To his indignant surprise it was in use by the kitchen maid, to whom a notice on the wall forbade any such privilege, and who was enjoying a long and pointless conversation with an admirer. He stood there fuming, consulting his watch in a marked manner and grimly clearing his throat while the hussy, taking no notice at all, squealed and wriggled with pleasure.

"Ah, gawn out of it!"

"The impudence!"

"Aren't you the boldest thing?"

At last, however, just as Andrew was enjoyably imagining himself in the act of throttling her, she reluctantly hung the receiver up and turned to him, glowing, with a "Oh God, Mr. Butler, and you waiting there this long time! What'll you ever be thinking of me?" uttered in tones of the deepest remorse. He had intended to quell her with a haughty glance, if not a sharp rebuke: now to his astonishment he heard himself replying on a similar

note of sincerity and warmth and with a faintly Irish in-
flexion, "Ah, for God's sake! Isn't there time enough for
us all?" The words had hardly left his lips before be began
to wonder if possibly he could be mad.

Having ordered the taxi and packed his things, he went
in search of Mrs. Mangan.

"I'm going to Dublin for a couple of days," he told her.
"But I'll keep the room on, if you please. I don't think my
business will take very long."

Mrs. Mangan had of course been aware of the process
server's impending visit and, on being tipped off that he
was in the village, had retired to her parlour.

"I wonder now," she remarked, "that a gentlemen like
yourself with money and his health to consider, would be
wasting his time in a place like this. Why wouldn't you go
on after Dublin, and see something else of the country?"

Andrew was gradually coming to understand the local
idiom.

"Don't you want me to come back here?" he asked.

Mrs. Mangan had, in fact, received an intimation from
Father O'hOgain that the continuing presence of her
troublesome guest was a matter of comment at the presbytery; and she winced, as she always did, at Andrew's de-
plorable directness.

"Yerra, what put that idea in your head?" she protested
indignantly. "Wouldn't a gentleman like you be welcome
anywhere? I was only thinking, oughtn't you see Killarney
and the Ring of Kerry? Or the Giant's Causeway up in the
north there? You'll be going home in a while and you'll
have seen nothing of Ireland at all."

"On the contrary, I believe I shall have seen a very great
deal," he told her gravely. "You get to know a country far
better by examining one small part of it in . . . in detail,
than by gadding about like a tourist."

"Oh save us, Mr. Butler! Is it worth the examining, then?" she sighed.

"It is as worth examining as any other place. But you have only to say the word if you want me to go."

Mrs. Mangan wanted it almost more than anything in the world, but at Andrew's gentle inquiry her eyes flashed with unwonted fire. "There've been some pretty queer fish in this house," she said, "and no one was ever turned from it yet. There was a fellow once kept a pack of beagles three weeks in his room, without any remarks being passed. Come on back when you please, Mr. Butler, and the fatted calf will be waiting."

At this moment it apparently came on to snow, as someone emptied a wastepaper basket from an upper floor onto the road outside. Mrs. Mangan darted to the window to deliver, in piercing tones, a message to the chambermaid who had done this thing and Andrew went outside to wait for his taxi.

The whole strange business of Pasty and Mr. La Trobe —for try as he would Andrew still thought of them in a separate way—had made a deep impression on his mind. He had never encountered anything of the sort in his life. Even the Congo, that fertile reservoir of comparison, failed to yield up anything like it. Not the least of the many surprising features in it was that he bore no ill will towards the culprit whatsoever. The flavour of the little man's personality lingered in his memory with the same gentle appeal as before, although blended now with a certain comic pathos. At the same time, in the perilous tasks ahead, he wanted to make no fresh mistakes: he saw that there might be a danger of falling in with a third manifestation, as it were, of Mr. La Trobe and of entrusting to those all-too-capable hands, with a child-like trust, his affairs. A clarification was what he urgently sought; and he determined to spare no pains in getting it.

On arriving in Dublin, therefore, he left his things at a hotel and went in search of Dr. Henry Muldoon. This was a scientist, working on nuclear fission, whom he had met in Oxford a couple of years before, whom he had greatly liked and had promised to look up were he ever in Dublin. It had seemed to him that Muldoon was everything an Irishman ought to be, gay, tolerant, humane, pleasantly subversive and, of course, free from English middle-class prejudice. He decided now to take him out to dinner, explain the difficulty in which he found himself and seek advice as to the best possible lawyer to approach.

The welcome he received went far beyond anything he could have expected. Although it was barely five o'clock when he reached Muldoon's laboratory, the scientist immediately downed his tools and insisted on beginning the evening right away. He would not hear of Andrew's giving him dinner but claimed him at once as a guest, remarking that in any case there was time enough to be thinking of food and there were more important matters to see to first. With that he led the way into the Shelbourne Rooms and, having comfortably installed them both in a corner, ordered large Irish whiskies.

"To start the blood circulating," he said. "It's the only thing that can do it."

They had not been in company long before Andrew became aware of several changes in this former acquaintance of his. To begin with, Muldoon looked older and more care-worn than when they last had met and he was much heavier, with the obesity of an habitual drinker. A nerve ticked steadily away below his left eye and his fine, scientist's hands were never still, now vaguely fluttering about his collar, now brushing invisible crumbs from his waistcoat, now making as if to run through his hair. Still more remarkable was the difference in his point of view. When Andrew politely told him how much he was enjoying his stay in Ireland and how much fun there was to be had in everyday Irish life, Muldoon looked at him sourly and the corners of his mouth drew down.

"Ireland isn't amusing at all," he said, with a final air. "She is ludicrous, which is not the same."

Andrew could scarcely believe his ears. If there was one subject in the world on which it was advisable to go easily with Muldoon in the old days, it was, precisely, Ireland: the greatness of her, the rightness, the dearness. Whenever he spoke of her there had crept into his voice a special tone, hinting at unutterable superiorities. He had at that time been working for five years past on a research station near Oxford, and, all were given to understand, eating his heart out. When Andrew first met him he was pulling wires all over the place to get the position in Dublin he now filled: which if he failed to do, the same poor heart must break. Muldoon then proceeded to astonish him further.

"Have you been to Oxford again?" he asked. "I wonder how Christchurch Meadows are looking just now."

For the next hour or two they talked of Oxford. There was no small corner of its life on which Muldoon did not wish to be informed. The news that there had been changes of staff at the Bodleian seemed to afflict him like a personal loss. He inquired tenderly after the dottier Fellows of All Souls one by one. He asked if morning coffee at the Cadena still tasted the same, and if the Warden of one of the colleges still had his terrible dog. He recalled in the greatest detail scenes in different Common Rooms that Andrew had long since forgotten, and spoke severely of various alterations in university procedure that had recently been discussed in *The Times*. At last even he fell silent, in his face a strange mixture of happiness and melancholy; and there followed a long pause.

"I must own up now," Andrew said, presently. "I've come to worry you with a little problem of mine."

He began to describe the events in Patrickstown and to explain his own attitude in the affair. As he went on, the twitching in Muldoon's cheek grew more pronounced and his hands leapt about in the air like those of a bookie. He continually glanced over his shoulder to see who was within earshot and once he broke in to beseech Andrew to lower his voice.

"You don't know who mightn't be at the next table," he said.

"So there you are," Andrew wound his story up.

"And are you really going through with it?" Muldoon asked, incredulously.

"I am, of course."

A savage gleam appeared in the other's eye, flickered and went out.

"You're mad," he said, sternly. "Listen, Andy, you don't know this country. It's next door to England and we speak the English tongue and all the while we are thousands and thousands of miles away. You'll be ruined. You haven't a snowball's chance in hell. And all for nothing, because no one in the place will have the faintest idea of what you are trying to do, or care either. And look here: supposing—it's impossible, but for argument's sake—by a miracle you won. You'd still achieve nothing. Slap one of those bastards down and a hundred spring up in his place. All the result would be that the unfortunate townspeople would have to fork out the money to pay the bill. It can't happen, of course. You're going to throw yourself away on an issue that, in this country, means absolutely nothing at all. Don't do it.

Say what the man wants you to say. It happens all the time here, and everyone will know it's purely a formula."

"I'm afraid that it wouldn't do," said Andrew, sadly.

Muldoon studied him thoughtfully for a while with a rueful look in his eyes that seemed to relate to his own position as much as to Andrew's. It was almost as if he were excusing himself for what he had just said, pleading with Andrew to understand how a man might be brought, by steady pressure on some inner weakness or confusion of his own, to affirm the contrary of what he believed. Or so it appeared to Andrew, himself unaware as yet of the basic nihilism of the Irish mind, and who imagined that what he saw in front of him was merely a defeated middle-aged man fast running to seed. Muldoon's cheek twitched now so violently that he seemed to be winking. All at once the gleam returned to his eye. "Oh God!" he cried, suddenly. "If you could! If somebody could! Just the once!" Immediately afterwards he threw one of his furtive glances round the room and went on in a low, suspicious voice: "But what do you want *me* to do?"

"Only send me to a trustworthy lawyer."

"And is that all?" Muldoon inquired, with a bitter laugh. "Wouldn't you like me to throw in the Holy Grail while I'm about it? A trustworthy lawyer, says he! In a case like this. You're a very good anthropologist, Andy Butler, but I'm not at all sure you ought to be let out alone."

"Is it going to be so very difficult?" asked Andrew, appalled.

"There's only one fellow would do it," Muldoon revealed, in a dramatic whisper. "To your satisfaction, I mean. And that's Felim Plunkett. He's a very devout Catholic himself, which is what you'd need. And he's a great one for freedom of speech and down with the censorship and all that. Oh, he's taken on dozens of tricky cases already. Some say he's an awful rogue, of course, but that mightn't be a bad thing either."

"Is he a resolute sort of character?"

"Oh, he is. The courage of a lion! And he'll need it," Muldoon said, gleefully rubbing his hands. "Why, this could ruin his practice entirely!"

"I don't think I want to ruin anybody," Andrew began, in new alarm.

"Oh, you'll ruin the lot of us before you're finished," Muldoon promised him lavishly. "You can't make an omelette without breaking the eggs!"

Andrew was pleased and touched by what he took to be the conversion of the scientist to his point of view, and thought himself lucky to have found the guidance he needed with so little trouble. He took out his notebook and asked for Felim Plunkett's address; but when Muldoon gave it to him, a faintly puzzled look came over his face.

"Isn't Merrion Square rather grand?"

"The best address in Dublin!"

"Then how does Plunkett come to be there? I mean," Andrew said, seeking to arrange matters in his tidy English mind, "if he takes on so many of these dangerous cases, and to his own detriment, how does he keep going at all?"

"Felim is above money!" the other replied, with the vagueness of an Irishman whom someone is irresponsibly trying to pin down to exactitude. "Let's have another drink."

They had a drink and then another and then some more. It was long past nine o'clock and all thought of dinner had been forgotten. The sight of an empty glass produced in Muldoon something akin to frenzy. His hair which, at the start of the evening, had been sleeked about his head like a fur cap now rode above his brow like a wreath of angry serpents. He launched into a string of

74

anecdotes about the clerics of Ireland, each more lurid than the last, and building up to a composite picture beside which the Inquisition itself appeared in the pale hues of an aquarelle. Ever and anon he would revert to Andrew's lawsuit, in which he now perceived the splendours of a holy crusade.

"And if you and Felim get that scoundrel down," he snarled, "let's have no dammed English nonsense about fair play. Kick him in the teeth: and while he's thinking it over, kick him again!"

With this little piece of tactical advice the party had to end, as the waiter signified his intention of closing the Rooms.

"We should never have gone there," Muldoon lamented, as they stood on the pavement outside. "This mania for closing on time! You'd think the British had never left the country at all. Meet me tomorrow in the Merrylea Lounge: we'll be safe till midnight anyway, and you'll tell me what Felim said."

Turning abruptly on his heel he stumbled away in the direction of Leeson Bridge. Once he wheeled about to roar *"L'audace! et encore de l'audace! et toujours de l'audace!"* before resuming his homeward way. The last of him Andrew saw that night was arm-in-arm with a lamp-post which he had recruited as partner in treading a measure. Singing, the Reader in Anthropology gaily retraced his own steps to his hotel in Kildare Street. On the way he passed a bare brick wall on which, in great white letters, some tortured soul had chalked the words —— *the Irish!* and, roaring with laughter, he paused to trace the word *Amen!* underneath them with his finger. As he fell in through the hotel entrance the manageress looked up with a friendly smile which turned to one of sympathy and approval as she noted the state he was in. His cheeks

75

stretched in a fatuous smile, he scampered up the stairs on all fours and dropped on his bed fully clothed: the darkness sparkled and blossomed before his eyes; and he very soon went off to sleep, thinking Dublin the jolliest place in the world.

The next morning he felt nothing like so well; and when, having telephoned to Mr. Plunkett's office, he learned that the solicitor would be in Court all day and could not see him before five o'clock of the evening, he decided that only fresh sea breezes could save his life. He took a bus to Howth and lay on the hill in the sun, the thudding of the waves on the shore below painfully echoed by that inside his head, and reflected in melancholy vein upon the situation into which he had so innocently stumbled.

On the stroke of five he mounted the snowy steps that led to Mr. Plunkett's impressive door and pressed the dazzling bell above the exquisitely burnished brass plate; and after spending a few moments in the waiting-room, with a box of expensive cigarettes open beside him and the current numbers of all the good magazines to choose from, he was shown into the presence of the intrepid campaigner himself.

"I expected you," said Felim Plunkett, rising to his feet with a flash of white teeth. "Harry Muldoon was telephoning this morning."

Felim Plunkett was a man to whom most people took an instant liking which they never afterwards, come what might, entirely lost. He was tall and handsome, with a manly frankness of expression and a ready, engaging smile: his whole personality radiated understanding and human sympathy. At the end of his arduous day in Court he was still alert and fresh as a daisy: he somehow made Andrew feel that all of his brain, experience and effort were unreservedly at his disposal. Indeed, the look he now gave his anxious client was one of such intense and friendly interest as to leave him in no doubt at all that he was apprised of the facts in the case and was already giving them consideration.

"I suppose he told you what it is all about," Andrew said, sitting down opposite him with a happy sense of coming near to harbour at last.

"He did, of course," said Felim, lightly. "But now I must have it all over again, in your own words, till I make a few notes."

He had, in fact, not the faintest idea of what brought Andrew to his door. At about nine o'clock that morning Dr. Henry Muldoon had rung him up at his private address and in blurred, wavering tones had announced that there was an English lunatic by the name of Andrew Butler at large in Dublin, with whom Felim should have nothing whatever to do. The said lunatic had only recently come out of a home for mental cases and was a prey to hallucination. He had some bee in his bonnet about a parish priest down in the country and had asked for the name of a lawyer. Muldoon had given Felim's, in order to calm the madman down, but he wanted it clearly understood that he took no responsibility at all in the matter; and if the fellow should quote him in any matter, he added, his voice rising almost to a shriek, whatever he said was a pack of lies.

"I'm afraid we lawyers are awful pedantic divils," Felim said. "May I first have a few particulars about yourself?"

"My name is Andrew Gladstone Butler. I am Reader in Anthropology at Edinburgh University and a Fellow of King's College, Cambridge; and I hold honorary degrees from Oxford and Paris," Andrew began.

"Ah, you see, Harry forgot to mention those," Felim

commented. "Thank you. And now let's have the story."

For answer Andrew passed him Mr. La Trobe's opening communication and his own reply, the Canon's statement of claim and the writ, all neatly tied together and already forming quite a stout little bundle. Felim glanced at them and threw his head back with a roar of laughter.

"Patsy rides again!" he exclaimed with delight.

"Do you know him?"

"Who doesn't?" The solicitor settled himself in his chair and began to read the documents carefully through, chuckling from time to time and pencilling an occasional note in the margin. " 'My defense will be that the words complained of are true,' " he quoted presently, looking up. "Have you anyone to corroborate that you saw the nuns leaping the bonfires?"

"You well may ask!" Laughing in spite of himself, Andrew explained the somewhat unusual status of the only witness he had; and the other man threw the papers down on the table and gave way to unrestrained merriment.

"There's no doubt of it, Patsy's a genius," he gasped. "You'd best get him to manage the case for you!"

"And I feel quite sure he would take it on!"

"Oh, he would. I remember once there was a frightful shindy over a will down there in his territory, with five brothers at each other hammer and tongs. And your man lending a hand to so many different parties, he ended by pulling a fast one on himself. He saw a chance to double-cross himself that was really too good to miss. But no one else ever succeeded in doing it." He resumed his study of the papers. "Now, Mr. Butler, we've got to be serious, though it mayn't be easy," he said at last. "First have patience till I give you some facts that may be new. From the fine bold style of your answer to Patsy, I'd say you were unfamiliar with the workings of Irish law."

The thing to bear in mind, he commenced, putting the tips of his fingers together in a judicial way, was that the issue of truth or untruth was irrelevant to the matter in hand. To begin with the Irish, an unmaterially minded people, had a subtler conception of what truth was than their Saxon neighbours, who were always the plodding slaves of fact. The question for the jury here was, who is bringing this case and who is defending it? The answer was, an Irish priest and an English writer. Those facts would speak for themselves, and they were the only ones worth considering. Because Irish law on paper was the same as that of England and because the long occupation by the English had thrown a kind of veneer over the country which only now was properly beginning to crack, the forms would all be preserved and the motions gone through. Andrew would seem to be fighting an ordinary case at law: in fact, the outcome was decided in advance. And why wouldn't the decent old boy get the little bit of money from the English fellow? Everyone knew the English were rolling. The alternative was not to be thought of. In the kind of Christian democracy that modern Ireland enjoyed, no verdict could ever be returned against a parish priest: because he was the cornerstone of society, because priests had had no end of an awful time in the Penal days and because the jurymen would ultimately have to account for themselves to their wives. If Andrew supposed that the whole established order of things could be placed in jeopardy on a frivolous point of did the nuns leap fires or didn't they, it was his Felim's duty to disabuse his mind of that, and bring home to him the unsoundness of his position.

"I hope," Felim said gently, "that you follow me."

"My poor brain is going round and round," Andrew replied. "What seems to emerge is, that you are on the Canon's side like everyone else."

"Ah no! I'm for you!" Felim cried expansively. "I share your feelings completely as a man; but as a lawyer I'm bound to clarify the legal issues."

"Clarify," said Andrew, putting a hand to his head.

"Well, and amn't I clarifying? Don't tell me you would have thought of all that by yourself!"

"Indeed no," Andrew agreed. "It is just a little beyond my range. But may I in turn attempt a clarification? As a scholar, I have spent my life in the study of facts. If you choose to call me their plodding slave, then do. Don't be offended, please, if I say something else. As an anthropologist, I have been in communities before now where fear and prejudice and magic had more to say than reason did, and it was not my experience that they were either the happiest or the most flourishing. I'm fully alive to the comical side of this affair and in days to come, looking back, no doubt I shall relish keenly. But in the meantime the fact that the nuns did leap fires, which strikes you as immaterial, will have at all costs to be maintained by me: because the alternative is the negation of absolutely all I believe in."

"And are you going to say all that in the box?" Felim inquired, with some little emotion. "Because I'll choke you if so!"

"I'm talking like a prig," Andrew smiled at him. "Not the least of Ireland's diabolical gifts is to make respectable people talk like prigs. Well, Mr. Plunkett, you mentioned the distressing quandary that Irish jurors would find themselves in, were they to decide in my favour. Think of me, won't you, lecturing next year to all those earnest pink-faced children in Edinburgh. What shall I tell them Father did, over there in Patrickstown?"

"You'll lose," Felim croaked. "It'll be five hundred

pounds at least. Have you got five hundred pounds to spare? Never mind the legal costs?"

"I have not, nor anything like it."

Felim brightened wonderfully. "Then you're in a very strong position," he cried. "You'll just tell them you can't pay!"

Andrew wearily shook his head. "I'm afraid," he said, "that it wouldn't do." If I stay much longer in Ireland I'll have to get a record made of that phrase, he reflected. "I'll raise it, don't worry. Sell something." My library, my little boat, my piano, he thought, with a pang. "So will you please set the wheels in motion?"

"Think it over again," Felim urged him. "We've the best part of a month before a defence need go in. What's the great hurry?"

"Because, as you see, the *Daily Packet* is in it too; and because someone by the improbable name of Lord Pulvermacher apparently finds the money burning so much in his pocket that he gives it away at once to all who ask for it."

Felim laughed heartily at this. "Ah, the English press! a great institution," he said, admiringly. "There's many a rogue in Ireland depends on it for whisky and cigarettes! Oh, we'd be lost without it."

"I take to you, Mr. Plunkett," Andrew said, firmly. "I'm delighted that Muldoon should have sent me here. I cannot however help noticing the note of reverence that creeps into your voice whenever you describe some particularly abominable piece of knavery. With the greatest respect, may it be understood that this case is to be fought in the stupid and unimaginative English way that might be expected of me?"

Felim's mirth broke unresentfully out afresh. "I'll be stupid and English to your heart's content," he promised. "Wasn't I at Trinity College? Before they made it a mortal

81

sin, of course. Now, I've told you the bad things; here comes the good. It's a thousand to one against this case of yours ever reaching the Court at all."

"How on earth do you make that out?"

"That's a long story and would only make your head spin again," Felim told him, comfortably. "But depend on it: the real issue is, whether yourself or the Canon is the first to collapse."

"Then I can only say, it will be the Canon."

"Ireland has a most insidious effect on the moral fibres," Felim averred, with a shake of his handsome head. "And she's like those viruses that mainly go for the strong. Oh, I'll be watching you, Mr. Butler!"

With that they shook hands and parted, in great good humour with each other.

As soon as he got back to the hotel, Andrew sat down and wrote a long letter to his friend and colleague, Guy Webster. He owed him a letter; indeed, he had been remiss, for Guy had written to him twice since he came to Ireland, letters full of concern for his health and of amusing gossip from Edinburgh. The sad condition he was in had led him to put off replying from day to day and week to week; and nothing could have said more for the tonic properties of litigation than the zestful way in which he now seized pen and paper. As he wrote, he seemed to see Guy's clever, sarcastic face relax in a grin of pleasure and to hear his wholesome, astringent comments. The miasma of Irish thought had begun ever so little to affect Andrew. The speech he had made in Plunkett's office, so emphatic and, as he now felt, sententious, was a proof of this. No longer able to feel that his rightness was self-evident, he had begun to argue; but now at the mere thought of Guy sitting at breakfast and smiling over his letter, all such imaginary mists were blown away. He described the affair to him as if it had been the funniest thing in the world, omitting all mention of his private terrors.

"Of course, this is going to cost me a pretty penny," he airily wrote, "and, as it happens, I've been thinking for some time of selling my boat. I'll miss our sailing trips round the western isles but really the upkeep is more trouble than it's worth. Don't go out of your way, but if you should hear of anyone being interested, you might let me know. I remember Hogg saying it would be just the thing for him: perhaps you could drop a word in that quarter?"

Determined to avoid the mistakes of the night before, he ate a substantial meal before setting out in search of Muldoon. The time had passed without his noticing it, and it was going on for ten o'clock when he left the hotel and made his way to the lounge where they had a rendezvous. The beauty of Merrion Square was heightened by the blue dusk gathering over it and he wished with all his heart that he was free to go for a quiet walk through the charming streets and along the canal. Until his meeting with Plunkett he had been too distracted to notice much his surroundings but now that peace of mind was returning he found his eye continually caught and soothed, by a fine building, by a tree, its leaves mysteriously romantic in the lamplight, by a sudden glimpse of shadowy hills on the horizon. But he reminded himself that Muldoon, to whom he owed so much, would be impatiently waiting for his news; and placing as ever duty before inclination he strode firmly on.

The bar was large and noisy, furnished with scarlet leather chairs with chromium-plated legs in a half-hearted attempt at modernity and smartness. Tobacco smoke hung over it like an evening mist and there were a number of shouting, swaying figures, in the midst of whom Andrew saw the scientist, in much the same euphoric state as when they had parted company. It became immediately clear, none the less, that an important psychological change had taken place in him. He turned as Andrew came in, stood lowering at him for a moment and then, with a shout of "There he is at last!" made an impetuous little rush towards him. Suddenly, again, he pulled himself up and inquired suspiciously: "Who are you, sir?"

"I'm Andy Butler," said Andrew, smiling at him.

"You don't look much like him, then," said Muldoon. "Have you brought your leprechaun with you?"

"What leprechaun is that?"

"The one you had in a bottle last evening."

"Don't mind him, Mr. Butler," said a foxy young man in a foxy tweed coat. "I think he's confusing you with someone else. My name's Bill Halloran. Have a drink. Have two drinks."

"Coming in here without his leprechaun!" the scientist bawled to the company at large.

"Wisha, Harry, be quiet now, there's the great fellow. Here, Mr. Butler, take this. We're some little way ahead of you, I can see."

Andrew thankfully took the glass, which was half full of what appeared to be neat whisky. The frequent need in this country for hasty mental reorientations was beginning to wear him down. A huge man with curly hair came up and laid an arm like a shoulder of mutton round his neck.

"I'm Michael Collins," he said, very tenderly, "and you're Andy Butler."

"I'm very glad to make your acquaintance."

"Michael Collins and Andy Butler," the other said, smiling and nodding. "Professor Michael Collins," he added, with a touch of haughty reproof in his voice, "not

84

the patriot fellow." His face clouded over. "The English shot *him*."

"I'm so sorry," Andrew apologized.

"Ah, go on away out of it, Mike! They did not!"

"Shot him," Professor Collins affirmed. "The murdering bastards." He set down on a bench rather suddenly, as if his legs had had enough of it, and stared into his glass. "I beg your pardon, Mr. Butler. There's no reflection on yourself."

"He's only talking," whispered Halloran. "He's a professor of Gaelic, if you follow."

The Professor raised his enormous head. "If you've any remarks to pass, Bill, let's have them straight out," he said, with dignity. "Only fair play here and gentlemen, like cricket. No stabs in the back, if you please."

"You'll be getting a strange idea of our Dublin manners, Mr. Butler," Halloran said, primly. "You're from Edinburgh, I think?"

"I'm at the University there. But a mere Sassenach myself, I'm afraid."

"Self-satisfied swine," remarked the Professor.

"I am a doctor of medicine," Halloran told him. "Are there a lot of doctors of medicine in Edinburgh?"

"I should think there are quite a few."

"There are an awful lot of doctors of medicine here," said Halloran, sighing heavily.

"Out there on the mountain alone," the Professor resumed, with tears in his voice. "Priests refuged him assolution!"

"I was to meet Dr. Muldoon this evening and tell him the results of an interview I had today," Andrew said. "But he scarcely seems in any shape to hear about it."

In fact Muldoon was leaning over the bar and wrangling with the barman, whom he vehemently accused of keeping

85

a leprechaun in a bottle under the counter, where honest students of nuclear fission could never clap eyes on it.

"You're a fine sort of barman," he was complaining. "I'll split you to pieces like an atom!"

"Please don't run away with the idea that we are always like this," Halloran pleaded. "You'd be getting the wrong impression entirely. Why, I don't suppose Harry takes drink twice in a year. That's the trouble really, he just isn't used to it. This was to be a party in your honour, you see, and we expected you rather earlier."

"I didn't know that, I'm awfully sorry," Andrew cried.

"Well, and how could you know? Wasn't it to be a grand surprise for you? Dublin hospitality, famous," Halloran said, with a wide sweep of his arm which carried a pair of glasses off a table. "Meet Peter Rooney. Meet Jimmy McGrath."

A lot of rather muddled shaking of hands took place. Dr. Muldoon now turned away from the bar and stood visibly collecting his powers for a fresh attack; and as soon as they had attained the necessary pitch he let a roar out of him like an angry lion.

"Andy Butler, is it? of course, it's the great Andy Butler! Andy Butler knows better than to believe in leprechauns," he shouted.

"Harry, would you ever stop it, for Christ's sake? Please don't mind him, Mr. Butler."

"Oh God, he's above all that! Not like us benighted natives!" the scientist continued.

"Wait now, Harry, will we go on to your home and let you get some rest? Will we do that, Harry boy?"

"Coming over to Ireland and setting us all to rights!" vociferated Muldoon, tearing his jacket off and dashing it on the floor, "Let me just hit him a crack, will you?"

"Murdering bastards," the Professor threw in.

Muldoon aimed a violent blow at Andrew's head; but he had miscalculated the distance by over a foot and, spinning round with the impetus, sat down on the floor. There he remained, attempting to canvass his audience to a proper view of Andrew's iniquity.

"The poor old man!" he said, now lowering his voice and speaking earnestly and sorrowfully. "The poor decent kind old man! Down there in the country. In his quiet happy little parish. What's he ever done? Just because Mister Bloody Butler doesn't believe in leprechauns. Not a word against the Irish priesthood, please. Best in the world. Brightest jewel in papal leprechaun . . . papal crown, I *should* say. Andrew Butler, have you no fear of God?"

And he lay back on the floor and composed himself to sleep.

"Now, sir, please," said the barman, unruffled.

"I really will have to ask you to excuse me," Andrew said, ominously, setting his glass down on the counter with a severe little tap. "And tell Muldoon, if it consoles him at all for the headache he will have tomorrow, that I think perhaps I shall soon believe in leprechauns, and fervently."

"Promise not to go off with the wrong impression of us, at least," Holloran begged him as he started to the door.

"I can promise that."

"And if you hear of an opening in Edinburgh for a doctor of medicine, please let me know. Dr. William Halloran, care of Merrylea Lounge, Dublin, will always find me."

EIGHT

Ever since Lord Patrickstown had learned that Andrew was staying in the village, he had been trying to pluck up his courage and pay him a visit. The fear of a rebuff had prevented his doing so up till now. Andrew had been in a very different set from his at Cambridge and even in those days had been spoken of as a superior intellect; and then, too, there was this troublesome matter of his own religious conversion which had separated him from so many people he would have been glad to see and which now seemed like a lasting barrier between himself and Protestant mankind. But at last he could bear to wait no longer. The burden of his solitary life in the great Hall had been increased by a temporary coolness between himself and Amanda Browne; and he felt that if he could not find some pleasant company soon, he should go mad.

As had been arranged between them, Miss Browne had come over to luncheon on his birthday, bringing an armful of flowers, some pots of her own honey and a signed copy of *A Very Parfite Knight*. Cat's-Eye O'Keefe had produced from somewhere, by his own inscrutable methods, a salmon:

there had been strawberries from the garden with cream and two bottles of champagne: and the whole affair had gone off delightfully. Amanda had not been able to clear up the mystery of the Reverend Mother's letter, but she told him enough about the rumpus in the parish to convince him that, for the time being at least, "They" had their hands full without bothering about him. He had decided to try and put the business out of his mind and wanted more than ever to see Andrew, for whom he now had a warm fellow feeling.

Unhappily for him, Amanda had just completed the manuscript of *His Sword, His All* and had not yet fairly got to work on *Yeoman of the Queen*. She was left with time on her hands and no profitable channel into which her abounding energy might be directed. There was thus plenty of it to spare for her friends; and bursting one day into Patrickstown Hall, and coming on Bertie knitting his brows over the bill which had just come in for the removal of the palisade from his beech wood, she had promptly determined to intervene.

At her dictation—for Bertie was always more scared of the power at his elbow than of that which invisibly waited beyond—he had written to the contractor, disclaiming all knowledge of the bill and all intention of paying it. It was vexing enough, he obediently wrote, to have this fence popping up and down on his land like a Jack-in-the-box without having to meet the cost of the exercise. He could only suggest the contractor apply to those responsible for it, and remained, his faithfully. Bertie rather enjoyed writing this letter, in such contrast to his own communications, and he felt very stern and brave as he posted it off; but once it was done, and Amanda's hypnotic presence removed, he was seized with a terrible fright.

He **was** too fair to blame her for what he had consented

to himself, but worse was to follow. She next decided the time was ripe for a move against the doctor, and started to collect signatures for a protest, to be headed by his own. But now Bertie struck. Quailing, he told her frankly he could have nothing to do with it. The young man's father had been a good friend to his, the boy himself was a tenant of the estate and, as a doctor, neither better nor worse than what was commonly found in the Irish countryside. Amanda had taken his refusal very hard.

"No worse, Hubert!" she barked, "No worse, when it's only by the mercy of God and the fact that the Maryville chemist was sober for once that I'm still here today! No worse, when never a week goes by without some further proof of his bungling incompetence! The man doesn't know the difference between a wart and a tumour. Only the other day he gave poor Mrs. Craig a bolus fit only for a constipated mule and when she was nearly destroyed with it, he told her offer the agony up! And it isn't only the Protestants he goes for. Why, he's been treating one of the nuns at the convent for a burn on her ankle, and now it appears it isn't a burn at all but a mosquito bite gone septic! Canon Peart was telling him off about it. Surely you won't stand out, when the Canon himself complains? The pair of them are usually as thick as thieves."

But nothing she said had any effect: for once the little lord stood firm, and Miss Browne had retired in dudgeon.

Thus it came about that Mrs. Mangan, glancing at the road from an upper window on the morning after Andrew's return from Dublin, saw a curious charade in progress there. First, the little figure approached her door at a snail's pace: then it stood outside, its head bent, making complicated movements with its hands: then suddenly it turned on its heel and trotted rapidly away, only to come to a halt some distance off and look back over its shoulder, as if irresolute. Then the whole caper was repeated from start to finish, and again, and still again, until Mrs. Mangan could bear to see it no longer and she threw up the window.

"Good morning, my lord!" she called down.

Bertie gave a violent start. "Ah, good morning, good morning, Mrs. Mangan," he mumbled.

"A grand morning!"

"Oh yes, a grand morning, indeed."

"Thank God!"

"Yes, indeed, thank God for it. Indeed, yes."

Mrs. Mangan felt that she had stretched her end of things as far as she could, and that the next move lay with him. She leaned on the window-sill and smiled affably down at the worried little person below.

"Is . . . is Mr. Andrew Butler inside?" Bertie, fidgeting, presently steeled himself to ask.

"He is, my lord, and waiting on you! You'll find him in the parlour there."

"Is he busy? Writing, I mean? or anything of that sort?"

"Not that I'd know. He's come down here for a rest!"

"Ah yes, to be sure, a rest. I'll walk in, if I may. Thank you, Mrs. Mangan."

Bertie took the plunge and made his way to Mrs. Mangan's parlour where Andrew, with an incredulous expression on his face, was reading the Irish morning newspapers.

"Goo . . . good morning, Butler. Don't remember me, do you? I'm sure you do not. King's you know, and so on. Sent down, of course."

Andrew had already risen to his feet. "De Bolleyn!" he said, with real pleasure in his voice. "My dear fellow, what brings you to Patrickstown?"

"I live here," the other said, blushing with delight.

91

Andrew had certainly never called him his dear fellow in university days. "So you remember me! Fancy that, after all these years. You haven't changed at all."

Nor had de Bolleyn himself, Andrew thought with amusement, except that he no longer wore the flowing, scarlet-lined cloak with which at Cambridge he had stamped himself on the public consciousness. He was dressed now in a suit of white banin with nothing out of the way about it except for the button-hole, a simple meadow daisy, executed in rubies and pearls. Apart from the change in apparel, however, he was the same tubby little figure with the bewildered look on its face that Andrew remembered.

"I suppose . . . I suppose you wouldn't like to come up to my place? We could talk about old times. And I've got some books, heaps of books. A roomful of books, though not all very good ones. Rather too many French novels of the Victorian period. My grandfather was a great reader," Bertie eagerly fluted on.

"I'd love to come," Andrew replied. "You are kind, de Bolleyn. I've nothing in the world to do. Except wait for Judgement Day!" he added, lightly.

"Ah, yes, yes, I heard something . . . very distressing. Don't let it worry you. Ought we to tell Mrs. Mangan?"

"Mrs. Mangan?" Andrew asked, losing the thread, as Bertie's friends often found themselves doing.

"That you're with me. Luncheon and things. And dinner, if you're not too hideously bored. I mean, we could punt on the lake after luncheon," Bertie explained. "That is, if you wouldn't be bored."

They stopped on the way out to put Mrs. Mangan in the picture regarding Andrew's arrangements and went up the village street, chatting together like old friends. In fact, between the hotel and the great iron gates of Patrickstown Hall, they probably said more to each other than in all the years they had been in college together, so glad were they both, for different reasons, of the company. But as Bertie turned aside at these gates and swung them back for Andrew to enter, he pulled up in surprise.

"Is this your place, then?" he exclaimed.

"Yes, quite right, you see, I live here. . . ."

"Then you are . . ."

"Patrickstown, that's it. Of course, you didn't know. I mean, I wasn't in those days. Welcome, and so on, you know," Bertie said, much pleased with the little effect.

They walked up to the house together in the cool shade of an avenue of great trees. Andrew allowed his friend to pipe away to his heart's content without interruption. He himself was deep in thought: from time to time a mischievous light danced in his eyes, ordinarily so solemn and calm; and if Felim Plunkett could have seen into his mind at that moment, nothing he found there would have surprised him at all.

Bertie led him up to the drawing-room and sat him down while he busied himself with decanter and glasses.

"We ought to have a little drink, you know," he chirruped. "I mean to celebrate and er . . . celebrate, you know. Old Irish custom, and that sort of thing."

"Patrickstown!" began Andrew gravely, when they had pledged each other's health.

"Bertie, Bertie!"

"Bertie, then," Andrew continued, in the same tone as before. "There is something that perhaps you ought to know. This is not the first time I've been in your grounds."

And he recounted the whole story of Midsummer Eve, while Bertie's eyes grew wider and wider and an expression of mingled annoyance and relief came over his face.

"Upon my soul!" he cried when Andrew had done, "that

was very wrong of La Trobe, very wrong indeed. What a naughty fellow he is! What a thing to do, with nuns in it, I mean. Everything in Ireland is tricky, but nuns are the trickiest of all. And they are entitled to our respect. I can't have my land used as a jumping-off place for insulting nuns, you know. And the results of it have been most unfortunate."

"To say the least," Andrew concurred.

"No, no, I didn't mean your affair, although that must be tiresome enough. But I mean, I got into awful hot water too, and I mean, I have to go on living here, what? Look at this," he cried, leaping up and running to fetch the file of correspondence with the Mother Superior: "see what I got into, all through that naughty fellow La Trobe. I couldn't make it out: I thought Reverend Mother was mad, or I was. In a way I'm glad it's all cleared up, I mean, from the point of view of one's sanity and so on, but it's a shocking affair all the same. And I simply can't fall out with them. You see . . ." he hesitated. "I . . . I . . . er . . . Andy!" he appealed, in tones of the deepest distress.

"Yes?"

"Did you know that I . . . no, of course you didn't!"

"Know what, chuckle-head?"

"That I . . . well, I mean . . . that is," said Bertie, somewhat reassured by the epithet, "I became a Catholic, you know!"

"No, I didn't know," Andrew agreed. "What of it?"

"*What of it?*"

"It's no one's business but yours, is it?"

"It seems to be everybody's business here. They'll hardly speak to me," said the little lord, piteously. "Then you at least don't mind?"

Andrew felt his brain reeling again, as of recent times had become its practice. "Of course I don't mind!" he cried in exasperation. "Why on earth should I mind? Is Ireland a gigantic lunatic asylum or what? I believe that never in my life before have I heard so much nonsense talked, or in so fervent a manner. Give me those letters," he continued, taking them out of Bertie's hand; but no sooner had he read them through than he flung them aside with a howl.

"Flesh and blood can't bear it," he said, forcing himself to speak calmly. "Not my poor Saxon flesh and blood, anyway. Fences going up and down. Vanishing bonfires. Nothing that is, is: all that isn't, devoutly believed in. Died for, probably. I'm going out of my mind."

"Have another little drinkie," Bertie suggested. "That's what we all do here. Well, at least, I can write to Reverend Mother now and explain it."

He was so happy to find that Andrew was not disgusted by his revelation that his other troubles for the moment receded.

"I think I've got a better idea," Andrew said. "Why don't you write to the Canon himself? Tell him what La Trobe did. Say how deeply shocked and sorry you are about it, and ask him to put things right for you with the Mother Superior."

The simple-hearted little fellow gazed at him with deep admiration. "I think that's very good advice," he exclaimed. "Let us do it at once and you can tell me what to put. I'm no good at all at writing letters: I always tend to say the opposite of what I mean, you know."

For the second time in a week his lordship sat down at this desk and penned a letter at someone else's dictation. The letter was short and civil but framed with an awful cunning so as to give the impression, without actually telling a falsehood, that Bertie had seen Mr. La Trobe on his wall with his own eyes. Andrew leaned over the back of Bertie's chair as he wrote innocently on, pausing now and again to ask how to spell a word, and at the end heaving a sigh of satisfaction.

"I could never have done that by myself," he said, contentedly. "Ineffectual, you know. I count for absolutely nothing here. Very different thing with my father. People shook in their shoes when he opened his mouth. That's him there," pointing to the portrait of a young man, with steely eyes and the jaw of a prize-fighter, wearing the full dress of the Household Cavalry, "rather funny, what? I mean, heredity and so on, all bosh, I suppose. He never thought much of me."

Andrew found the simplicity with which he made these admissions curiously moving. At the same time he became aware of the changes Bertie had undergone since they had met. The blithe dotty little character of Cambridge days, a familiar joke even to lots of people who had never actually known him, had given place to another, still absurd and engaging but with a new and melancholy sweetness of its own. This difference was felt the more sharply because of the setting in which Andrew now saw him. He had never been one to interest himself in the family histories of other undergraduates, and to find this little figure of fun in the role of local bigwig had greatly surprised him. Bertie seemed physically lost in his surroundings, mentally at sea in the circumstances of his life, and the pathos of his gentle acceptance of the situation aroused Andrew's compassion.

"There are different ways of counting, you know," he suggested.

"Now Andy, I wonder if you are right? Not as regards this country, I think. If you want to count in Ireland, people must be afraid of you and," Bertie revealed, "no one was ever afraid of me. Of course, I don't want them to be. And for my part, I am terrified of almost everyone. I suppose it's a complex or something of that sort."

Andrew could think of nothing to say to this, and Bertie went on, "I am so fond of the people here, you know. Of course I know there's nothing to be said for them, but it doesn't seem to make any difference. I should love to help them all if I could. . . ."

But now an appalling din broke out in some far-away quarter of Bertie's ancestral home and, with a cry, he sprang to his feet.

"Luncheon already!" he cried. "Do you mind if we go in at once? I've got my old nurse stopping here for a few days, and the poor dear lives for her food, you know. If I'm only a minute late, she says it's too bad of her to upset my arrangements and something on a tray would have done very nicely. So come on, Andy, there's a good fellow," he urged, fleeing towards the door, "I mean, we've trouble enough, haven't we? Without vexing poor Nannie, and that kind of thing?"

NINE

THE golden sunlight continued to pour down on the little village. Day after day the skies were free of cloud; everything danced and shimmered in the heat: the dogs moved uneasily from patch to patch of baking ground or lay on their sides with dripping tongues and heaving flanks. Some of the young men had gone so far as to walk about stripped to the waist in a most unchristian manner, and all the people were burned in a lovely range of colours from honey to bronze. With these external changes, moreover, had grown apace and still more markedly those inward ones, so profoundly disquieting to authority, which have already been noted. There was a gaiety in the air, a spirit of lightness and mockery abroad, quite alien to the Irish soul, a damp and melancholy thing, lover of darkness and confusion.

It revealed itself horridly in the affair of Cat's-Eye O'Keefe and the ghost. Returning to rest one night after saying the rosary together with a few old friends, Cat's-Eye had seen a ghost coming out of the parish hall. Such, at least, was his account of the matter. In fact, he had been very drunk indeed, more so than usual, blundering along by the cold white light of the moon with the road rising and falling before his eyes like the waves of the sea. He had paused to admire his reflection in the duck-pond, and to address a few dignified words of greeting, as one patriot to another, to the statue of Corney O'Malley; and it may well have been that one or other of these images translated itself in his heated brain to emerge as the white-clad figure that, he was to insist over and over again, he saw flitting down the steps of the Canon's hall. He could give no very exact or coherent description of the ghost beyond that it was like the man in a Greek statue, but as to his having seen one, he would admit of no argument.

In this, he was simply playing true to form. Cat's-Eye was known in the village both for the odd things that happened to him in his cups and for the sturdy way he clung to his interpretation of them after he sobered up. A famous example of this, and one still narrated with glee, was when he offered to fight the village pump for refusing to tell him the time. Cat's-Eye would never agree he had been mistaken in this and would always adduce to the yarn a piece of evidence that struck him as final.

"Pump, is it? and didn't the feller say, loud as bells, 'I haven't me watch about me and if I had, 'tisn't you I'd be getting it out for!' " he would snort contemptuously. "Didjever hear a pump come out with a mouthful like that?"

The awful thing in this latest adventure of the detrimental O'Keefe was the attitude of the village. To a man, it accepted the ghost entirely. That sedate and reliable matron, Bridget Foley, informed Father O'hOgain of the occurrence with a perfectly straight face: with even a little breathless nervousness in her manner of speaking which showed her the possessor of real artistic gifts. As far as the inhabitants of Patrickstown were concerned, the Canon's hall was officially haunted; and it followed from this that simple Irish peasants like themselves, barely able to write their names, could not be expected to attend a dance in it. Apart from a dozen obligingly bought by his lordship, the tickets remained unsold; and the Canon all but foamed at the mouth.

He was never the man to allow the grass to grow under his feet. No sooner had he determined on the dance than all was put in train for its preparation. The tickets, the posters were printed: the application for an extended license was in: Paddy McGuire's band was bespoken, and it was a fresh proof of the temporary ascendancy of Satan that the Canon had not after all been able to get it for nothing. Ten guineas for Paddy, whether the band played to an empty hall or no; a printing bill for over five pounds: not a penny piece coming in and, worst of all, a kind of general suppressed hilarity over the whole affair that the Canon sensed without being able precisely to track it down.

"That's what comes of making concessions!" he thought, grimly, and resolved to be wiser in future.

He preached on the matter, with his customary vehemence, the Sunday after it happened. With a prudent eye to his weekly supply of trout, he forebore to denounce O'Keefe himself in the way he deserved; but he gave his flock an impartial basting for their ignorance and credulity. He bid them think shame of themselves for being no better than black men and heathen. How often must he tell them they were to eschew all superstitions, save those approved by Holy Church? So there was a ghost in the parish hall, wasn't that right? And did they really suppose that a ghost, that knew what was good for it, would venture to set foot in a building that belonged to himself? Wasn't he between them and all harm? It grieved him to say so, but the parish was going to the Devil as fast as it could. He would continue killing himself to save it, but doubted it might be too late.

This sermon, like the other, had no effect at all. In truth, his Reverence had gone a little too far; he had somewhat over-egged his pudding. And, although not a soul in the parish realized it, there was a curious private reason for the extravagance of his words. The poor Canon was horribly frightened of ghosts himself. He railed at his subjects for a weakness he was all too conscious of sharing and could never, from that day on, pass the hall after dark without involuntarily quickening his steps and feeling his pulses hammer; and even at times, safe in the parochial bed, he would suddenly think about it and dive underneath the clothes.

As if this sea of troubles were not enough, there must needs arrive on the top of it the letter from Lord Patrickstown. It was nothing less than a bombshell. The effect of it on the Canon was all that Andrew had foreseen that it would be; and could Bertie have somehow been present while he read it, he would never again have complained that he counted for nothing in local affairs. It was bad enough that something had happened to put his lordship out of humour, for the Canon saw the day approaching fast when he would have to seek a little special assistance in that quarter. But what was worse, what really terrified him even while it did not surprise, was the realization that La Trobe had been up to his tricks again and that there was more, although he could not imagine what, in the convent business than he had been allowed to know.

Small wonder, then, if the Canon began to feel like some noble stag at bay, facing a pack of snarling, worrying curs. But, except when ghosts were in it, he was a man of firmness and courage, and he rallied himself almost at once.

First he went stamping up to the convent and tackled the Reverend Mother. Up to the present time he had not discussed the law-suit with her, nor did he intend to do so now. He had deemed it sufficient to inform her that there had been no leaping of bonfires in her garden on Midsummer Eve: he had further, to tie up the loose ends, corrected the doctor's diagnosis, and indeed the patient's own, in the matter of Sister Conception's ankle; and that, he reckoned, would have to do.

"I've a letter here from Lord Patrickstown, complaining of certain matters," he began. "Perhaps, Reverend Mother, you'll tell me how you came in correspondence with him."

"I wrote to him, certainly, Canon," she replied, nervously. "I'm responsible for the convent, amn't I? I couldn't have him up on the wall, spying on the nuns and laughing at them?"

"And when did he do that? What did he laugh at?"

The Mother Superior hesitated. A nice problem of etiquette presented itself: she knew now, as a matter of doctrine, there had been no leaping of bonfires on Midsummer Eve, but she did not know how the matter should be discussed between themselves.

" 'Twas the night the nuns didn't leap the fires," she faltered at last.

The Canon took the point at once. "But what made you think it was his lordship, Reverend Mother?" he asked, a shade more kindly. "Was it his own voice at all?"

"I never heard his voice in me life, Canon," she answered with dignity. "But whose else could it have been? There on his own wall? I wrote to complain him, all right: I'm sure I'm very sorry if I did wrong."

"It seems to have been a trespasser from the village all the time," the Canon informed her. "Didn't he tell you so in his reply?"

A bewildered look passed over the nun's face as she remembered the letter from Bertie.

"I couldn't make head or tail of what he told me, Canon," she admitted. "There was nine pages of it and divil a word of sinse. He seemed to think he had done harm all right, but that I was mixed up in the time of day. Will I show you the letter?"

"Ah no, it's done now, Reverend Mother," the Canon said. "Don't mind him! But he's a good friend to us all, isn't that right? Could you send him a bit of a note, you're satisfied there's been a mistake?"

"I could, of course, Canon," the Mother Superior agreed at once. "And 'tis glad enough I'll be to do it. His lordship's a good friend, all right. Now everything can go on as before."

As soon as Canon Peart had left her, the good soul went to the chapel and, falling on her knees, asked pardon for her hasty judgement and gave thanks that she had been mistaken in it. She entreated the Blessed Virgin not to let her go making a fool of herself again and spoiling the convent's chances. Then she retired to her office and wrote immediately:

DEAR LORD PATRICKSTOWN,—The Canon is after visiting and told me of the mistake I made in regard to yourself, for which I most humbly ask your forgiveness. I am giving instructions, the fince can go up as before. No doubt the contractor will agree to a favourable price, as we've been putting quite a bit of work in his way!

All here will continue to pray for you.

Having finished this and sealed it up, she dropped a line to the contractor.

The Canon next went to call on Mr. La Trobe at his house. It was too far to walk in the sun and he did not want to get his motor out; and so he hailed young Malachy Lynch, whom he caught in the act of driving away with his milk-can to the creamery. The half-witted youth was overjoyed at the suggestion that he wheel about and drive six miles in the other direction. They jogged off together in silence, the Canon having first spread a large white handkerchief over his head and neck and clapped his biretta on top of it. Slowly the milk turned to cheese in the baking can.

Patsy lived in a pretty Georgian house with his mother, to whom he was tenderly devoted. The house was large enough to serve both as dwelling and office, and the solicitor had his plate up beside the front door. It bore the legend: La Trobe, La Trobe, Finkelstein and La Trobe: or rather, had borne it, for two thick lines had been engraved across the name of Finkelstein. When Patsy had finally seen that Mr. Finkelstein did not quite come up to the requirements of the firm, he would not have a new plate made but simply crossed the offending name off the old one, where it stood, a shameful testimony to its owner's incompetence.

Patsy was out in the garden now, helping his mother to pick the caterpillars off the cabbages and drop them in a jar of salt water. His fingers were green with their juice, and every now and again he would trot over to the old lady as she worked her row and proudly show her the number he had collected. A little cloud passed over his sweet face when the maid came out to say the Canon was waiting inside. He was not in the mood for talking business, particularly business that wasn't going any too well.

There still had not been a sign of life from the *Daily Packet,* not even a formal acknowledgement of his letter. Their lack of courtesy pained and shocked him. On the other hand, he had received from Felim Plunkett that

morning a short note to say he had been instructed by
Dr. Andrew Butler in the suit between the Canon and
him, and that a defence would be entered in due course.
He at once got on to Felim by telephone and asked if he
knew that his client was a lunatic. Felim cheerfully replied
that the same was true of all his clients: no one went to law
unless he was deranged.

"Ah go on now, Felim, seriously!" Patsy had urged. "The
man's after coming out of a Home!"

"Then he ought to do well in Ireland!" came in Felim's
gay voice.

"Yes, but Felim dear! listen, man, for your own sake.
You'd be wise to leave this case alone," Patsy went on.

"And why would that be, Patsy dear?"

Patsy thought quickly. "I've reason to think," he said,
lowering his voice to a portentous undertone, "that His
Grace himself is interested in the matter."

"Is that right?" Felim inquired. "Well, that's a pair of us
anyway: for, just between ourselves, so am I."

With that he hung up, leaving Mr. La Trobe a prey to
the darkest misgivings. Was it possible, he wondered, that
the English writing fellow was not such a fool as he looked?
How had he come to fly, as a bird to its nest, to the one
solicitor in Dublin that Patsy dreaded to see against him?
What powerful, subversive interests could he be in with,
to put him on a bold stroke like that? Was he a Mason!
Would someone put up the money? The Orange Lodges?
Could it be that this case was not going to be the straight
easy ride home he had promised his reverend client?

There were other anxieties as well to darken the horizon
for Patsy. On receiving Butler's impudent note, he had
set to work, in a purely tentative way, to draw up a list of
witnesses. Half a dozen should do, he thought; and all that
was required of them was to swear in the box that they had

never heard of any bonfires at the convent and to declare that, if there had been, it was impossible it should not have come to their ears. They would also of course be expected to say that a better priest than the Canon never trod shoe leather, but that was a secondary matter. Was it so much to ask, in the cause of religion? But to his amazed disgust, the villagers had proved very sticky. They had displayed a passion for absolute truth he had never observed in them before. It wouldn't be well for them, they demurred, to be saying things like that, and the Holy Name brought into it. Patsy had been obliged to cross out the names of the six leading citizens he had written down and replace them with six of inferior calibre: these in turn had proved a disappointment and he had gone on working methodically down through the village. At present there were only two names on the list: one, a man of whose farm Patsy held the mortgage, the other, a drunken idler and good-for-nothing who agreed for the sake of a ride to Dublin. A nice state of affairs for a Christian parish! And the trouble was, he could not afford to coerce them, for the elections were coming on and he had determined to stand for the Dáil.

He rose to his feet with a sigh. "The Canon's here, Mammy, I'll have to go in," he called across to the old lady. "Will I keep him to dinner afterwards?"

"You will not," replied Mrs. La Trobe briskly, without looking up.

By the time Patsy had washed his hands, combed his hair and changed his jacket, he was his confident happy self again. He came with elastic tread into the office where the Canon, with a brow of thunder, was tearing the petals from the marigolds in a bowl on the table and scattering them on the floor. Knowing himself no match for the other when it came to finesse, the priest decided to take the bull by the horns.

"Well now, La Trobe, this is pretty work!" he began explosively. "What were you about on the convent wall on Midsummer Eve?"

The solicitor seated himself and, taking up an ivory paper knife, gently patted his left palm with it: it was as near as he ever came to betraying uneasiness.

"Surely, Canon, you'll not mind everything that writer fellow says?" he remonstrated. "Because he'll say an awful lot before we finish him."

"Who said anything about the writer fellow?" retorted the Canon, swiftly. Years of experience in the confessional had given him a certain adroitness in examination. "You were seen there by Lord Patrickstown himself."

Patsy looked startled, but recovered at once. "May I ask how you know that?" he queried, sweet as honey.

"Didn't I get a letter from him this morning?"

"This morning? Three weeks after it happened? That's interesting, very interesting. Because I happen to know that the writer fellow spent the whole of yesterday up at the Hall. Would it be some kind of put-up job between them, now? Ah, but don't let it worry you, Canon," Patsy said in his most soothing manner. "When it comes to the point, his lordship will never speak against us."

"You and I wouldn't know what gentry will do," said the Canon, with brutal frankness.

"He's a Catholic, Canon!"

"He's a convert, you mean," amended the Canon, sourly. "God knows what he mightn't get up to. He might think it was his duty or some such tommy rot. And you still don't answer me, La Trobe. I want to know why you were there."

Patsy laid the paper knife down, folded his little hands and gave his client a long look that was positively angelic in its innocence.

107

"Shall we say, my dear Canon, I was just satisfying myself that the nuns were not leaping fires?"

"We will not!" roared the priest. "The article wasn't written then! The point never came up! God bless us, they *could* have been leaping fires at that time, for all I cared!"

"Yes, Canon," Patsy said, very blandly indeed. "So they could!"

The Canon glowered across the table like a truculent bulldog.

"I am not satisfied, La Trobe!"

"Then Canon," said Patsy, with real sorrow in his voice, "I can only suggest I withdraw from the case."

"The sooner the better!"

"Very well, Canon. If you'll kindly name my successor, I'll make the necessary arrangements. But while I'm still advising you," Patsy continued, regretfully wagging his head, "I'm bound to warn you, your position becomes much more difficult."

"How so? How so, La Trobe? How does it become more difficult, eh?"

"Because, once I'm out of it, the other side will be free, if they so desire, to call me as a witness."

The Canon all but leaped from his chair. It really seemed to him as if the gates of hell had opened and he could hear the dreadful laughter of the fiends inside: a sensation as familiar to the clients of Mr. La Trobe as to his adversaries, or even, perhaps, more so.

"You'd do that, La Trobe?" he asked, thickly. "Speak against me? Me own solicitor?"

"But I wouldn't be your solicitor, Canon. And the law is the law."

"The law is the law! A grand way for a Catholic to talk!" But the Canon knew he was beaten. He was yoked in frightful matrimony to this monster until the end of the road.

His great grizzled head was slowly sinking, like the head of a bull in a *corrida* too fast and furious for him. When next he spoke it was in a tone, for him, strangely subdued.

"And what'll we do then, La Trobe? What'll we do?"

"May I take it, you wish me to continue acting for you?"

The Canon lifted his two enormous hands helplessly in the air and let them fall again.

"Well, now, Canon, there's any number of things we can do. And first I'm going to make a little admission. I'm not perfect," Patsy very fairly owned. "I'm not infallible, Canon. And 'twas a bad mistake I made there, letting you join the writer fellow in the action. Oh, I ought to have known the scribbling fraternity better. Gestures and attitudes and nothing behind them, so they've nothing to lose. But when you've made a bad mistake, what do you do? Why, you put it right, of course. And that's what I'm going to do now, with your permission."

"You mean, we should climb down?"

"Settle, Canon, settle," Patsy corrected him, wincing a little at the crude expression. "You give me a free hand with the fellow and I'll settle him on the best terms I can get."

"And he mayn't agree at all."

"He will, the way I have in mind. I know writers," said Patsy, basing this belief on an occasional evening spent in the journalists' bar in Dublin. "He'll be delighted. Oh, I'll have him out of this before you can turn round! And then, as regards the paper, Canon. We'll have to give them a bit of a prod. They think they can laugh at yourself with the Irish Channel between us! I'll have to get leave in the High Court to serve a writ outside the jurisdiction."

"Another writ!" moaned the Canon.

But his powers of resistance had come to an end: he was wax in the monster's hands. Before he left the solicitor's office, he had signed instructions to Patsy to make the application in the High Court: better than that, he had promised a further cash payment with a few days and even, in a kind of delirium, complimented the little man on his handling of the affair. In the hall he hovered as long as he could, his nostrils tickled by a most delicious smell coming from the kitchen.

"And you didn't bring your car!" Patsy marvelled, looking up and down the road outside. "And there's divil a yoke that might bring you back! It's a bit of a walk you have in front of you, thirsty work in this weather. I only hope, when I'm your age, I'll be half the man you are, Canon."

And shaking him warmly by the hand, he gently closed the door.

"And what did the old boy want wid ye?" asked Mrs. La Trobe, tucking her napkin under her chin, as they sat down to luncheon.

"God help us, the usual blether," Patsy replied, busy with the carving knife. "Will I give you the wing or the breast, Mammy? The breast looks lovely today. And wait till I cut you some more of the ham. There now, eat away at that. Sure, we need all our strength in shocking times like these."

TEN

THE following day was signalized by a gathering of the brothers La Trobe. Patsy was the head of this flourishing practice, his house the nominal headquarters; but in fact the two brothers Brendan and Kevin had sub-offices of their own at strategic points in the county, whose affairs among the three of them they had nicely tied up. On grave occasions Patsy would send for them, remarking that three heads were better than one; and the news that they were converging never failed to strike a chill into even the stoutest hearts in the neighbourhood.

The interesting thing about their conclaves was that so little was actually said. Among three spirits so wonderfully attuned to each other, discussion was almost unnecessary. They merely exchanged glances out of the beautiful, dreamy eyes that all had in common. The conference today was no exception to this rule. Patsy outlined the position that had arisen over the Canon's lawsuit and explained that the English fellow was to be got out of it; and there was a little pause.

Brendan was the first to speak. "A half," he said.

There was another pause, and Patsy said, "Kevin?"

Kevin cocked his head to one side and answered, "One-third."

Another short silence followed, and Brendan declared, "'Tisn't the moment for paring cheese."

Patsy turned it over in his mind and then, in his capacity of chairman, gave a ruling. "Start at one-third, and you may go to the half." He appointed Brendan to see to the matter, gave a few more brief instructions, and the meeting was over.

A few days later Patsy entered the Four Courts in Dublin to make his application to serve the writ on the *Daily Packet* in England. He was again spruced up in black jacket and striped trousers, with a flower in his buttonhole, and he was dealing out to left and to right the winning smiles that made him such hosts of temporary friends. The application came before Mr. Justice (Heigh-ho) D'Arcy, an implacable anticlerical and the brother of a Bishop. No sooner had the learned gentleman grasped who the plaintiff was than he knew it would have to be granted. For this reason he made great play with the documents, reading them through very slowly and carefully with a comical look of importance on his monkeyish face and raising a little point wherever he could.

"Isn't it rather early days to be taking this step, Mr. O'Sullivan?" he inquired, peering at Counsel over the rims of his spectacles.

"My lord, it is nearly a month since we sent the newspaper our letter," Mr. O'Sullivan replied, bowing so low that he nearly fell over.

"Twenty-four days," said the judge, glancing down. "Perhaps the editor is too busy to open his correspondence?"

A burst of sound greeted this remark, the sort of high,

throbbing, wailing cry that used to come floating out of dental surgeries in the days when laughing-gas was used. It issued from Mr. La Trobe who had chosen in this way to mark appreciation of the judge's wit. Mr. Justice D'Arcy smiled his thanks, and continued.

"At all events, we should hardly expect the editor to attend to the matter himself. In the circumstances, I cannot think that the period elapsed constitutes any unreasonable delay."

"My lord, we have not had so much as the courtesy of a formal acknowledgement," said Mr. O'Sullivan, emotionally. "And my reverend client has a reason for wishing the matter dealt with expeditiously."

"I never knew a client, reverend or otherwise, who hadn't," observed the judge, stealing a look at Patsy who rewarded him with another hideous outburst.

"My lord, this whole affair has been a terrible grief to him; and he is no longer young," cried Mr. O'Sullivan, his voice trembling.

"What age a man is he?"

Mr. O'Sullivan turned to Mr. La Trobe and frantically whispered something: Mr. La Trobe feverishly whispered back.

"Sixty, my lord."

"That's very young indeed these days," said the judge sharply, adjusting his wig in a self-conscious manner.

"My lord, he has all the care of a parish on his shoulders," Mr. O'Sullivan proceeded, throwing his shoulders back and clutching the sides of his gown. "He is the best type of Irish Catholic priest, humble, zealous and charitable, loved by all in the parish and, indeed, far beyond its confines. He enjoys the absolute confidence of His Lordship the Bishop. In all his long years of toil in the cause of religion, none has ever dared . . ."

"I'm sure, Mr. O'Sullivan," the judge interrupted, "I should be greatly indebted to you for this statement, had I not seen the papers. As it is, perhaps you will take my word for it that I am able to read."

Mr. La Trobe's falsetto throbbed out again, wilder than ever; and Mr. Justice D'Arcy's severe expression relaxed.

"Leave is granted," he announced. Then, in a milder tone and with a sidelong glance at the reporters' table, "I wish to say, however, that in cases of this sort precipitation is to be avoided. Defendants must be given time to consider their position and we must be particularly sensitive in the matter when the defendants are foreign. It is no exaggeration to say that, when it comes to scrupulous fairness, our Irish Courts are an example to the rest of the world: let us, therefore, always be jealous of the high renown we enjoy in this respect."

Having noted with satisfaction that the reporters were all busily writing, he coughed and made out the order.

"Got 'em!" thought Patsy, and having wrung Mr. O'Sullivan warmly by the hand, he left the court in high feather. He walked happily across the Liffey to the Dolphin, where he enjoyed an excellent steak and some claret, and two helpings of tipsy cake, a dish of which he was inordinately fond. Next he went to a shop in Grafton Street where he set about choosing, with great care, a new hat for his mother. He narrowed the choice to two, one of honey-coloured velvet with pink roses peeping roguishly from under the brim, the other, more serviceable but not so attractive, of brown felt with a kingfisher's wing riding a-top; and he told the assistant to put both aside, the final decision to be made, after discussion with the interested party, by post. Then he looked at his watch to see what time remained before he must catch the train home. Will I go to a fillum? he mused: or will I do the Stations of the Cross instead?

He thought that if he went to a cinema it would be running things rather fine, and he turned into the Carmelite Church. Seeing the rapt expression on his beautiful face as he knelt before the first Station, an old lady who had dropped in for a few minutes to take the weight off her legs fumbled for her rosary, pledging herself at once to lead a better life.

One of the guns for Patsy's new attack was thus nicely mounted in Dublin; and down in the village no efforts were being spared to bring up the other.

The day had begun for Andrew with a telephone call from his solicitor.

"How's the Reformation progressing down your way?" Felim greeted him.

"We are doing well," Andrew replied, and went on to describe, with some complacency, his brilliant move in the matter of Lord Patrickstown.

"And his lordship actually wrote to the old boy?"

"I dictated the letter," said Andrew proudly. "Shall I tell you what we said?"

"Fire away."

Andrew recited the letter word for word as he had composed it; and from the other end of the wire came confused and smothered sounds as Felim strove to master his merriment.

"Look here, Butler! Wasn't it very naughty of you to suggest, as you clearly did suggest, that Patrickstown had actually seen your man at his wicked work?" he asked, as sternly as he could, writhing in his chair with delight meanwhile. "How's he ever to stand up to cross-examination?"

"Oh, we can't drag poor little Bertie into the thing. My idea," Andrew explained, "was simply to spread alarm and despondency in the enemy ranks."

"Listen to me, Machiavelli," said Felim, trying hard to

keep his voice steady, "there's to be no more of your ruses without prior consultation with myself, d'you see? The crookery of it! And no more correspondence, either. Understand?"

"Very well, Plunkett," said Andrew meekly. "But wasn't it rather clever of me?"

At this Felim broke down entirely. "You're coming along nicely," he crowed. "I thought you would. Ah, but I'll not rub it in! But see here, is there any chance you might be in Dublin again soon? because there are one or two things I'm none too happy about."

"What things?"

"Nothing I'd want to discuss over the telephone. But there's the question of Counsel."

"That's your business, isn't it? Engage him. I've every confidence in your choice."

"Engage him, says he!" cried Felim, bitterly. He had spent five whole days endeavouring to do just this. It was quite remarkable, how very busy the various members of the Irish Bar that he approached turned out to be, as soon as he explained the nature of the case to them. Mr. O'Sullivan, his best hope, had already been snapped up by Mr. La Trobe. "We may have to make do with a Protestant."

"Well, why not? All the better, I should think."

Felim groaned. "Why not, God help us! Well, will you come to Dublin?"

"Why don't you come here? Come for the week-end. It's looking lovely."

"All right, so. I can't manage the whole week-end. I'm going to see a yacht I'm thinking of buying on Saturday morning. But I'll drive down on Sunday morning and we'll talk things over then."

"Au revoir," said Andrew, and hung up.

So Felim was going to buy a yacht just when he, Andrew,

was trying to sell his. Andrew retired to his room with another mystery to brood over, namely, that of Felim's finances. This mystery had puzzled a number of first-class brains in its time. Felim was well known in Dublin, and indeed to all Ireland, as a man ever ready to do battle on behalf of unpopular things. He believed in justice for Protestants and fair play for Jews and nonsense of that kind: he defended writers, trade unionists and other riff-raff: he took on cases involving the clergy and really fought them. He was well aware of the dangers in what he did. "I've a case coming up now," he would sometimes ruefully remark, "that'll lose me five hundred a year, I suppose. But it can't be helped." Shortly afterwards the news would go round that he was removing to a larger house. Presently he would strike another resounding blow for truth and justice, cost him what it would: and the next thing, his friends would be receiving postcards from Monte Carlo, whither he had retired for a month or so to rest. There was no catch in it. Felim was all that he seemed to be: it simply chanced that truth and justice paid very handsomely, no doubt because he had the field more or less to himself.

Andrew's thoughts wandered on to his own little craft. There had been no acknowledgement yet of his letter to Guy Webster: very likely Guy was busying himself in the affair and when he wrote it would be to say a purchaser had been found. There would be no more of their trips then up the west coast of Scotland and round the islands. Andrew remembered the days they had spent together. He thought of the green and purple seas, the crisp sound of the boat cleaving the water, the lick-lick-lick of the ripples against her side as she lay at anchor, the play of light over the mountains on shore, the kind foolish faces of seals popping out of the sea in their wake at sundown, the fish they caught and cooked for themselves, the siestas on deck in the sunshine, the soft voices of Hebridean shoremen: all gone, he reflected, because he had been mug enough to do a good turn to a Mr. Esmé Pearl. Or rather, simply, because he had been a mug. Andrew did not always display the same keen intellect in dealing with worldly matters as he did in his work, his wits being somewhat dulled by whiggery and high principles. There was, he bravely recognized, quite a streak of the mug in his composition and now it had brought him to grief. Looking back, he could not see he had much to reproach himself with, but he had fallen innocently into a trap which the illiterate but warier Mr. Pearl would have seen and avoided. He must not put the blame on anyone else but simply carry things off as best he could to the end. But preach to himself as he would, the thought of his little boat and the happy times he had spent with her still tore at his heart all the morning.

After luncheon he retired to one of his favourite haunts, a tree on the bank of the river, where he lay on his back in the grass idly watching the patterns the foliage made against the sky and listening to the murmur of the stream as it flowed past. He was thinking of nothing in particular but simply enjoying the cool shade and the amenity of the place when all at once he found he was not alone. A man was standing beside him, with hands clasped behind his back and a look of the utmost benevolence on his face. That face, Andrew thought, he knew: it was one he should never forget: but what brought him up smartly, and with a clear sense of nightmare, to a sitting position was that it was placed a good three inches higher from the ground than memory told him it ought to have been. He stared at it in real distress for a moment, and then hesitatingly said: "Ah . . . Patsy?"

The man gave him a smile of ineffable sweetness. "Brendan!" he said. "Patsy's me brother."

"Aha!" said Andrew, much relieved. "So Patsy has a brother."

"There's three of us," answered Brendan. "Would you have an objection at all, Mr. Butler, if I was to sit down a moment with you?"

Without waiting for permission, he sat down with his back against the tree and, removing his hat, fanned himself with a meditative air.

"Isn't it glorious weather we're having, thanks be to God?" he proceeded. "Oh, I never remember anything like it before. You'd think we'd all got to Paradise already. And the countryside looking a picture. It takes a lick of the sun to bring out the colours in it. I imagine you're a bit of an artist as well, Mr. Butler, or am I wrong?"

"Have you made your way out here to satisfy yourself on the point?" Andrew inquired.

"Oh. you're sharp all right," laughed Brendan. "As a matter of fact there's a little matter we ought to discuss. I'm only waiting to catch me breath again."

"If it is anything to do with that brother of yours, he must approach my solicitor," said Andrew, primly.

"Wait now, let's not be in too much of a hurry," Brendan reproved him, with unruffled calm. "The little conversation we are about to have is entirely without prejudice."

"Anything your brother undertakes is singularly free from that," Andrew replied: "but if you were a solicitor yourself, you would know there is a form in these matters."

Brendan chuckled triumphantly. "I am a solicitor, so!" he said. "I've the laugh of you there, Mr. Butler. All three of us is solicitors. Now will you hear me out?"

"Well, I oughtn't to, but go ahead."

Brendan took out a gold case and offered him a cigarette.

"Ah come on now," he urged, as Andrew shook his head, "these are good fags all right. Did you think there was drugs in them? But please yourself. Now, in reference to this shindy about your article. You've probably got the wrong idea altogether about the sort of man me brother's client is. That man, now, he wouldn't harm a hair of a living soul if he could help it: he'd rather die! Why, I could tell you stories—true ones—of his kindness and goodness from now until kingdom come. And what's worrying him no end just now, between ourselves, is that you may have the impression he wants to be hard on ye."

"I haven't given the point a moment's consideration."

"Ah, don't be all stiff and English about it. We'll look at this in a sensible kind of a way, will we? He's been thinking the whole thing over meanwhile, the money 'twill cost you and the worry you'll be having—and you not long out of an institution—and says he to himself, 'How's this going to look on the Day of Judgement? The fellow's a human being for all he's a Protestant and a writer!' "

"I presume," said Andrew, in a classroom manner, "that this attractive preamble is leading to something?"

"Indeed, it is: and I'm coming to it," Brendan cried, eagerly, "we've a little suggestion we'd like you to think over. Let me emphasize again, *entirely without prejudice*. It's simplicity itself, that's the cream of the whole thing. Just do nothing at all: take no further steps in the matter: and you'll never hear another squeak about it till the hour of your death."

He leaned back against the trunk of the tree, beaming anxiously at his companion.

"You surprise me a little," Andrew informed him. "You just told me (and I confess I shivered to hear it) that you three brothers are all in the law. Must I really break it to a member of so distinguished a legal family that things are

120

not so easy as all that? You have served a writ on me: it's got to be answered one way or another. There's no dead letter department in the High Court, as far as I know."

"This is Ireland, Mr. Butler," said Brendan, with a patronizing air. "You'd be surprised what we'd do, when we put our minds to it."

"I wouldn't," said Andrew, "but I've noticed in Ireland a sensitivity—a remarkable sensitivity, when you think it over—to the outward forms and proprieties. What will you say? How shall you account for my absence from the suit?"

"Sure, we'll say you couldn't be found!"

Andrew clutched his head as his brain began to reel in the familiar fashion. "With me living here right under your noses?" he demanded, in a voice which held an unmistakable touch of awe.

"I'm not saying 'twouldn't be as well for you to move away!"

"I've listened to you, Mr. La Trobe," Andrew said shakily, "more from a professional interest in your modes of thought than anything else, I fear, but I have listened. And here is my crude, English reply. I will not leave Patrickstown nor will I change the instructions given to my solicitor. In due course the action will be fought. If your brother's client is unwilling to proceed with it, he must withdraw the proceedings against me and pay the expenses incurred up to now. I'm sorry if you are disappointed, but that is my last word."

Brendan was not disappointed at all, for it was just as he had expected it to be. He had been told to chance his arm in this way in case the English madman were cracking up, but his main argument, his trump card, was still to come. Now, leaning forward and lowering his voice to a honeyed murmur, he produced it.

"And what would you say, Mr. Butler," he cooed, "if we made it worth your while?"

"What on earth do you mean?"

"The paper isn't going to fight us, we know that. We've heard from them. There's three hundred pounds coming in! What would you say now to a hundred of that?"

Andrew stared wildly round the sunlit meadow, wondering if he were asleep. Then, feebly, he shook his head. "In the unlikely event of your really having just said what I think I heard you say, the answer is no."

"A hundred and fifty, then? A clean hundred and fifty? We'll pay your man off for you."

Andrew gave the same helpless wag of his head as before. "I should want the whole kitty, Mr. La Trobe!" he told him, very gravely indeed. "And a full apology to myself for the annoyance, in the local paper, on the front page and printed underneath a photograph of the Canon and the Reverend Mother side by side!"

"Oh I could never get you all that!" Brendan mourned. "We're trying to hush things up a bit, do you see? I might raise the money a bit, but not without further consultation. I was told not a penny piece more than one hundred and fifty. And I must say, Mr. Butler, you're a little unreasonable all the same. It's the fairest offer I ever made: fifty percent of the takings and, mind you, none of the bother!"

He gazed lovingly at Andrew with his head on one side, looking more like Patsy than ever. For the twentieth time Andrew wondered why these creatures did not disgust him quite as much as they ought. Brendan horrified and amused and touched him all at once in the same curious way as his brother did: they seemed to him like malignant children who yet possess an innocence all of their own: and when, pulling himself together, he spoke, it was as a father might, more in sorrow than in anger.

"After my first encounter with your brother, Mr. La Trobe," he said, kindly and steadily, "I truly believed I had struck rock-bottom. I thought I had plumbed depths of human infamy of which, until then, I had no conception. It seems I was wrong. A whole new layer remained beneath, waiting to reveal itself at a suitable moment. I shall be interested to see what fresh strata of roguery disclose themselves in the future."

"Yerra, that isn't a very pleasant way to talk, Mr. Butler!" Brendan complained, looking ever so slightly nettled. "And to the man's own brother, too! Ah, but don't let's be quarreling," he cried, with a sweet, confiding little air, "why wouldn't you do it, itself? Sure, we're trying to help you, and you won't be helped. Me offer still stands. Why won't you take it? Why?"

His bewilderment was perfectly genuine.

"Because, Mr. La Trobe," Andrew cried back, his voice rising to a shout of despair, "because—I'm—afraid—it—simply—wouldn't—do!"

He fell back on the grass exhausted, his long frame shaken by spasms of mirth. With a melancholy look on his face Mr. Brendan La Trobe got to his feet and silently moved away. Once he turned back to remark: "Without prejudice, mind! and of course if you were ever to mention this little talk of ours, we should have to deny it." With that he was gone. Andrew lay in a kind of stupor, with mad thoughts racing through his head faster and faster like waters gathering above a weir. The afternoon wore on and the shadows began to lengthen; and towards evening a passerby might have heard, coming from under the boughs of the tree, little occasional bursts of almost demented laughter. The impact on his mind of the little scene had been tremendous: he had made the small transition into a new mental state that many do who stay long enough in Ireland, had crossed over into territories of the soul from which, looking backwards, the familiar landscapes would always from now on wear a somewhat different and crazy aspect.

ELEVEN

THE morale of one of the principal characters in the drama was thus in very poor shape; and that of the other was fast tottering to a collapse. As a result of Patsy's brilliant two-pronged stratagem, the Canon first had to be told that it was no go and Andrew declined absolutely to retire; and almost immediately afterwards he found that he himself had become overnight a national figure.

The newspapers seized on the story of his action with the greatest delight. After months and months of drouth, of the bickerings in the Dáil, of remarks by visiting American senators about the iniquity of Partition, of rises in the cost of living and of pictures of newly ordained priests blessing their mothers, the pagan nuns of Patrickstown and their aggrieved defender fell on the parched columns like a delicious shower of rain. What editors lacked in the way of detailed information, they made up for by the size of their headlines and the prominent position they gave to the story; while the comments they dared not make were expressed in the manner of presentation. The observations of Mr. Justice D'Arcy were everywhere given in full; and a Protestant newspaper contrived, by a judicious use of heavy type at certain moments of Mr. O'Sullivan's pleading, to convey a world of skepticism and subversive glee.

When they had sucked the orange dry at the Dublin end, they dispatched photographers to the village. Then the public took to driving out there in the evenings with its supper in a basket, and the place was full of laughing strangers asking the way to the convent. As if by magic, a number of bees quietly biding their time in the national bonnet sprang to life with an angry hum. Parties in favour of stopping the sale of English newspapers in Ireland resumed their campaign with fresh spirit. Gaelic enthusiasts pointed out that if Ireland were only Irish-speaking, no one would understand what the English newspapers said and their cruel blows would fall on space. A nationalist body called for a law to be passed making it obligatory on all English visitors to wear a distinguishing mark, such as the Star of David once worn by Jews in Germany; and a confraternity in Limerick telegraphed the Prime Minister demanding that the clause in the Constitution which guaranteed equal treatment for all religions and creeds be amended. In Dublin two well-meaning ladies collecting signatures for a Peace Petition were stoned, amid furious cries of "Remember Patrickstown!": extra police were mounted at the British Embassy: and a thousand schoolchildren marched to the Archbishop's Palace, where they knelt and recited the rosary. Editorials appeared in pietist newspapers urging the faithful to remember the Penal Days and denouncing the intelligentsia. Publicly, all Ireland was up in arms: privately, all Ireland was hugging its sides.

The mystification that such behaviour gave rise to in Andrew's mind was deepened by the numerous letters he received, all of them except one, which asked for the loan of a hundred pounds and gave name and address in block capitals anonymous. Roughly, half of them were on his side and half on the other. There were a dozen or so simple, straightforward threats of murder. One frantic correspondent compared him to Judas Iscariot and informed him he would be better employed in calling off his Black and Tans, a pamphlet describing their atrocities, dated 1922, being enclosed. Another writer invoked the blessing of Heaven on him and uttered a fervent prayer that he would shortly deliver a slap in the gob to some more of those "smug, big-bellied bastards of Maynooth." Another urged him to go gravely and steadily forward in his great crusade, sparing no effort and regardless of the expense: this communication came, as a matter of fact, from the pen of Mr. Pasty La Trobe, but Andrew was not to know that. He sat in his little room, mulling them all over with a dazed look on his face and counting the moments till Felim should come to take care of him.

The Canon's post-bag was also heavy, and his letters too were divided in two camps as Andrew's were. He ploughed through them all, complacency alternating with rage, until he came to one (likewise from Mr. La Trobe) accusing him of "simony and jansenism." This unexpected, wanton and capricious attack was suddenly too much for him, pulled down as he was by the weight of publicity; and he informed his housekeeper, in an angry roar, that he was unwell and should keep his bed. She was to make him a basin of gruel for his dinner and he would see no one, absolutely no one at all, did she hear?

"Will I send for the doctor, Canon?" she faltered.

"Have sense, woman!" he thundered. "I said I was ill, not that I wanted to die!"

He stormed upstairs to his bedroom and slammed the door.

In the afternoon, however, he recovered himself suf-
ficiently to send for Father O'hOgain and discuss with
him a plan of campaign. It was agreed that the news of
his illness should be fed to the delinquent village in easy
doses. Today, it would be simply announced that he was
indisposed and that the curate was taking over the care
of the parish. Tomorrow, the intervening night having
been pain-racked and sleepless, he would be much worse:
the day after, his condition was to give rise to anxiety;
and on the following Sunday the charitable prayers of the
faithful would be solicited at both Masses for his recovery.

So much for the progress of the disease and the bulletins
concerning it. Besides attending to these, Father O'hOgain
also had a delicate work of propaganda on hand. The
whole must somehow be laid at Andrew's door; not content with insulting their nuns, the parish must understand,
he now was bent on hounding their priest to his death.
The curate set about his work with a will and his lanky
black figure was seen all over the place, with a whisper
here and a significant nod there, with innuendoes where
he was not too sure of his man, with forthright denuncia-
tions in quarters believed to be safe. But the little collective smile that played over the face of the village only
grew wider.

In despair, Father O'hOgain looked in on the Sergeant
of Guards. He found him in his office, with his tunic un-
buttoned and his feet resting on the table, reading a book
on the care of the Pig. At the interruption he looked up
in annoyance which changed, when he saw who the visitor
was, to assumed cordiality and genuine wariness.

"I'll not keep you a minute," the curate promised, "I
only wanted a word about the English fellow at Mangan's.
The feeling against him here is terrible!"

"Is that right, Father?" the Sergeant asked, in a wondering tone. "I wasn't hearing that at all."

"Ah, the people would talk to me where they mightn't to another," Father O'hOgain told him. "And I was thinking, hadn't you better get him out of this? For his own good, before there's any real trouble?"

"There'll be none. There's always people who'll look for mischief in any town," the Sergeant said, comfortably, "but I'll quench them! The fishing is at the divil with the hot weather and it's left them nothing to do but talk. But you don't want to mind them, Father. Sure, the people of Patrickstown don't believe what they say themselves!"

"All the same, I wish you'd get the fellow out of it."

"How in the world could I do that, Father? He's done nothing at all," said the Sergeant innocently.

"Nothing at all!" roared the curate, in a passable imitation of the Canon. "Don't you read the newspapers, man?"

"I do not. I'm rushed off me feet as it is!"

"So I observe," retorted the curate, looking at the Sergeant's great boots with sardonic amusement.

"If anyone breaks the law I'll hear of it fast enough," the Sergeant replied, unmoved, "But it's good of you all right, Father, to be so concerned for the fellow's health. An Englishman, too! I'm sure he ought to be grateful."

Father O'hOgain swept out of the room without another word, and the Sergeant happily took up the care of the Pig where he had laid it down.

As perhaps has emerged, the Canon's temperament was at no time of the more placid sort; and by now the reverses he had sustained in battle, the horrible and unforeseen consequences of Patsy's *démarche* in Dublin and, above all, the diet of arrowroot to which for the sake of appearances he was adhering, had transformed him into something like a demon. He lay in bed all day with the curtains drawn across his window panting with heat, the jacket of his mauve-striped pyjamas wide to display the tangle of fur on his great barrel of a chest, and roaring objurgations at his housekeeper in language anything but clerical. At the close of the second day Father O'hOgain timidly apprised him of the uphill work he was having with the parish and entreated him, for all their sakes, to see the doctor.

"He needn't be let do anything, Canon," his curate said, "but it might impress the people. They're in a queer old mood all right."

The proposal met with a further storm of complaint and abuse, but in the end Canon Peart gave way and the doctor was summoned.

"Mind now, he's not to stay more than a minute!" the patient growled.

The doctor came and sat respectfully on the edge of a chair while the Canon briefly explained the nature of his illness and his intentions regarding the course it should run. It happened that on this occasion his medical adviser was perfectly sober and brisk and aching to practise his art; and the attitude of his reverend patient disappointed him very much.

"Will I feel your pulse now, Canon?" he asked hopefully.

"You will not!"

The doctor sighed. "How do you feel in yourself? Are the bowels working?"

"It's no concern of yours if they're not!" the invalid barked. "And anyway there's nothing in them!"

"I hope you're not losing strength too fast. No food and no sleep together, that's a dangerous thing. You'd best let me give you a sedative, the way you'll be getting some rest," the young doctor urged him. "We don't want you falling ill."

"I am ill, I tell ye!" the Canon bellowed. "Seriously ill!"

"The more reason, so. Look, Canon, you sent for me and you should take my advice," the doctor said, boldly. "There's me reputation to consider, after all!"

"Well, all right, all right, be quick about it."

The doctor sprang at his bag and swiftly produced a vial of fluid and a hypodermic needle. Having carefully wiped a patch of the Canon's arm with disinfectant, he gave the injection with neatness and despatch, and, taking a step backwards, surveyed his handiwork with the greatest satisfaction.

"There now, I think that should settle you!"

As it turned out, he was perfectly correct in this surmise: for the Canon sank at once into a coma and did not come round again for forty-eight hours. It occurred to the doctor, when he was anxiously called again in the evening, that something very similar had happened to him once before. He could not account for it at all, unless he had mixed the doses up, but of one thing he felt quite sure and that was that no very great harm would result. All the big men in Harley Street were using deep narcosis now for nervous conditions: or so, at least, he had been given to understand.

"He'll be wonderfully quietened when he comes out of that, it wouldn't surprise me," he remarked, looking down at the unconscious figure on the bed. But in view of his patient's importance, he said it might be as well just to take a peep at the medical books; and he promised to visit again when this had been done.

The news streaked round the village that, as a result of having the doctor in, the Canon was now really ill; nor did it long remain in this simple unadorned state. The story that next went about was that the doctor had inadvertently given their priest a shot of a new Protestant drug for easing the pains of childbirth; and the smile on the local face grew to something very much like a grin.

Things had come to the pitch where it looked as if, for the credit of religion, the Canon would seriously have to think about passing away. Then something unforeseen took place which altered the picture and sent the little ship off on a fresh tack altogether.

Canon Peart regained his senses two days after the injection was given and, at eight o'clock in the evening, was sitting up in bed reading some comics that had been seized from the boys in the national school. He was somewhat bewildered by his involuntary vacation from life but on the whole, as his physician had foreseen, he felt wonderfully rested. Without consulting him, preferring to depend on her woman's instinct, his housekeeper brought him at tea-time not the prescribed bowl of slop but an ample and delicious meal of scrambled eggs, soda bread, barmbrack and honey; and this had induced in him a mood of serenity. When she suddenly reappeared in his room looking flustered and unhappy, he greeted her with something as near to a benevolent smile as his features could manage.

It vanished at once when she told him the Sergeant of Guards was below, was sorry indeed to intrude on a sick-room but must absolutely see him without a moment's delay. The Canon did not love the Sergeant, as being the representative of a power not spiritual and whose interest more than once had been successfully maintained against his own. In view of this urgent message, however, he sent word for him to come upstairs; and it was immediately plain to him from the man's demeanour that he had not exaggerated.

"I'm after getting a telephone call from the town, Canon," he said, with none of his usual, faintly ironic deference, "I'm afraid there's bad news all right. The

O'Shea boy's had a bit of ill luck. He fell from a scaffolding up at the works there this evening. They say his back might be broken, and that."

A hush fell on the pair of them when he had done speaking. The boy was the only child of his parents, who had married late in life, and he was everything in the world to them.

"A broken back, is it? That's an awkward kind of a thing to have," the Canon said, slowly.

"It is. They're not sure yet, we'll hear more in the morning," the Sergeant replied. He hesitated, fumbling with his cap. "The old people will have to hear something about it, of course. Will I go on up there, Canon? 'Tis a shocking long way. You'd never be able to stir in the condition you're in."

The Canon lay back on his pillows, his soul the field of a violent and terrible conflict. The path of his duty was clear before him: he must get up at once and go climbing the mountain to where, furthest from the village of any, the O'Sheas had their cabin. By so doing, however, he would avow to the whole parish the fraud that had been practised upon them. Father O'hOgain's carefully spaced-out bulletins would be seen and reviled for the shams they were. The gathering tides of ridicule, which he feared more than any hatred, would swell to a mightly flood and sweep away the remnants of his authority forever. He would take his place, with the doctor and Cat's-Eye, in the repertory of stock parish jokes. The warring impulses with him made him feel quite weak; it seemed to him impossible that he should go, equally impossible that he should stay.

"'Tis a shocking long road, Canon," the Sergeant repeated, avoiding his eye, "and with the condition you're in."

The Canon roused himself, like an old war-horse at the trumpet's call.

"Never mind the condition I'm in," he growled. "They've a right to hear it from me, I suppose?"

"Oh, God bless you," said the Sergeant. "I was hoping you might say that."

"Then go to hell out of this, would you?" his spiritual director requested, "till I put on me clothes."

"Will I walk with you as far as their door?"

"You will not. I've been out on me own before this."

The Canon dressed and, waving the remonstrances of his housekeeper aside, left the house. Before him was a climb that would take at least three hours, over some of the roughest ground in the country. He walked up to the top of the village street and struck off up a boreen that went for a bit and then petered out as if discouraged. After that he had to make do with the narrow rocky footpath when he could see it or stumble awhile over the tangled scrub and sharp stones until he found it again. The unwonted exercise made his heart pound and his head swim, and his clothes stuck damply to him: darkness fell before he was halfway up and although he had a torch the way in front was so strange and featureless he thought he should never arrive at his goal. His feet pained him from continually stubbing against the bits of rock: in spite of the long dry spell the mountain was soaking, and as the way is with Irish mountains, the higher he went the wetter it grew, until he found the water gurgling about his ankles and seeping over the top of his boots; and more than once he missed his footing and measured his length on the prickly ground.

A mood of intense self-pity took hold of him. Ah, he was good enough for them in a bit of trouble. They'd send for him all right to get up from his bed and meet his death on the mountainside when he was needed. But would they stand by him, when he wanted a bit of help in his turn? Not at all. As long as all went well for themselves, they'd never mind him in the world. He was only there to spoil their sport and make himself disagreeable. Bridget MacCarthy now, the boldness of her! Did they imagine he enjoyed hunting a bit of a girl that? Was it that that had turned them against him? He had to think of the good name of the parish, had he not? Wouldn't he just as soon be chucking her under the chin with the rest of them? But no sooner was the thought in his mind than, appalled by it, he asked forgiveness and recited a Hail Mary. The Devil was out and about all right, trying to grab him, in the desperate state he was in. All the same a priest's life was hard enough, a lonely, bitter thing and there wasn't a soul alive he could tell his troubles to.

As if in mockery, a bramble shot out a long, hooked, thorny arm and ripped his face. The Canon jumped with the pain and dropped his torch, which rolled away down the hill for twenty yards or so. Down he had to go after it and, coming on it at last, kicked it furiously where it lay. Snatching it up again, he found he had knocked the life out of it. There was nothing to guide him now but the light of the moon which was slowly rising over the distant hills. Panting and groaning he fought his way up again, and the same wicked bramble lashed out and caught him once more. He was almost ready to cry with rage and exhaustion.

But now he had come to a twist in the path and all at once these tormenting worries of his vanished and were forgotten. There above him not very far off, its white-washed walls gleaming pale in the moonlight, was the O'Sheas' cabin. With its lighted windows it had a happy, contented little air as if no one inside it could ever dream that sorrow was on the way. Canon Peart thought no more of his bleeding face, his aching limbs or his swollen tender feet. He stood for a moment or two staring ahead of him and passing a dry tongue over his lips: and then slowly and reluctantly he went forward. Outside the door he stopped again, and for longer; then, very softly he rapped on the door.

His task came even harder than he had expected and, if the truth is told, he did not make a wonderful job of it. He was more used to giving orders, making complaints or issuing reprimands and, in spite of the prayers he had offered just now in the darkness, he could not easily find the words he needed to bring comfort to breaking hearts. But he did the best he could, and the people in the cabin knew it and were grateful that he should have thought them worth the trying.

"One of us'll be up to you in the morning," he told them, finally. "We'll be coming with better news for you then, please God."

Old Mrs. O'Shea took down the china jar from the chimney-piece where she kept her poultry money and started feeling inside.

"Father would you . . . would you ever . . ." she began, in a trembling voice, but he at once and with impatience interrupted her.

"Put it away, put it away for God's sake," he muttered, almost savagely. "I can say a bit of a prayer without that, I imagine."

"There's the boy's bed all ready," O'Shea said. "Will you not stay the night with us? It's a long way all right to go twice in the evening."

Canon Peart hesitated. "I won't," he said at last. "You're best by yourselves just now. Father O'hOgain or myself'll be coming tomorrow. Good night for the present, and remember, they're not at all sure about him yet."

He shut the door and started limping down the painful road that led to home while, as soon as he had got a little way off, the first terrible cries of lamentation that Mrs. O'Shea had kept back in his presence came to his ears.

TWELVE

Wᴴɪʟᴇ Canon Peart was toiling up the moutain in the cause of duty, all at Castle Knock was joy and pleasure, mirth and song. The quarrel between Amanda Browne and Lord Patrickstown had been patched up, for the reason usual in small communities, namely, that the parties needed each other too much to continue it. For many years Amanda had published with the same firm in London and had always corresponded with a Mr. Angus Ferguson; and now she had received a note from this gentleman saying he was on holiday in Ireland and should very much like to call. He had proposed himself for tea on a certain date and she had written back at once, in the traditional style, to say that he must certainly stop with her for a couple of days.

Miss Browne was not the woman to squander her imaginative powers, which she reserved for her historical works. Beyond a vague speculation as to whether Mr. Ferguson were a brawny Highland chief who might presently be used as a model, she made no attempt to visualize the man who for so long had promptly and courteously, if also a little primly, answered her letters. She was at first taken aback by his appearance. He was a slender, youngish person with long white hands and a high-pitched giggle: his face was thickly coated, like that of an old actress, with a powder that seemed brown in some lights and purple in others: there was some doubt if the greenish tint of his eyelids was real; and he had a tendency to ramble on about Proust. His conversation and manners alike were something new in her experience, and she was at a momentary loss as to how to deal with them. Hardly, for example, had he been in the house for an hour when, on her asking, "May I show you round the place, Mr. Ferguson?" he had replied, with his giggle, "My dear, do call me Anguish, won't you? My friends all do."

Amanda saw there was nothing for it but to send for Bertie to come over as soon as convenient.

For his part, Anguish was highly delighted with what he found. He had been quite sure he knew what sort of lady Miss Amanda Browne would be and, before leaving London, had wittily entertained his cronies with impersonations of her. "Castle Knock" he took to be the name of a trim little villa with a small and carefully weeded lawn in front of it: Miss Browne herself was an intense and hungry maiden of forty-odd, surrounded by cats, dressed in handspun material and decorated by strings of coral beads acquired on holiday in Rapallo. When therefore the "natives," as he naturally called them, directed him to the massive ancestral home of the Castle Knock Brownes, and he noted the beautiful park, the flowerbeds, the stables, the walled garden crammed with delicious fruit: when he had had time to look about him inside the house and to savour its lavish train of life: and when, above all, he had been able to study the personality of his hostess, rakehelly as one of her own heroes, he decided he could not do better than spend the rest of his holiday here. He would dine out on it all over London on his return: for the time being, he was prodigal of compliments and assiduous in little attentions, such as the careful and exquisite arrangements of enormous bowls of flowers. By the time that Bertie, dressed up in his dinner jacket of midnight blue, arrived beaming for the party, Amanda was over her first surprise and Anguish was well dug in.

The evening was one of the most uproarious that even that seasoned old dwelling had witnessed for many a year. It was odd that it should have been so, for the ranks of the little party were swelled at the last moment by Amanda's cousin, Major "Fruity" Barlow. He had driven over à l'impromptu from Connemara and was not really the type of gentleman to harmonize with the other guests. Looking at his firm red face, short grey hair and military moustaches, one might have feared uncomfortable pauses at the dinner-table. But by one of those happy social accidents, he took to the company as if it were the kind he preferred above all others. Silent indeed he mostly was, apart from mighty roars of laughter and exclamations of "No, I say! dash it! that's a bit thick!" but his silence was of the jovial sort, proceeding rather from a close attention to victuals and drink than from disapprobation.

As the invitation had been for eight o'clock, Bertie of course appeared at twenty minutes past nine. Anguish was not familiar with this old Irish custom and, believing that time was short, helped himself liberally to the whisky that the butler handed round before the meal. When the little lord at last arrived, he was in a mood to be enchanted with everything and the information that this new guest had ridden over in his evening clothes sent him into ecstasies.

"My dear, you *haven't!* How absolutely splendid," he

chortled. "Oh, I think Ireland's too wonderful. Do you *always?*"

"Well yes, out to dinner, you know," Bertie replied. "The horse understands about getting me home, and things."

This revelation sent the publisher into fresh transports, while Fruity embarked on some reminiscences of the horses he had known and their sagacity in ticklish corners. Presently they went in to dinner. Miss Browne was an impressive sight at the head of her table, in a satin gown of peacock blue, her muscular arms bare to the shoulder and diamond rings in her leathery ears. One of her small eccentricities was a preference for dining always by artificial light. The curtains were drawn to exclude the fading gleams of day, while overhead the chandelier blazed and all down the long room the side-lights glowed under their rosy shades. On the sideboard was a magnum of champagne in an ice-bucket, with reinforcements drawn up behind in pleasant array.

"Glad to see that, Amanda," said Fruity, with the liberty of a relation. "Never saw champagne in a bottle till I got to England. Never saw claret in anything but a cask."

The dinner faithfully adherred to the accepted pattern of dinners in Irish country houses. To begin with, there was a nameless soup which defied all attempts at analysis and which was followed by an interval of twenty-five minutes. It was during this, with the champagne flowing freely, that Anguish sounded the Major for his views on art.

"Art? A bit out of my line, that sort of thing," said Fruity, with a doubtful shake of his head. "Don't even know what I like." A gale of merriment swept the others and, encouraged, he added in a choking voice, "Don't even like what I know!" Burying his face in his napkin, he laughed so much and his short neck deepened to so alarming a shade that Amanda was relieved when the butler reappeared with the next course and forced him to pull himself together. She was convinced that sooner or later one of Fruity's jokes would prove fatal to him and was most anxious that nothing should spoil her party tonight.

Now they had a salmon, for the obtaining of which the resources of the indispensable Cat's-Eye had once more been brought into play. It was followed by roast ducklings; but here again a hitch occurred, as the lights failed, according to local practice, just as the butler was handing the potatoes to Fruity. Patiently he waited, meanwhile resting the dish on Fruity's head; and when at last the service was restored and the lights went up, there Fruity sat, his honest red face crowned with Wedgwood, while the butler gazed upwards as if expecting a *fiat lux* from above. This little tableau created such a furore it hardly seemed anyone would have the strength to continue his dinner.

Only one awkward moment arose during the meal and it was quickly smoothed over. Fruity, assuming that he was with gentry, made a disobliging remark about Catholics and the little lord, in spite of urgent signals from his hostess, bravely piped up to say that he had joined them.

"You haven't! my dear, you haven't!" wailed Anguish, in tones of the deepest horror.

"Yes I have," said Bertie, miserably wondering if he must lose this scintillating new friend already.

"But it's no longer the thing at all!" Anguish moaned. "It's Vedanta or the Church of England now, no two ways about it. One or the other, or you're *absolutely out.*"

Fruity coughed. "Vedanta," he said, severely, and recalled a fella he'd known in India, long-haired type, never cut out for a soldier, went in for the Hindu stuff, left the regiment, deserted his wife and upset the commanding officer (decent a chap as ever drew breath) no end. But soon it all passed off in a fresh tide of champagne.

The ducklings were followed by a vast bowl of tipsy cake, into which both sherry and rum had been so unsparingly poured that merely plunging a spoon into it released a bank of gas sufficient to cause them all to lean back in their chairs. After that, and another long wait, the butler came in, looking sheepish, with a baking-tin in his hands full of a grisly, curdled, smoking mess.

"What's this at all, Michael?" asked Amanda, grimly. "Didn't I order a cheese soufflé?"

"You did, Miss Browne, of course, but the cook never made one before in her life."

"And why couldn't she tell me that?"

"Well now, you see, she's one to take a chance where another wouldn't," replied the butler equably, poking at the mess with a spoon.

"Oh, *Heaven!*" gurgled Anguish.

"Take it away" commanded the mistress of the house, "and bring on the brandy."

The brandy travelled steadily round the table and the night wore gaily on. Deep in conversation with Bertie, with whom she was privately overjoyed to be friends again, Amanda failed to notice that her other guests had fallen strangely quiet. When next she gave them her attention, it was to find Fruity fast asleep and breathing heavily, and Anguish in a heap under the table; and a look of stern disapproval came over her face.

"I knew the English couldn't drink," she snorted, "but I thought better of me own cousin. Well, Bertie, I suppose it's a day. How about your horse?"

"Oh, I left him saddled," Bertie said. "Always do, you know. Only thing to do."

"Then I'll say good night. I'll get little Lord Fauntleroy up to his bed. Fruity'll have to shift for himself."

Striding round to where Anguish lay senseless on the carpet, she hauled him out, swung him up over her shoulder in a fireman's lift and made easily for the door, declining the butler's offer of assistance. So many of her evenings closed in this way that she knew the procedure backwards.

Bertie tripped away to the yard where his horse was patiently standing, tied to the gate. He was feeling as jolly as could be, not drunk, by no means drunk, but absolutely in tune with the Infinite. For the time being he had quite shed the load of helplessness that numbed his faculties as a rule: rather, he felt capable tonight of bold and splendid decisions. No more sapient head, no firmer, more resolute hands could have been found in Patrickstown, as it seemed to him, to direct and arrange its affairs. Singing a snatch of a popular chorus, he carefully mounted and clapped the horse's sides with his heels: whereupon, to his great disappointment, his steed moved slowly and cautiously backwards.

"Come, Billy, you ought to know better than that!"

As the retrogressive movement unaccountably continued, he leaned forward to give Billy an encouraging pat on the head, only to find that it had gone. "No head?" he asked, wonderingly. He lay back on the saddle to think things over when, to his surprise, his own head came smartly to rest on the horse's neck. Elated as he was, he grasped the situation in a flash.

"Why, you're back to front, you old silly!" he laughed.

Slowly and gravely he dismounted, and walked round to the other side of the horse, where he made preparations for climbing up in the same position as before. But he had reckoned without the horse, a steady, respectable animal who had been long years with the Family and disliked anything in the nature of a liberty. He now concluded the time was ripe to teach Master Hubert a lesson and, with a whinny of valediction, trotted off down the drive by himself, deaf to his owner's entreaties.

There was nothing for Bertie but to make his own way home. He was so happy he did not mind it a bit. He capered along, now playing an imaginary fiddle, now throwing both legs up sideways and kicking them together in the air. Sometimes he paused and clapped his little hands for very glee. Anon he sang or, gratefully recalling his unlooked-for reconciliation with Amanda and the brilliant new acquaintance he had made that evening, he knelt in the roadway and piously gave thanks. Then up again and off, with a hop, skip and a jump. In this delightful way the distance was easily covered and in no time at all he found himself outside Mangan's Hotel. He bethought himself then of a private word he had for Andrew's ear.

"Andy!" he bawled, at the top of his voice.

There was no reply at all, not surprising as it was now long after two o'clock. Bertie stooped and dragged up a hank of grass by the roots and hurled it at Andrew's window.

"Andy!" he howled again.

At last a light went up and Andrew's sleepy, wrathful face appeared at the window.

"Who's there? Is that you, Bertie? What on earth's the matter?"

"Andy, Andy! The fince! The fince!"

"What fince, you frightful ass?"

"The Mother Superior's fince! Between ourselves," said Bertie, screaming with laughter, "it's up again!"

"Will you shut up? Do you want to wake the village?"

"No," said the little lord, very humble.

"Then go home. Go to sleep."

"I don't quite remember where home is," Bertie confessed. "And I must say, I thought you'd like to hear about the fince. Up, down, up, down, like a seesaw, you know. Very rare in a fince." He sat down suddenly and remained in that position, chuckling to himself like a pleased baby.

"I'm going to dress and take you home," Andrew informed him. "You must sit there and not make a sound until I come. Do you see?"

"Just as you like, of course," said Bertie, suddenly rather distant and formal.

Andrew closed the window and started looking about for his trousers; but almost at once there was a thud on the window-pane as Bertie hurled a second projectile. Andrew flung the window up.

"What did I say?" he hissed, furiously.

"Yes, what did you? That is what I wanted to ask."

"I'm-going-to-take-you-home!"

"Yes, hooray. But I mean, before that, what did you say?"

"Just that I'm going to dress."

"I thought it was that, you know. But Andy," said the little lord, in a reasonable, helpful sort of way, "why do you? Dress, I mean. Such a bother for you."

"Be quiet, cuckoo."

Hovering between annoyance and amusement, Andrew dressed himself and, pausing only on the landing to listen for sounds of alarm in the house, crept slowly down the creaking stairway in the dark and carefully opened the front door. Here he pulled up short with a cry of amazement, for the seated figure of Bertie, small enough to begin with, appeared to have shrunk almost to nothing. Then he discovered with horror that it was not Bertie at all, but Bertie's clothes, evening jacket, trousers, shoes, socks, frilly white shirt and, he noted with ever deepening dismay, his underpants, all folded together neatly in a little pile as Nanny would have liked to see them. Glancing round sharply, he saw the little fellow darting away at full speed, his plump form flashing in the moonlight like a minnow, in the direction of the parish hall.

Andrew set off at once in pursuit of the runaway, but his shoes and clothes slowed him up. Bertie had a good start and, on reaching the hall, he turned up one side of it, looking back roguishly over his shoulder with a cry of Coo-ee! and the pair of them commenced a most undignified and protracted game of round-and-round-the-mulberry-bush. Now Andrew would pin his hopes to a sudden spurt: now he would creep stealthily round in what he hoped was an unexpected direction, meaning to catch his prey from behind: now he simply drew himself up against the wall and held still, on the chance that Bertie would walk right into him; but it was all to no purpose. Bertie eluded him easily every time and was enjoying the romp far too much to wish it ever to end.

It was at this unsuitable moment that the Canon's path crossed theirs. He came hobbling up the road, miserable and footsore, and so weary he hardly knew if he were asleep or awake. His mind was fixed on nothing but reaching his bed as fast as he possibly could. Even the sight of the haunted building as it came nearer and nearer could not intimidate him as it usually did. But then all at once, as he slowly drew level with it, he saw a sight that chilled the blood in his veins and drove even his excruciating sufferings out of his head. There, unmistakable in a patch of moonlight, stood the naked figure of a man! That ghost which, as now vividly came to his mind, O'Keefe had described as being like the man in a Greek statue! It saw the Canon in the very same moment as the Canon saw it and, clapping its hand to its heart as if even ghosts knew what it was to be startled, flitted off in the direction of the hedge at the further end of the hall without a sound.

For a moment the Canon stood transfixed in terror and then, as the full import of what he had seen sank in, he let out a cry like the screech of an owl.

"Oh Jesus and Mary love me!"

Now Andrew came creeping round the further corner of the hall, bent almost double, his hands tensed ready for the catch. Once again he was trying his dodge of stalking round in what he divined must be the opposite direction to Bertie's, since only a few seconds ago he had been just in time to see the chubby back disappear round a corner ahead of him. He had made up his mind that, drunk or not, Bertie should be soundly spanked on capture, and his mouth was watering freely at the prospect of it. It was just then that the Canon's bloodcurdling cry smote on his ear: in the same moment he too observed the little silvery figure dive for the shelter of the leaves in the hedge: and seeing a man fully clothed at least ten yards nearer to it than he was, he shouted: "After him! Get him, for God's sake!"

Before the words were fairly out of his mouth, he had both recognized his enemy and realized the nature of his emotion. There before him on the road, gibbering with fear, the dupe of his own monstrous propaganda, was the ignorant bully, big-mouthed and weak-minded, who held the hundreds of his fellow beings in this little place in subjection by a system of threats and promises never to be made good. Was it really possible even in this crazy country, Andrew thought, almost suffocating with rage, that anyone should take seriously this ass? that he himself should have spent night after troubled night in apprehension of what this pitiful zany might do?

"You blithering idiot, you!" he snarled, as much to himself as to the Canon, and plunged off down the lane in the wake of the ghost.

But the Canon was far beyond any feelings of resentment. Andrew might have reviled him to the top of his bent and he would never have answered a word. He stood, trembling and muttering and twitching for a few seconds longer and then, suddenly finding his legs, went lickety-split for home. His boots twinkled over the ground as if he never was up the mountain at all; and he hardly drew breath until he was safe down near the foot of his bed with the clothes tightly wound about his damp, palpitating old skull.

THIRTEEN

The following day brought the news that young O'Shea was almost sure to live, that his injuries were not so grave as had been feared and that, although it would be a long business, a complete recovery was not impossible. The village received the verdict with the mingled pleasure and regret normal in such communities, and the young doctor averred that such had been his own opinion from the start. Immediately the Sergeant got the message, he went down to tell the Canon. The change in the priest's appearance struck him most disagreeably. He was a kindly man and, seeing Canon Peart pale and haggard, with great shadows under his eyes, the thought came to him that perhaps the illness had not been feigned after all. Having promised to leave word at Father O'hOgain's lodging that he was to bring the glad tidings up the mountain without delay, he went off again and soon was spreading this view round the parish.

The Canon lay in bed, in a dreadful turmoil of spirit. He was sincerely glad for young O'Shea. But, why could they not have found it out at once, so that he might have been spared that dreadful walk and its still more hideous ending?

Thank God, the parish knew nothing of that, but they must even now be making intolerably merry over his sudden recall from the doors of death. Not only human beings but the very events of life seemed to join in conspiracy against him. As for Andrew Butler, the poor man could not think of him without wincing and groaning aloud. Up to the last he had clung obstinately to the hope that the rascal was only bluffing. But a fellow who was not afraid of a ghost would hardly be afraid of anything else. A fellow not only unafraid of a ghost, but actually seeming to have some kind of a hold over it! What's that he'd said? "After him! Get him, for God's sake!" Did anyone ever hear the like of that in his life? Was that the way to approach the supernatural? Wouldn't you think it would be enough to get the man struck dead?

He groaned again and nervously shifted his aching limbs. The ghost was the very last straw. He had seen it, might see it again, it was a reality. His attitude to the supernatural in religious matters was curiously matter-of-fact and businesslike; he could not be said to disbelieve it, but it was simply there to accept and use as a means of government. He would terrify his flock with vivid and, as it were, eye-witness accounts of the torments of hell, but he never lost a moment's sleep imagining that one day they might be his. What really struck home to his peasant mind was the fear of the human dead, the swarming invisible presences of the night, beings he could not control and who mocked and threatened him. What was to be done? He must send for La Trobe, have a long talk with La Trobe. La Trobe at least was flesh and blood; and La Trobe must see the writer fellow and get to the bottom of the mystery.

The next day was Sunday, and still the Canon remained sunk in despair. Even when Father O'hOgain, pink in the face with excitement, came in with the news that the collections at the two Masses had doubled themselves, it brought nothing but a sardonic gleam to his eye.

" 'Twill be from those tourists the newspapers sent us," he said bitterly. "At least they've the decency to pay for their amusement."

It was true that the influx continued, had indeed greatly increased over the week-end. What with motor-cars, bicycles and pony traps, the little main street of the village looked, as one inhabitant put it, like Piccadilly Circus. Some of the village boys were earning shillings and sixpences by taking the strangers round on a kind of conducted tour, taking in the Convent, the Canon's house and Mangan's Hotel, and supplying a stream of colourful misinformation. At about half-past twelve a beautiful sleek Daimler drew up in front of Mangan's and the rumour buzzed about that a Bishop was visiting. In fact, fresh evidence of the soundness of justice and truth, it belonged to Felim Plunkett.

"What do you say I drive you out of this and we'll get a bite somewhere?" he said, gaily. "I don't want you growing morbid."

"I've promised Mrs. Mangan we'll eat here," Andrew told him, regretfully. "It's a question of her lunch trade, you know. All these people want to see me, among other local objects of interest. Mrs. Mangan thought if we didn't mind staying in, she might get some custom at last. I think we should: she was very good to me in the lean times."

"What it is to be famous!" Felim marvelled; but he submitted with his usual good nature.

They sat down in a room like an oven to a meal of roast mutton with mashed swedes, Spotted Dick and carageen jelly, and mouse-trap cheese. As the astute proprietress had foreseen, the hotel was full to overflowing, until at last tables had to be spread in the smoking-room, the parlour and out in the yard behind. The air was full of suppressed enjoyment and muttered comments.

"That's him, that fella there!"

"The one in the ritzy suit?"

"Not at all! The one with a class of hair like an old nest."

"He's cool enough."

"Ah, sure, the English are cool all right. Look at Dunkirk."

"And who's the boyo with him?"

" 'Tis a famous Q.C., specially over from London."

"Is that right? Jasus, he's eating mutton like you or me."

"Well, I'm sure I don't know what to say to you," Felim remarked, taking a pull at his stout to wash the taste of the gravy away. "Will you be satisfied, when you've the whole country upside down?"

"I'm the one to be upside down. I feel as if I were walking in my sleep," Andrew confessed, and he told Felim of his discussion with Mr. Brendan La Trobe on the banks of the river. Felim laughed so much that he nearly choked.

"Oh, Patsy, Patsy! God forgive me, I love that man!" he cried. "And did you close with the offer?"

"Not at all!" The words were out of his mouth before he could stop himself.

"Not at all!" Felim mimicked him. "Oh, Butler, Butler! I tremble. I'm watching."

"Sure, dey hadn't even de money! It was a little previous, wasn't it?" Andrew inquired, with an innocent look on his face.

"Ah, it won't be long now, with the writ turning up in England. But as far as your part is concerned, I don't know why I sit in that stuffy office of mine sweating away at your documents. The wheels are slowly grinding to a standstill," Felim told him.

"Are you sure of that?"

"Positive. You know, this has all been a storm in a tea-cup. The poor old Canon was just trying, in a very human way, to get a few pounds together for some purpose of his own. That's the beginning and the end of it. The last thing in the world he was looking for, was real trouble. How could he ever guess what an awkward customer he'd hooked? Oh, I can feel for him."

"You arouse my interest," Andrew said, "by your tender allusion to the poor old Canon, I mean. I feel I am watching the birth of a legend, and of course, legends are very much up my street. A kind of dream personality is being gradually built up around this old crocodile that will soon acquire a life of its own, like the characters in a good novel. First, Patsy in the exuberance of his imagination tosses off a pen portrait of a saintly old man toiling away for the good of his parish: then it's solemnly taken up by this Mr. O'Sullivan, as if it in some way corresponded with the facts."

Felim laughed again. "Ah, Tom O'Sullivan! Don't mind Tom. He's the best in the world," he said. "I tried to get him for ourselves, you know: too late. If I had, he'd have been barking away in the other direction."

"There's another interesting thing," Andrew continued, "in fact, it's really quite fascinating. In a courtroom everything becomes quite different from what it is. I've always greatly admired, for example, the sheer intellectual achievement of a good summing-up. But it comes to my mind now I've heard litigants say, when you know what really happened it sounds like the ravings of delirium. You lawyers are not appreciated: you're the great creative artists of the age!"

"Well, thanks very much! I hope you're sincere," Felim said. "I think I can promise you anyway you won't recognize your own story by the time we finish with it. But let's go on up to your room, will we, and look the documents over? After that, whether you like it or not, I'm driving you out in the country. I've a little treat for you."

The defence Felim had prepared was very short, its lapidary style in great contrast to the ebullience from the other side. The defendant stated that his article did not refer to the plaintiff, of whose existence he had been un-aware, and that the facts concerning the nuns were true in substance and in fact, while for the comments on them the plaintiff was referred to *The Golden Bough,* chapter 63, page 646 (inter alia) of the Abridged Edition of 1922.

"I don't like you giving the reference like that," An-drew complained. "Make them work! There are twelve volumes in the standard edition."

"Ah, the poor decent man! Are you human at all?"

"None of that. Make them work," Andrew repeated, firmly. "And it isn't quite accurate to say I was unaware of the plaintiff's existence. No one who spent a single day in Patrickstown could be that. Could you change it to, 'unaware of the plaintiff's connection with the convent'?"

"Right you are," Felim said, pencilling in the margin. "But I tell you, my old bones say you are not going to need this anyway."

"Well, get it in tomorrow all the same, will you? The brooding silence of the great Pulvermacher is sure to be broken before long. If they're worried, let's keep them worried."

"I can see you're a born litigant," said Felim, with fatherly pride.

"And now what about this little treat?"

Felim explained that he was about to see yet another facet of the coruscating personality of Mr. Patsy La Trobe. At a village some twenty miles away a political meeting was to be held that afternoon, at which Patsy would address the citizenry as the Sons of Erin candidate in the coming elections. Until you had heard Patsy speak on the political situation, Felim declared, you could not really hope to get the full flavour of the man. Andrew was not sure if he really wanted to get it, but he could see that Felim was longing to go, and so he agreed very cheerfully. They climbed into the Daimler and slid easily away down the street, while a dozen or so enthusiasts leaped for their vehicles and followed in their wake.

"I'm sorry if I must leave this little affair of yours just as it grows really interesting," Felim said presently, as they drove along. "I don't know what follows when a P.P. is downed in front of his parish by a foreigner. Imagination boggles at the thought. In fact, it's so unthinkable that I don't believe it will happen. You'd best mind yourself, Butler, or he'll have the laugh of you yet."

"Oh, I think I've trimmed his claws," said Andrew tranquilly.

"It's easy to see you've no experience of Holy Church's claws," Felim told him, reverently lifting his hat as they passed a chapel of ease. "You'd never be talking in that airy way. Depend on it, the tables will turn somehow. And they won't care how they do it, either. Oh, there's a shot or two in their locker yet."

"You sound like Muldoon."

"Ah Muldoon, God help him!" chuckled Felim. "That was terrible work you did there. He was off to Lough Derg as a penitent next thing, to starve three days and walk barefoot on the stones and beat his breast."

"Is he religious?" asked Andrew in wonder.

"Religious!" said Felim kindly, as if to a child. "He thought it would get round that he was a friend of yours. And there's probably five who'd be glad to get his job if they could."

"You bring out the most staggering propositions as if they were simple matters of common sense," Andrew complained.

"You're long past being staggered," Felim assured him. "And you'll be going rapidly downhill yourself from now on. Look, isn't that our political genius over there by the trees?"

This was the first big public meeting that Patsy had held on his own behalf and it was to be a milestone in local affairs, as marking the occasion when he finally came down on one side of the fence. He had always intended, for the furtherance of certain projects of his own, to become in due course a member of the Dáil; but up to the present he had found it difficult to decide which of the two major parties, Irishmen All or Sons of Erin, should enjoy his allegiance.

Lest it be thought he was a man of no sincerity, it must be made clear at once that the programs of the two parties were identical. Each bravely took its stand on the plank of Ireland Catholic, Gaelic, Republican and Free, the last desideratum being of course a reference to those six counties in the North, cruelly torn from Erin's arms by a freely negotiated treaty, and now experiencing the horrors of a police regime compared with which the excesses of Hitler and Stalin had been as naught. While out of office, each party assured the voters that only by the speedy return of itself to power could these objectives be reached; but when it was in, they seemed in a mysterious way to become all at once shadowy, remote and unattainable. Then the party would settle down to the real business of government, which in the first place meant sweeping the grafters from public life and replacing them by deserving brothers and cousins and uncles of its own; and in the second, hanging onto power for the three years that were necessary if Ministers were to qualify for a pension. At the end of this period, dead beat, they would promptly resign on the first issue to hand, even, if need be, a matter of principle.

On the whole Patsy had been inclined to favour Irishmen All, since rather more than half of his richer clients were of this party. It would also be easier to get himself adopted by the committee, since their present man was weak and had no national record, while the Sons of Erin representative was immensely popular and had once shot a British Tommy from behind a hedge: a feat which the processes of time had transmogrified into the holding off, with his bare fists, of six drunken Black-and-Tans who were seeking to murder some Irish women and children. Patsy could offer nothing like this, as he had been a small boy in the troubled times; but he thought perhaps he could do something with a rousing call for a new spirit in Irish politics and a break-away from the sterile hatreds and feuds of the past. He was working hard on the possibility when, to his great relief, the Sons of Erin fellow dropped dead: a happy and timely act, the more auspicious in that he was a bachelor and there would be no need, following the kindly Irish custom, immediately to return his widow. Patsy could hesitate no longer. The Sons of Erin had it: not only would he inherit Mr. Keating's good will but he could also conveniently silence hecklers at meetings with a cry of "And now, boys, hats off for the dead man!"

The Sons of Erin had set up their tribune in a meadow some little way from the village. The tricolour of the Republic waved proudly from an improvised flagpole beside it and a banner inviting the electorate to "Vote for La Trobe and a New Deal" was tied securely round its base. The meeting was none too well attended, as the cream of the citizens had gone off to see the fun at Patrickstown; but those who had no means of transport and found the day too hot for walking had turned up as an alternative to the usual Sunday entertainment of standing at the crossroads and hoping for a motor smash. Some hundred persons only were now assembled, dressed in their hot Sunday black, on their faces the determination not to be impressed by any guff that might be doled out to them; and it was therefore impossible for Andrew and Felim to mingle discreetly with the throng as they had intended. As they walked over the grass, Patsy was just rising to his feet, and he at once acknowledged their presence with a courteous inclination of his head. He then paused for a few instants, while his practised eye raked the audience for emissaries from Irishmen All or the agents of Mr. Finkelstein, formerly his partner, now his implacable foe. Then, in simple, sincere, manly tones he began his speech.

"My friends," he said, "I stand here this afternoon with feelings of the greatest humility, with a deep sense of my own unworthiness. When I think upon the man, God rest his soul, who stood here before me: remember his glorious record in our national resistance: reflect on his achievements as the servant of our people, both in small local matters and broad national issues: and when I consider the esteem he justly enjoyed among the excellent citizens of this neighbourhood, the question I put to myself, quite simply, is this: Who am I, that I should take his place?"

"Yes, who?" came from a saturnine individual on the edge of the meeting.

Patsy made a swift mental note of the danger point and went on. "Yes, who?" he repeated, sweetly. "A man still young, known perhaps to some of you but, in the political arena, still untried. A man debarred by the fact of his age from having played any part in the establishing of this young, vigorous nation whose tremendous strides in the social and technical field are the wonder of Europe. A man who, nevertheless, and by the very fact of his youth, the freshness of his outlook, may have a contribution to make by introducing a new spirit into Irish politics and helping to clear away the sterile hatreds and feuds of the past.

"O please don't think," he exclaimed in a sort of wail, raising both hands as if entreating silence, "O please don't think that it is my wish to decry those glorious figures that tower above the recent history of our beloved land. Far from it. I yield to no man in my reverence for them. I will go further. I will say boldly and I will say advisedly, in the presence of you all, that not half enough has been done for them. Why! there must be some listening to me this afternoon who, if they had their rights, would be drawing their thirty shillings a week from the State which owes its very life to their self-sacrifice. And, my friends," he said, putting his hands on the table and leaning on them, while his voice sank to a dramatic half-whisper, "if it should be your pleasure to send me to the Dáil, I pledge myself to do my utmost to see that Justice is done."

Some of the older members of the audience began to look thoughtful.

"And what'll you do just?" the danger point wished to know.

"I will come to details in due course," Patsy continued, wondering if Finkelstein or politics were behind this nuisance: "for the moment I crave your indulgence while I map out the main lines of me policy. I referred, friends, to sterile hatreds. It is time now that these vanish from our political life. Hatred never got anywhere yet: only love (for I hope all are Christians here) can ever be a real success. Oh, I'm not saying it's always easy. And I know what is passing in your minds now. How can we put hatred away, you ask, while our brothers in the North are groaning under the same bitter yoke that, after seven hundred years of indomitable struggle, we ourselves threw off? How can we sleep quiet in our beds at night, while England's cruel red still blows over a great part of our fair green land? I sympathize, friends, I know how you feel: indeed, we all must feel the same, for whatever differences there may be among us, in politics or religion or some little thing, we are all Irishmen!"

He broke off at this, waiting for applause; but none came. The audience, which slept very soundly on the whole and never bothered its head about the North from one end of the year to the other, was losing interest. It would greatly have preferred to hear something more about Patsy's scheme for a wider allocation of pensions. To make matters worse, the danger point felt called on to pipe up again.

"Is that right?" it asked, sarcastically. "Wasn't it Irishmen All two minutes ago?"

A rumble of laughter rose from the crowd as it took the point. Patsy gently mopped his brow with a handkerchief and cast another fly. He sensed that the meeting was not behind him and he dreaded a failure with Felim and the English fellow there to enjoy it. Unwisely, he decided to turn the tables on them by an appeal to popular sentiment and a reference to local events.

"I say, we are all Irishmen," he proceeded, "and as such, we want to keep our great traditions alive. We want to safeguard that purity for which Ireland's name has been honoured through the ages. We want no filth pouring in here from the presses of foreign countries. We want no tabloids, no cheap yellow Fleet Street gutter clap-trap. We must build up a wholesome literature of our own, on Catholic Gaelic lines: we must boycott foreign newspapers!"

He was quoting verbatim from an editorial in one of the Catholic papers and felt sure it would do the trick. Purity was always safe for a round of applause, and it was unlikely that any of his hearers would dare object to anything so much along the official line of the moment. But once again his judgement was at fault. A spirited rejoinder there was, and one proceeding from a source that was itself as greatly astonished as Patsy, the moment the words were spoken.

"Is it boycott the foreign newspapers?" bawled Andrew now. "Sure, and don't we all know you make your living from them?"

A shout went up, as the meeting at last came alive. Andrew stared round him, thunderstruck. He thought it was the most extraordinary thing that had happened to him in his life. He had had no intention of speaking whatever: the words had burst from his lips unbidden and where, pray where, had he picked up that perfect intonation? It was a stranger surely who had taken possession of him; but a stranger who seemed to wish him no harm, for Patsy was crimson in the face and shaking, and he saw nothing but laughing, friendly faces whichever way he turned. At the ludicrous expression of amazement on his respectable, scholarly face, the laughter grew louder still; and when some local Know-All passed the word round who he was, it swelled to a mighty roar. Far away, Patsy could be heard screaming, "And now, boys, hats off for the dead man!" but no one minded him; and in fact, by that one stroke, his political career was suspended for years to come.

Felim was seated on the ground, apparently enjoying a quiet cry.

"Most improper! most improper!" he sobbed. "One more like that out of you, and I retire. Sacred Heart of Jesus! These English! Come on away out of it," he commanded, scrambling to his feet. "You've done enough for the evening. I'll run you to the hotel and then I must get to Dublin and a telephone. There are parties whom it would be criminal to keep in ignorance of this a moment longer than need be.

"I must say, I'm surprised at you, Butler," he said, reprovingly, as the car bounded off with them. "A man of your sort, to stab the poor hoor in the back like that! Surely, the British Empire was never built up in that kind of spirit? Didn't it repose on solid foundations of probity, straight dealing and fair play?"

"Nothing of the kind," said Andrew, complacently. He was disposed now to pretend to himself that the whole thing had been a brilliant, premeditated manoeuvre. "The Empire succeeded because Englishmen knew how to meet a given situation in the manner it called for. In a manner that harmonized with the inner rhythms—I borrow the expression from that Church which its members, I imagine playfully, describe as Holy . . ."

Felim help up a warning hand. "Silence!" he said. "None of that. I'm a devout Catholic. I'd be down the drain tomorrow if I wasn't."

"I apologize," Andrew said. "I only meant to say, the Empire reposed mainly on the fact that Englishmen knew how many beans make five."

He leaned back in his seat with a look of dignified self-approval on his face. Felim drove along in thoughtful silence, breaking now and again into helpless giggles. As Andrew got out of the car at the hotel, he drew out a small book bound in Russian leather and passed it to him. He had the serious, humble air of a small boy approaching some revered pugilist or footballer.

"We all have our little weaknesses," he said, "and I have a childish habit of collecting autographs. I know it's silly. But would you give me yours? You see," and his voice wandered away up the octave again, "I never thought I would live to see Patsy bested. I never dreamed it was possible!"

And Andrew gravely put his name under that of the papal nuncio.

FOURTEEN

THE amenities of Mangan's Hotel were more of a spiritual than a material nature. A visitor could be sure of a warm welcome, a lively interest in his personal affairs, sympathy in his disappointments and excellent advice in his perplexities; on the other hand, he could not depend on the bath-water being hot, his bed being aired or his meals being anything more than just eatable. This dualism revealed itself most clearly when a guest ventured to make some little request or suggestion that would tend to his greater comfort. At once Mrs. Mangan would assent to it with enthusiasm, reproaching herself bitterly for not having thought of it first: after which, as if her energies were exhausted, all would continue as before.

Soon after Andrew had arrived, he had intimated that his usual breakfast consisted of tea, toast and two boiled eggs. Mrs. Mangan had examined him closely on the subject of the eggs, pressing him for an exact statement as to the number of minutes he wished them to boil and whether he preferred them always to be hen's eggs or whether he sometimes would consider the eggs of a turkey or a duck. Andrew had been very pleased with her attitude, contrasting it favourably with the indifference of hotel-keepers in England; and when next morning the rashers and fried eggs appeared again, he was more amused than anything else and gently reminded his hostess of their arrangement.

Mrs. Mangan reviled herself fluently for having a head that was no more use than a boiled potato and begged him not to lose heart, as all would be put right on the morrow. But rashers and eggs were served again; and, after a few more attempts, each one a little feebler than the last, Andrew had resigned himself to the situation.

When, therefore, he seated himself at the breakfast table and saw two beautiful brown-speckled eggs boiled ready for him, carefully muffled in knitted cosies, he sensed immediately that something was up. The idea gained on him when he found that the tea was hot and the toast freshly made; and when Mrs. Mangan came hurrying up to inquire if all was as it should be, he could doubt it no longer. He was also aware, unresentfully, that the aims of the landlady rather than his own interests were being in some roundabout way advanced.

"Come now, Mrs. Mangan, what's the fuss?" he smiled, for he had still not cured himself of the habit of coming to the point.

"There's no fuss at all, Mr. Butler," she replied, blushing. "I was hoping the breakfast was to your liking, that's all. Is that enough for you, now? There's some lovely boiled prunes in the kitchen, if you'd try them."

"Lovely boiled prunes!" echoed Andrew, in dismay.

"Or some of the carrageen mould?"

"G'wan out of it," he said, kindly. "My dear lady, I know you well enough by now. There's something troubling you. Let me hear what it is."

"Oh God, Mr. Butler," Mrs. Mangan said, in a sort of little moan. "I'm sure I haven't made you comfortable here at all. It's been a difficult time for me all right, with the weather and the place standing empty. I couldn't blame you a bit, if you walked out of here tomorrow!"

"But aren't things looking up a little? And I'm not going to walk out of here tomorrow."

Mrs. Mangan looked down at him with a timid hope in her eyes. "Is that right?" she asked.

"Of course it's right. There's never been any question of it. What put that idea into your head?"

"Joe O'Leary, that leaves the milk, is after saying you're going up to Patrickstown Hall to stay with his lordship," she faltered.

"Then Joe O'Leary is after dreaming. I am slowly growing accustomed," he cried, with a sudden burst of irritation, "to the local people knowing what is to befall me before I do and, if I may say so, being apprised of the contents of my post before I receive it. It is surely going too far when they settle my future movements by divination."

"It's not true, then? Joe O'Leary was never wrong before," she demurred, torn between the two sorts of probity.

"Mrs. Mangan, I give you my word it is not true."

"I'll not deny that with things as they are, you're a bit of an asset!"

"If it will assist you," he pledged himself, "I will sit outside in a booth all day, ringing a bell and shouting, 'Walk up! Walk up!' "

"Sure, I'd never ask a gentleman to do that," said Mrs. Mangan quite seriously; and, looking much relieved, she left the room.

No sooner had Andrew eaten the first of his eggs than she was back again, wearing an expression as near to malicious enjoyment as her pleasant face could manage. Carefully closing the door, she drew a chair up to the table and, seating herself, whispered: "Patsy La Trobe's brother Kevin is here outside! and he'd like a private word with yourself."

"I was expecting something of the sort," Andrew said calmly. "But I won't see him. Big chief make palaver with big chief. If Patsy has something to say, let him come here and say it."

"He'd never do it. I doubt if Patsy'll be going about much today, after the way you quenched him there!" Mrs. Mangan opined.

"So you heard about that? From the milkman, I suppose?"

"Not at all. Sure, no one's talking of anything else. And what message will I take to the brother?"

"You may please tell him," said Andrew, decapitating his second egg with the air of Napoleon signing a decree, "that I will see Mr. Patsy La Trobe in your bar at six o'clock. Should I be a few minutes late, he may wait for me. If Mr. La Trobe is in any doubt as to which bar I mean, it is the one in which I first had the pleasure of making his acquaintance."

Mrs. Mangan clapped a hand over her mouth. "Oh God!" she said, happily, and tripped out of the room again.

There was to be little peace this morning. The next visitor was Lord Patrickstown, smartly dressed in a suit of Italian silk shot blue and green, and looking altogether much jauntier than Andrew had seen him before.

"Forgive my barging in, and so on," he said cheerily. "Haven't you finished breakfast yet? You are lazy! It's ten o'clock, I mean. How are you? It's ages since we met."

"Is it?" asked Andrew, in surprise.

"Why, yes. I haven't seen you since the day we had luncheon. And we wrote that letter, you know. By the way, everything's all right. Reverend Mother isn't angry any more, and they've put the fence up again. Not quite what we wanted, but still very jolly. I had the bill for it this morning. I ought to have told you before, but I've been rather busy and things."

"And what brings you here? Have some tea?"

"I won't, thank you very much. I've had an idea," Bertie confided. "That is to say, Anguish had the idea, but I think it's very sensible. Won't you come and stay up at the Hall? You might be more comfortable, and Anguish says you'll be safer. I told Anguish all about you and the Canon at dinner last night, and Anguish says the *jacquerie* will soon be here, howling for your blood and so on. Up at the Hall we could bar all the doors and sell our lives as dearly as we could, I mean. And those cannon my people brought back from the Crimea, you know. Anguish says we could prime them up. Of course, that's all frightful rot. A joke, really. But do come to stay, Andy, won't you? For as long as you'd like?"

"But, Bertie dear, what would the Canon say?"

"To hell with the Canon!" spiritedly exclaimed the little lord. "Well, of course, that's rather rude. But Anguish says, he's a silly old nonsense. And in a way, if you come to think of it, so he is."

"Before we go any further," Andrew begged, "do please tell me who this Anguish is."

"My dear! he's Amanda's publisher. Oh, such fun! I met him there at dinner, at Castle Knock, you know, Amanda's place. We had such a capital evening, I don't really remember how it ended. Billy, that's my horse, brought me home afterwards and I think the sagacious animal must have put me to bed. I woke up on the sofa in the drawing-room, with the hearth-rug over me, and my clothes all neatly folded on a chair beside. The only funny thing was, my backside was terribly sore. And the colour of crushed raspberries. I must have come an awful cropper at some moment and never noticed it. I mean, drink, and all that. It seems to act as a kind of anaesthetic after a certain stage," Bertie warbled on, and listening to the open-hearted little fellow Andrew had a pang of conscience; "well, be that as it may, but then Amanda turned him out of the house. Too bad of her, really. Said he was a white-slaver. She does rather leap to conclusions, you know, especially when she's in between books. All Anguish did was ask two of her maids if they'd like to go to Tunbridge Wells. His aunt had particularly asked him (he's her heir) to look out for two Irish maids for her. But Amanda said it was a likely story. Said no one in her senses would want one Irish maid, let alone two. Unfortunately, you see, Anguish had asked her to go to Paris with him just the evening before. All quite pure, I need hardly say, but Amanda saw it as a corroboration. She'll come round presently, I expect, but for the moment Anguish is staying with me."

Andrew looked at the happy little face across the table and felt all of a sudden strangely moved. "Do you know, I believe you're a saint," he said thoughtfully. "I think you may well justify Patrickstown yet."

"Oh my dear boy, much obliged, I'm sure, but that's a bit steep, isn't it?" Bertie chuckled. "What on earth made you say that?"

"Just the way you trust everyone and share everything," Andrew said. "Yes, Bertie, I'm fey this morning. I see it all inside my head. I'm not clear as to the details: but I see you, as in a mist, rising up and saving us all, including the Canon: uniting us, unlikely as it may appear, in brotherly love."

"Oh, don't start having visions, I do beg," Bertie cried. "They are the bane of the country, that and miraculous apparitions. Not that I deny the miraculous for a moment, you know. Only some of the things that happen here are beyond everything. And you've no right at all to horn in on that department, you dear old cynic."

"It's Ireland, I suppose," Andrew sighed. "The bog water is rapidly rising in my brain, or what I used to think of as such."

"You're not letting the Irish get you down, are you Andy?" his friend anxiously inquired, "Because you mustn't, you know. I never let them get me down. Not quite down, you understand."

"You're Irish yourself, though, aren't you?"

"Good Heavens, no! I'm an Alien Usurper," Bertie explained. "We've only been here about four hundred years. They'll hunt me out of it presently, I daresay, and then I shall live in a flat in South Ken. To tell you the truth, I can hardly wait. But we're getting away from things. Do promise to come and stay with Anguish and me, won't you?"

"I'd love to, my dear fellow, but it's impossible," and he told of the trade boom at Mangan's and the role he was expected to play in it.

"Oh well, of course then, your place is here," his lordship promptly agreed. "But Mrs. Mangan will give you some time off now and again, won't she? Then you must come straight up to us. You'll adore Anguish, I'm certain. He's teaching me how to embroider."

He flitted away, like a gorgeous dragon-fly in the iridescence of blue and green, and Andrew resumed his meal. A few minutes later the door slowly opened again and round it, on a level with the door-knob, came a face heavily powdered and wearing the expression its owner described to himself as Startled Fawn. At the same time a sprightly voice announced: "It's only little me!" Then the face abruptly rose to its correct position and the voice said petulantly, "Drat the boy, where is he? I was to meet him in here." Without waiting for an answer the phenomenon retired, and there were sounds of a light body scampering away down the passage; and Andrew was left to marvel anew at the warmth and capacity of Bertie's heart.

He spent the day looking over his Irish notebooks and generally tidying up his affairs. He sensed, as Felim did, that the lunatic adventure in which he had been involved was drawing to a close. As a passenger in an aeroplane becomes aware of a change in the sound of the engines as the craft begins to lose height for the landing, so he felt now, by the kind of sixth sense he had developed, a slackening of pressure in the air round him. He looked forward merrily to his appointment with Mr. La Trobe. That Patsy would come he felt certain, but what new infamous inducement he would offer, he could not conceive. The proposal brought to him by Brendan could, he thought, scarcely be improved on but he still had the greatest faith in Patsy's inventive genius. From five o'clock onwards, he found himself constantly glancing at his watch.

At a minute or two after six, Mrs. Mangan ran up to inform him that the solicitor was in the bar below. With relish she narrated the manner of his entry into it. He had strolled in with an armful of sweet peas which, he said, were a tribute from his mother to Mrs. Mangan, a lady for whom they both felt the greatest esteem. Having handed the flowers across the bar and suitably inquired after her health and prosperity, he turned to the stool in the corner that Andrew normally occupied and fell into an attitude of delight at the coincidence of his happening to be there. Noticing, a split second too late, that the stool was empty, he turned back to the proprietress with a look of comical dismay. She told him soothingly that he was expected, and she would find out this minute if Dr. Butler were disengaged. She had left him, very subdued, pensively sipping a large glass of whisky.

But when at half-past six Andrew, unable to restrain himself longer, came down to the bar, Patsy had fully recovered. He was of those choice spirits whose greatness shines out best in defeat. In his loving welcome, his eager plying of the enemy with drink, he made it clear that all was completely and finally forgiven. He was the same cherubic Patsy that Andrew, it seemed now ages ago, had met one evening with those ramifying consequences to himself.

"Now, Patsy, I've a great deal to do," Andrew began, trying to sound aloof and severe, and failing entirely. "So you must come to the point at once."

"I will, of course," Patsy cried. "Amn't I here for that? But it's a queer old point all the same for two grown men to discuss, and in broad daylight too. Honest to God, I'm embarrassed. I hardly know where to begin."

"At the beginning," Andrew suggested.

Patsy laughed heartily, as if this were a brilliant joke. "Oh, you're sharp all right," he said, with genuine respect in his voice. "You've been too many for us, that's the truth of it. I've always said the English were not such fools as they looked. Ask anyone, if I didn't."

"To the point," Andrew said, gently.

"My client now, Mr. Butler," Patsy obediently began, gazing down into his glass, "is a spiritual man, leading a spiritual class of life. He sees things in a way that you or I mightn't see them. He's a point of view that's beyond us altogether, I suppose. The invisible world is as real to him as this bar here is to you and me. Do you follow?"

"Not in the least," replied Andrew, "but go on."

"You may have heard," Patsy continued, "that there's something strange at the parish hall. Oh! of course I don't believe it, nor do you. But you see, my client does. And the people do, at least they won't go anywhere near it. Now the parish hall is the hub of our cultural and social life. It stands in a temporal way for what the Church does in a spiritual, if you understand."

"Both are pretty little sources of revenue for your client, if that's what you mean," Andrew remarked brutally.

"Ah, now, now!" Patsy said, indulgently. "We won't quarrel. To put the thing in a nutshell, Mr. Butler, my client believes there is a ghost at the hall: and somehow or other he's got it fixed in his head that you have some connection with it. It's a fantastic idea all right but, well . . . he believes you'd have a control over it!" And he tilted his head at Andrew with the amused yet complacent look of a parent relating the sweetly silly remarks of his child.

It is painful indeed to have to record the answer that Andrew made. Up to this minute, it may be thought, after all little human frailties have been taken into account, he it was that stood on the side of the angels. A prey to weakness, fear, unworthy concern for himself and uncharitable thoughts towards others, he may have been; and yet he did, even if tremulously, bear aloft the little flickering torch of human sanity. If in the saga of Patrickstown there was a hero at all, it was surely he; and now with one wild move he cast all virtue aside and joined the forces of darkness.

Looking Patsy straight in the face, he blandly inquired: "And wasn't he right?"

Patsy's beautiful eyes widened. "I beg your pardon, Mr. Butler?" he stammered.

"The Canon is perfectly correct in his assumption," Andrew repeated in English. "He is much better informed than you are." With that he took a dignified pull at his glass, as if the matter were closed.

Patsy studied him in silence for a while, and very slowly there dawned on his face such a look of humble admiration as perhaps it had never worn before. As a knight of the Round Table glimpsing the Holy Grail, so had he for one instant an ineffable vision of his own brass plate with the name of Butler where Finkelstein's had stood. It faded at once, leaving him to grapple with the grim realities of the present.

"My client was wondering," he resumed, reverently, "if we couldn't persuade you to get the ghost out of there. He's ruining everything, the way it is."

"I see no reason to interfere," Andrew replied. "He's perfectly inoffensive and well-conducted. He hasn't broken anything, has he? Well, then."

"I'd say it was trespass, all right."

"Then sue," said Andrew promptly. "Serve him with one of your famous writs."

Patsy chuckled appreciatively. "I needn't say, this unfortunate little misunderstanding of ours would all be forgotten. Wouldn't that influence you?"

"Not at all. Why should it? I've made my position clear, I think. Of course . . ." he broke off, frowning, and ruminated a while. "Look here, Patsy. The ghost has his rights as well as anyone else. He's taken a fancy to the Canon's hall and why not? But he does pay a certain amount of attention to my views. There's quite an attractive parish hall over at Maryville; and if you were to tell me that your client had withdrawn his action not only against myself but against the newspaper too, I might be able to get the ghost to transfer."

"Oh God, Mr. Butler!" Patsy wailed. "What's that you're saying? The newspaper too! Why, that's me client's last hope! He's looking for a walkover there!"

"I daresay he is," said Andrew sternly. "But so he was with me. He'll be equally disappointed in both cases. The paper will fight him tooth and nail. The Canon may be no end of a dog in things spiritual but in worldly matters he doesn't know enough to come in out of the rain. What! the great Pulvermacher, to bow to the grotesque pretensions of an ignorant, superstitious, benighted witch-doctor from the bogs! Oh, don't interrupt me!" he roared, as Patsy raised his hands in terror: "Pulvermacher, controller of a thousand destinies! shaper of great events! Pulvermacher, at whose dread name Cabinet Ministers shake in their shoes! Pulvermacher, whose *Ethics of Journalism* stands on every editorial desk throughout the civilized world! Patsy dear," he said, lowering his voice to a compassionate murmur, "did you really think you'd get away with it?"

"We have before this!" Patsy faltered miserably.

Andrew looked at him and slowly and sorrowfully shook his head. "Patsy La Trobe," he said in a half-whisper, "I think you must be mad."

Patsy heaved a mournful sigh. "Well then, Mr. Butler," he said at last, "the suggestion is, you will withdraw your ghost and we will withdraw our action."

" 'Twould strengthen me hands . . ." Andrew began at once, and then broke off. Looking down his nose he went on, primly: "It would strengthen my hands with the ghost, you know, if I could tell him the action was already withdrawn. In other words, it's your move."

"And we've only your word for it then, you'll see to the ghost!"

"Just so: because otherwise, you see," Andrew explained sweetly, "I'd have only *your* word for it you'd wind up the action."

"I think I see what you mean," said Patsy, nodding. Then all at once a great bitterness flooded his soul. "And all the time there's no bloody ghost at all!" he cried.

"Isn't there, though!" said Andrew, smiling.

The little man drained the last drops from his glass and got to his feet. In a curious way he seemed to have aged in the last five minutes. "I think you've won, Mr. Butler," he said, with a fine, sad dignity. "I've no doubt at all that my client, with the way he is in, will instruct me in the manner you wish. There is only one little observation I have to make. To most of us over here, in spite of our grievous history, the name of England has hitherto stood for straight dealing and fair play. If anyone had told me an English gentleman could ever behave as you have done, I should have said, 'Stuff and nonsense, sir! Stuff and nonsense!'"

"Ah, it's a queer old world," said Andrew, amiably.

Patsy passed from the bar with every line of his small figure quivering in righteous indignation. Mrs. Mangan at once hurried up from the other end of the bar where she had discreetly been busying herself.

"Oh God, you sorted him! Oh God, you'd the best of it there," she said gleefully. "Did you see the face on him as he went out? 'Twould have soured the milk." And then a look of horror came over her face. "Sacred Heart of Jesus, Mr. Butler, what will you ever say to me?" she gasped, laying a plump hand on her bosom. "There's two telegrams came for you days ago! Look," she said, fishing the two little green envelopes out of an empty pickle jar standing beside the till, "didn't I plunge them in there meself, the way I'd remember to give them you? And the rush we had put it right out of me head. Oh Lord, Mr. Butler," she quavered, "suppose it's something important?"

Andrew took them from her and opened them. The first was from his friend Guy and ran,

MY DEAR BOY HURRAH FOR YOU DON'T BE SILLY SELL YOUR
BOAT WHAT NONSENSE CHAPS ALL RALLYING ROUND PAGET IS
IN CHARGE AND WILL GET IN TOUCH GOOD SHOW MORT AUX
VACHES

WEBSTER

The second was longer and said:

ALL HERE WISH EXPRESS ADMIRATION YOUR COURAGEOUS
STAND AGAINST FORCES OF OBSCURANTIST TYRANNY STOP WE
PLEDGE ALL SUPPORT FULLEST EXTENT OUR CAPACITY STOP
CAMBRIDGE WISHES BE ASSOCIATED IN THIS ALSO DURHAM WE
ARE NOT YET SURE OF OXFORD STOP THEREFORE HAVE NO
FEARS FOR FINANCIAL SIDE STOP WILL COMMUNICATE FURTHER
AS PLANS MATURE STOP MEANWHILE WE SEND WARMEST
SINCEREST REGARDS SIGNED COMMITTEE.

PAGET

FROBISHER

WINTHROP

MENZIES

TOMBS

"No, dear Mrs. Mangan," said Andrew, placidly. "It's
nothing of any importance whatever."

He had plenty more drinks and then supped and retired
early to bed, where for the first time for many many
nights he enjoyed the kind of deep, refreshing slumber that
little children have, and the very good, and the very
wicked.

FIFTEEN

N̲ow at last the weather began to show signs of breaking. There was still not a cloud to be seen and the sun beat down as pitilessly as ever, but the sky changed from clear burning blue to the colour of ashes. No breeze ever stirred the leaves, and the place became airless and sticky and oppressive. The feel of an impending storm weighed on the little village, whose inhabitants at once began to show signs of jumpiness. A number of peculiar things happened one after the other, and several people behaved in a mysterious or reprehensible way.

First, a milk-white she-ass appeared from nowhere and ran wildly up and down in the neighbourhood, as if seeking something she had lost. No one in the country, as far as was known, had ever possessed such an animal and the occurrence therefore had all the marks of a portent. In no time at all there was a spate of nervous rumour and speculation. The matter was brought to the notice of Canon Peart, who refused to interest himself in it, remarking that his parish was full of asses and one more, of whatever sex or colour, could make no difference to anyone. The beast appeared twice again, with always the same lost, bewildered, agitated air, and there were those who asserted that her being was supernatural. On the third and last occasion, however, she was seen by Mr. Wimbush, the Protestant Rector, and the legend died at birth: it could be safely assumed that anything Mr. Wimbush saw had a natural and wholesome explanation behind it. But the little mystery was never cleared up and continued for some days as a favourite topic of conversation.

It soon paled into insignificance beside the amazing and inexplicable affair of Cat's-Eye O'Keefe signing the pledge. When the announcement of it first was made, there was such a torrent of talk as even the Canon's lawsuit had failed to release. The mere thought of Cat's-Eye in association with the schoolmaster, the sacristan, Malachy the village simpleton and the four or five other pallid and spiritless individuals who carried the banner of temperance in Patrickstown, stirred the local intellect as might have done the news of some stupendous natural upheaval or even the approaching end of the world. It was something almost beyond the compass of the human mind. In fact, Cat's-Eye never signed it. When the time came for him to go up to the church where Father O'hOgain was complacently waiting, he was seized with a sudden attack of faintness; and he naturally took this as a hint that he was following a course unacceptable to the Divine Will. But for a long time to come the finest local brains were teased and vexed by the very idea of his having contemplated so rash and deleterious a step.

All this, again, was as nothing to the sudden and determined assault of Father O'hOgain on Lizzie O'Rourke. Lizzie was the Scarlet Woman of Patrickstown and all attempts to redeem her had long since been abandoned: nor did the police molest her since, a native of Connemara, she would plead her cause in Court in such pure and racy Irish as shamed the Justices into letting her off. A gay, voluptuous, handsome creature of thirty or so, she was celebrated for the looseness of her behaviour and for the fact that, alone in the parish, she was not in the least little bit afraid of the Canon. The reason for this was that, when all was said and done, Canon Peart was a Man, and Lizzie knew far too much about Men ever to fear one. Before her laughing gaze the biretta and the soutane, indeed, the Bishop's hat and the judge's wig, nay, purple robes and crown themselves, all the various outward symbols of male importance somehow dwindled and vanished, together, it must be feared, with the rest of the victim's coverings: never did those amused green eyes see anything more than the sorry little posturing object within. From one end of the year to the other she never set foot in the church or paid a penny piece for the support of the clergy. It was useless to coax her with the promise of Heaven or browbeat her with the threat of Hell: Lizzie had heard even wilder babble than that from Men in her long and pleasurable experience. For years now she had lived in the tranquil immunity of those who refuse to be frightened, peddling her wares with a minimum of concealment and perfectly content with her lot. If she had one wish, it would have been to see a little more of the world: Men, she was fully aware, were exactly the same in London or Paris as in Patrickstown, but she would have been glad to see how other women dressed. But the opportunity had never come and on the whole she was satisfied to remain as she was, the joy and relief of the men for miles around, and a thorn in the Canon's flesh.

This weathered stronghold of iniquity Father O'hOgain now resolved to take by storm. He did not consult his superior beforehand, as he wished the whole thing to come as a joyful surprise. With the parish in its present grievous state of laxity and insubordination, it seemed to him that by wiping out this one persistent blot he could stay the downward trend altogether; it would be a blessing to all the faithful and a feather in his own cap. Fortified, then, by the twin armour of innocence and anæmia, he lost no time in putting his plan into action, and presented himself at the door of Lizzie's cottage with the request for a few moments' chat.

That first interview lasted an hour and a half. The curate had never spoken to Lizzie before in his life and even when passing her on the road had always hastily averted his eyes with a muttered prayer. He had vaguely expected rudeness, mockery, blasphemous outcries: he found only a pleasant welcome. It was a long time since he had enjoyed anything half as much; and when at last he dragged himself away, it was with a promise of returning on the morrow with some pious works for her to study. He hurried back to his lodging with psalms of thanksgiving on his lips, confident that a breach had been made in the enemy wall.

Left alone in her trim little kitchen, Lizzie gave herself up to unrestrained and unholy merriment.

Punctual to the minute on the following day the curate was back, with copies of *A Key to Heaven, From Counting-House to Cloister* and *A Life of the Little Flower*. Lizzie was waiting with half a dozen bottles of stout. Father O'hOgain did not drink as a rule, as he did not much care for the taste of alcohol and it took very little to turn him giddy. But with Lizzie's immortal soul at stake he was prepared for every sacrifice. As often happens when we firmly resolve on an act of unselfishness, it came more easily to him than he expected. One bottle followed another and at last all six were empty.

It must not be supposed that the time passed in mere roistering. Father O'hOgain spoke to what he believed to be his new penitent with an eloquence he had never dreamed could be his. He was a man inspired: ideas, images, parallels, sentiments dashed through his fertile brain and fell from his tongue in honeyed cascades. He reminded Lizzie that the sins of each of us open the wounds of Our Saviour afresh. He bade her reflect, none the less, that the door never shut. Hope never ended nor were the wells of grace ever dry. He himself, unworthy as he was, ventured to believe that the purity of repentance brought more joy to the holy angels than the purity of virtue. Love, he concluded, was all that mattered: love, love and more love! Anything else was dust and ashes. Dust and ashes! he repeated sternly, wagging a finger at her.

He then bethought him that it was really time to go. But, on endeavouring to rise, he made the appalling discovery that his legs refused to carry him. Twice he made the attempt and twice he fell back in his chair. At the second time he burst into tears.

"Oh God, Lizzie, I'm done for!" he sobbed. "I should never have taken the old stout!"

"Arrah, be easy, Father dear. I'll help you," she replied. "Sure, I know this game like the back of me hand."

The poor young man felt most bitterly conscious of his fall from grace. All Lizzie could see in it was the spectacle, a recurring one in her life, of a Man in drink. She settled him as comfortably as she could and drew the curtains across the window, lest any prying eye should see what didn't concern it. Then she brewed up a hellish black tea and, while he gulped a cup of it down, stood over him fanning his brow with *A Life of the Little Flower*.

"Now listen, Father," she said in a motherly way, when the worst of the crisis seemed to be over, "the tay will get you as far as your home and not a step further than that. Be getting some rest now, that's the great boy. Go on up to your house and lie down on your bed, and never mind anything till it passes off. It's good advice I'm giving you!"

Like a lamb the curate struggled to his feet and tottered out of the cabin. As Lizzie told him to do, he turned his steps in the direction of home. But then it passed through his blurry mind that the Children of Mary were waiting below in the national school; it was the day of the week that he always instructed them. Was he to fail a second time in his duty? Wheeling about, he stumbled off down the road once again but, as Lizzie had forecast, the restoring powers of the tea were spent. Before the dozen or so surprised little faces that were pressed to the window-panes in the school, he went on reeling blindly past and out of the village altogether. After another hundred yards or so, he selected a comfortable ditch and laid him down to sleep.

It is a curious and diabolical fact of life that a sincere wish to do good can be more productive of mischief than almost anything else. Paddy O'hOgain had started out with such high hopes, such pure intentions, and if there had been a tiny drop of human vanity in it, it was no great matter: now he lay for all to see, dead to the world and snoring like a pig. It need hardly be said that every step in his campaign had been followed by the village with the keenest relish, and this latest development filled it with ecstasy. The turning of the tables on the high-minded aggressor by the redoubtable Lizzie struck it as one of the neatest jobs in the history of man. Only one thing was lacking to round it off to perfection: accordingly, with no mean or vindictive purpose but simply to squeeze the last little drop of pleasure out of a memorable incident, an anonymous telephone call went through to the parish house.

The curate slept on in his earthy cradle, sweetly dreaming of Lizzie. After a time the delectable visions that flitted through his mind disappeared, to be replaced by others of a different sort. Now, he dreamed, a mule was vigorously kicking him in the ribs and his ears were filled with a mighty roaring like that of an angry sea. The dream persisted and gradually it became plain to him, confused as he was, that it was not a dream at all. He was lying on the ground, he could not think where, and some rude fellow was shouting at the top of his voice and jabbing his sides with a stick. It seemed to him his best plan was to take no notice whatever. With an angelic smile of forgiveness, he settled himself to rest again, pillowing his cheek in one hand like a baby.

"Me parish a kip!" the voice was thundering, "and me curate a sot!"

Father O'hOgain whispered the words over to himself, and decided he could make nothing of them. It was an ignorant way to roar all right, that the fellow had. My parish! My curate! That was impudence, all the same. Only the Canon had a right to talk like that. Slowly and indignantly he opened a sticky eye to quell the bold stranger and hastily snapped it to again.

"Oh I see!" he whispered, fervently. "Yes, I see."

The shouting now stopped and was followed by a silence that was a hundred times more terrible. The curate decided that the only thing for it was a frank man-to-man discussion of the whole affair: he was still tipsy enough to believe this approach to be feasible. With difficulty he struggled to a sitting position and, reaching for his hat which had rolled a little way off, he set it on his head.

"You'll be surprised at finding me here like this, Canon," he commenced, with child-like candour, "but the truth of it is, I'm after reconciling Lizzie O'Rourke."

"Is that what you'd call it?" riposted the Canon. "It's

a grand expression I'd say, for carousing in houses of ill fame."

"I've brought her back to the fold," the ass proceeded, with a maudlin note in his voice. "You'll see her at Mass on Sunday. Wasn't that worth the little bit of bother? A soul reclaimed? For each of our souls is of equal and infinite value in the eyes of Heaven. And we must make her welcome," he cried, the facile drunkard's tears starting to his eyes, "much will be forgiven her because she loved a terrible lot, or words to that effect. Think of Mary Magdalen. Remember the woman found in adultery. Let him who is sinless, eh, Canon?" A severe attack of hiccups made it impossible for him to continue.

The Canon listened to this farrago with the sour expression of any responsible Churchman who hears the Gospel seriously quoted.

" 'Tis plain the drink isn't dead in you yet," he commented. "I'll talk to you when it is. I'll just tell you the one thing now, Paddy. You'll be off to Mount Melleray in the morning."

"Mount Melleray, Canon!" cried the poor fellow, starting up in horror. "Sure, you'd never do that. I'd be shamed forever. Mount Melleray! Why, 'tis only for incorrish . . . incoggir . . . for hopeless drunks!"

"And what else are you?" his master demanded. "Let you pack your bag the minute you're home, for I'll telephone the Lord Abbot this evening, we've a heavy case for him."

There was a pause, broken only by intermittent hiccoughing. Then Father O'hOgain painfully got to his feet and raised both hands like a prophet of old.

"Nayshig . . . Ignius . . . Ignatius Peart!" he declaimed, "I do believe you are Satan himself!" His wavering eye travelled down the Canon's person and came to rest on the toes of his enormous boots, splaying out under the hem of his cassock. "God Almighty!" he shrieked. "The cloven hoof!" With that, overcome, he pitched forward and lay quietly on his face.

The next unusual sight to meet the entranced eyes of the village was that of the Canon escorting his delinquent curate home. He had slipped an arm round him in what appeared to be a most amicable way and was half dragging, half carrying the inert figure over the ground at high speed. Fortunately, it was the middle of the week and the tourist trade had for the moment slackened a little; few strangers were there to witness the calamity and these few assumed that the young man had been taken ill. A reporter from the *Catholic Pillar,* who had been assigned to Patrickstown to write a series of vignettes on its happy, Christian life, immediately drew out his notebook.

"I only wish that some of our sneering, carping, *soi-disant* intelligentsia," he wrote, "could have stood beside me this afternoon, to see this same old Canon, so cruelly pilloried in the foreign press a week or so ago. I wish they could have seen, as I did, the fatherly love with which he assisted his ailing curate: stricken by age, bowed by suffering as he was, carrying the boy in his arms like a baby and murmuring words of comfort in his ear. Let the high-brows mock me, if they will: I am not ashamed to say that my eyes were wet. . . ."

The Canon adhered to his plan of sending Father O'hOgain to the monastery. In the ordinary way he would have called the doctor and acute indigestion, overwork or a murmuring heart would have been diagnosed in the twinkling of an eye; but in view of his own recent illness he judged the time inauspicious to follow the normal routine. It could not have happened at a worse moment, for he needed his curate as never before. Someone had got to spread through the usual channels the true, official, *ex cathedra* version of why he was not proceeding with the libel action. He had not yet fully made up his mind as to what this version should be but he expected to do so shortly, and it was important then that it be promulgated at once, before that lying atheist at Mangan's got to work on his own account. For duties of this kind, Paddy O'hOgain, with all his faults, had ever shown an aptitude bordering on genius: it was beneath the Canon's dignity to do it himself; and he saw with despair that he would have to rely mainly on the efforts of Patsy La Trobe and the housekeeper. There was no help for it, however, and he packed the curate off early next morning, deaf to his anguished entreaties.

Mrs. Mangan had lost no time in broadcasting to the village a faithful, indeed an almost verbatim, report of Andrew's business discussion with Mr. La Trobe. Not a soul in the place but knew that the Canon was not proceeding further, as well as the singular grounds for his coming to this decision. The rustication of Father O'hOgain now lent colour to a view gradually forming among the people that their priest was a little strange. The fact that he believed in ghosts was not so bad: sure, a man who believed the things he said in the pulpit every Sunday would believe anything in that line: but if he really believed that Paddy O'hOgain was addicted to drink, then it was getting beyond a joke. The thought of Paddy, who could never take a sip at a wedding without making a face over it, being kindly and firmly weaned away from the bottle by the good monks, was too much for them. They began at last to ponder their responsibilities.

It was characteristic of the inhabitants of this little village that absolutely nothing was said. Each knew what was in the mind of others without any remarks being passed. The matter of Father O'hOgain was never again alluded to: jokes about bathrooms, lawsuits, haunted halls, mysteriously dropped from the local repertory overnight. Every man became a closed vessel as wordlessly and collectively all felt their way towards a solution. Removed from them as he was, the Canon yet felt a change in the mental climate and deduced that they were plotting some fresh devilry. His griefs, his humiliations, his financial worries, had destroyed for the moment the mainsprings of his confidences. Since the night of his awful climb up the mountain, the Sunday collections had gone steadily up, more than once a village lad had come to ask might he dig in the garden, and chickens, baskets of eggs and pounds of butter had been left at the presbytery door. All this was done, the Canon reasoned, to lull him into a false security while they contemplated something more horrible than all that had gone before. And while the village brooded, he was nerving himself to confound it.

It was then that Malachy, the simple fellow, saw his vision.

SIXTEEN

Lord patrickstown's estate divided itself roughly into two parts. To the right of the great house and behind it, marching with the convent grounds and falling down away to the river, were all the wooded lands, while to the left there stretched acre upon acre of hilly terrain, some of it covered with grass and some with scrub and fern, where beasts had their grazing and the herds of deer their home. Here and there a knoll was crowned with a ring of trees: some half mile from the house was the lake, covered with trailing weeds and little white flowers; but for the most part it was bare, rough land, open to the view and untouched by the labour of man.

On one rising point, however, invisible from the house, stood unexpectedly an exquisite little Folly of a sort that might have been more appropriate in the park at Versailles. It had been put there by one of Bertie's more dashing ancestors, and it was a Folly not in the English sense of a costly, useless structure, but in the French, of a little rustic retreat in which to give oneself up freely to diversions calling for quietness and concentration. In this sense the noble lord himself had conceived and enjoyed it, and the tales of his extravagant carryings-on had long since passed into the lore of the neighbourhood. It was in reality no more than a pavilion, consisting of one beautifully proportioned room and possessing a domed roof, with slender marble pillars on each side of the entrance. The ground had been levelled before it to make an approach and two lines of marble figures stood there forming a guard of honour: to the right, naked youths, bold and amorous, to the left, maidens, shyly looking down but equally naked. Although nobody had since put it to the use for which it was intended, the little place was still cared for to this day.

Malachy had been helping himself to a few of Lord Patrickstown's rabbits, as was the local custom. Early that morning he had set his snares in a choice place of his own; and now after nightfall he had been the rounds collecting his booty up and setting the snares again for the morrow. He was on his way home, with a vacant grin on his face and half a dozen rabbits in either hand, when for some reason the gleaming white marble figures, that he had seen a hundred times before, attracted his cruising eye and struck his capricious fancy. Later on he was to assert that one of the maidens had beckoned to him but this detail, after careful examination, was tidied away as weakening the major part of the story.

He left the path and walked to the edge of the smooth cropped grass that led up to the Folly. There he stood between the two lines of figures, staring ahead with his zany's grin, when all at once the door of it opened. He distinctly heard the click as the catch was pulled back, so there was no question of its flying open by itself; but this detail too, one of the clearest he could remember, was also later suppressed. For a moment or two he saw nothing but the yawning blackness of the room behind. Then suddenly a white figure appeared, framed in the doorway: it paused for an instant and, very slowly, began to move forward.

There was a half-moon in the sky, but it no longer gave a clear white light as in recent weeks. Obscured by the moisture now charging the air, it shed a pale fuzzy gleam in which only the bare shapes of things stood out. The impression that Malachy's feeble mind received was that of a man about to go for a swim, but he did not stay to verify it. With a wolf-like howl he dashed his rabbits to the ground and made for his mother's house as fast as he could. He thus could not see the shadowy figure dart for the shelter of darkness again with an alacrity equal to his own.

Mrs. Lynch was entertaining some friends of her brother-in-law, the postmaster, with an evening cup of tea. The widow of a man who had drunk first his farm and then himself out of existence, she would not have enjoyed the place she held in local society without this powerful relation; but as it was, the cream of Patrickstown was glad to gather under her humble, leaking roof. Mr. Purcell, the land agent, was there, and Mr. Treacy, the richest farmer: Mr. Mulligan, the grocer, who had amassed a small fortune by rendering his accounts to the gentry only once a year, in the sure knowledge that they were too lazy ever to check: her brother-in-law, and two or three other serious and reputable members of the community. Not one of them trusted the others across the room, but together they formed a cohesive little body of opinion and were, in secular matters, the moral and intellectual leaders of the parish.

As Malachy, his eyes starting from his head with terror, came bursting in and sobbed out an incoherent account of his adventure, it dawned on them all that something of the greatest importance, something entirely and utterly removed from the everyday run of things, had occurred.

Each came to this conclusion independently of the others: not so much as a glance or a nod passed between them. Only the trend of their interrogation revealed how absolutely they were at one. Under the soothing influence of their kindly presences the boy gradually calmed down and under their gentle but persistent questioning he began to sort out his muddled ideas and remember the scene more clearly. By the time they had finished with him, he knew beyond all doubt that what he had seen was a beautiful lady in shining white raiment, under whose pure feet, as she walked slowly forward to bless him, a host of tiny starlike flowers sprang out of the earth in homage.

Satisfied in having at last prised the truth from this unpromising subject, they set to work to make much of the boy. They assured him the holy men in Rome would have given their eyes for his chances: they plied him with cups of tea and slices of cake: they insisted on his going at once to bed and taking it easy. Mr. Purcell felt that to mark the gravity of the occasion the doctor ought to be sent for, but here the widow Lynch was adamant.

"The boy is all I have," she said.

When Malachy, now leering with a fatuous self-importance, was bedded down, they lingered on awhile in an atmosphere that was hushed with awe. Their minds were working too fast for any real discussion to be desired but an odd remark now and again showed the sense of the meeting.

" 'Tis a great thing, that, a great thing indeed for the boy, Mrs. Lynch," said Mr. Treacy.

"And for the town as well, mind you," remarked Mr. Mulligan.

"It's a number of years since it happened in Ireland," Mr. Treacy went on.

A pause followed, and then Mr. Lynch expressed what

was in the hearts of them all. "And isn't it the perfect answer," he inquired, "to those that wanted to cry us down?"

There was nothing for it after that but to recite the rosary with widow Lynch, as the glad genetrix of a possible beatification, giving it out to the rest of them. Anything less would have shown a grave want of manners, and left the evening incomplete. Their crafty peasant faces composed in tranquil devotion, they kneeled on the stone floor and chanted with a will. If now and again from under reverently downcast lids they shot little sidelong glances at each other, it was no more than the prudent habit of years. Then, with profuse expressions of esteem and congratulation, they took their leave, their minds still humming away like so many dynamos. Late as it was, they found time to pay a few calls before they went home to bed.

The convent chapel next morning at early Mass was crowded out, with long lines of kneeling figures on the grass around it. Then the village went to work with a will to present a smiling face to the world. Flowers, blue, white and yellow, appeared in every little window, and clean curtains too wherever it was possible. The windows themselves were polished until they shone, the space before each cabin door was swept and tidied, ducks and hens were forbidden the use of the kitchens. Boys ran about picking up bits of paper, empty tins and bottles and other rubbish and tipped them judiciously into the stream. The Lady Chapel in the church was transformed into a bower of lilies, begged or stolen from the gardens of the big houses around. The mummified blooms before the Patriot's statue were replaced. The shops were closed and, in a spontaneous act of devotion, every man jack in the village abstained from work.

While these preparations went steadily forward, the

reporter from the *Catholic Pillar* was racing up and down like a hysterical beagle. As soon as he judged that his chief would be in the office, he telephoned Dublin and, in a voice trembling with excitement, began to pour out the story. To his immense chagrin, however, the man at the end of the wire sounded none too pleased.

"It's a good story all right, Seumas, but I wonder can we use it," he said hesitantly.

"God Almighty, Mr. Kavanagh, it's the biggest break for years! Our Lady Herself, appearing to rebuke the scoffers . . ."

"I know, I know, sure I know," interrupted the editor, wearily. "But we'll have to hold it all the same until we get a clearance. The high-ups are pretty down on these apparitions. There was one out in the Wicklow Mountains a year or so ago that they scotched altogether. You're too young to remember, Seumas, but in 1935 or thereabouts a girl in County Clare had a vision, and it was allowed, and she went off to New York and became a fashion editress."

"There's no danger at all of that happening here. The one who saw it is a simple, saintly youth."

"Yes, but an experience like that makes them cagey," the editor told him. "One can see their point of view. I'll do my best for you, Seumas, but don't be too optimistic. In the meantime, there's no harm if you start on the build-up. Patrickstown's Answer to Malign Critics. Unswerving Devotion to Our Lady. Affecting Scenes at Convent Door. Local Feeling Runs High. The usual gup."

"I'll do it," promised the faithful Seumas, mastering his disappointment.

While they spoke another conversation, similar in its trend, was being carried on between the parish house and the Palace. It was with great trepidation that the Canon took up the receiver and asked for the Bishop's number.

Inexcusably he had failed to consult His Lordship before calling the action off, feeling that his grounds for doing so were beyond his powers of exposition; and he feared that the matter would now be referred to. The Bishop had telephoned *him* when the story broke in the newspapers and had been inclined to crustiness over the whole affair. What he would say when he learned that, after so much undesirable publicity, it had been cancelled without his leave, the Canon shuddered to think. But there was no help for it, as the rule was clear: all apparitions, saintly interventions and miracles to be reported without delay.

The Bishop, like the editor, was far from delighted.

"It sounds very much like *enthusiasm* to me," he grumbled. "Frankly, Canon, your parish is altogether too much in the limelight these days."

"What can I do, my Lord?" pleaded the Canon. "I've spoken to the boy and I'm sure he's telling the truth. He's got the details of it far too pat to be making it up. And the people are all mad for it. That is the situation at present. What is to happen next, of course, is entirely within Your Lordship's discretion."

"What about this Malachy Lynch? Is he a good boy?"

"There's no harm in him at all."

"Confesses and communicates regularly?"

"I wouldn't say that," the Canon replied. "His mother, now, she's most assiduous. But the boy himself . . . well, he's a bit simple."

"Do you mean to say he's an idiot?"

"Ah, there's a hard word," the Canon said. "But I'm bound to tell you, he's none too bright."

"I don't like the sound of it, Canon."

"Nor do I, my Lord," the priest admitted. "But I've told you now what has happened, as it was my duty to do, and we await Your Lordship's direction. If you tell us there's a mistake, of course, there's nothing more to be said."

"I won't do that," said the Bishop, peevishly. "I've had experience of these matters. It can be very dangerous, once the people accept a vision. They'll be starting a cult on their own if we don't mind ourselves and then the next thing will be, a whole crop of unauthorized miracles."

"What does Your Lordship wish me to do?"

"Nothing for the moment. This is not a question for us. I'd best drive up to Dublin and put the case to them there. Meanwhile tell your people to keep calm, and you hold special devotions every day until further notice."

"I will, my Lord," and the Canon hung up. Worked off me feet, I'll be, worked off me feet, he reflected, bitterly.

The Bishop had shown a nice understanding of the village mind. As if aware that attempts might be made to baulk it, it proceeded steadily throughout the day with demonstrations that grew all the time in fervour and intensity. Little bands of singing people made their way to the Folly where they knelt, they backs scrupulously turned to the marble figures, and recited the Litany of the Blessed Virgin Mary. The main street was bedecked with flags and bunting, while streamers embroidered with the slogans "Salve, Regina Coelis!" and "Welcome, the Queen of the World!" were stretched across it from window to window. From morning to evening the church was packed with the faithful all in their Sunday clothes, prominent among them, and cold sober, being Mr. Cat's-Eye O'Keefe.

"They are such good people, you know," Bertie said, with emotion, to Andrew. He alone of the Canon's flock had no clear idea of what was to do, but the sight of them all going about it stirred him to the depths of his being. The two friends were lazing in deck-chairs in the rose garden at Patrickstown Hall, idly watching a parliament of rooks who were holding a stormy session in an elm tree near by. Mrs. Mangan had decided not to to share the news with Andrew for the present, and he had strolled up to try and find out from Bertie what was happening. They had pooled their scraps of informations and were little the wiser; but they both agreed it was very mysterious and rather lovely.

All at once the little lord sprang to his feet and darted away to the furthest rose tree in the garden. Bending over one of the crimson flowers he carefully removed a small insect, as if instinct had warned him of its detrimental activity just at that moment. Slowly he returned towards his chair, then halted and wound one ankle about the other. His round face grew slowly pink and his pale lashes fluttered up and down as if the light of day were too strong to bear.

"It makes me feel so utterly ashamed and unworthy!" he burst out. "Oh, Andy, there's such a weight on my mind."

"Tell me," his friend said, sympathetically. He was feeling happier and more at peace than he had for a long while past. It was not simply that the awful prospect of the lawsuit had been removed. Since the report of his knavery in respect of the ghost had gone round the village the people, although firmly behind the Canon in all essentials, had begun to regard him with genuine esteem and affection. They looked on him now as almost fly enough to be one of themselves, and the sense he had of taking a real place in the community at last was very agreeable.

"Oh, if I could! I'm sure you wouldn't be hard on me. It's the old story of Jekyll and Hyde, if you see what I mean," Bertie faltered, sprinting away to pick up a few brown leaves.

"Surely not as bad as that?"

"Oh yes, it is. It's a frightful compulsion I've got, you know. Well, compulsion . . . I mustn't use that word now I understand about Sin. But before I joined the Church, I went to an analyst about it. A horrible person, from Vienna or somewhere of that sort. It went on for months and cost me hundreds of guineas. And do you know what his opinion was, after all that expensive tomfoolery? *He couldn't see that it really mattered.*"

"I expect I shall agree with him," said Andrew, comfortably.

"Oh, you won't. With your principles, I mean. I do so look up to you, Andy, if you don't mind my saying so," the little fellow went on, his eyes fixed on the other in mingled hope and dread.

"Well, out with it and we'll see," Andrew told him, closing his own eyes and folding his hands across his stomach.

Bertie made a sudden dash at a blackbird on the lawn, whose peaceful search for grubs he appeared to consider intolerable. Having driven it off, he once more came back to his place with hanging head and, sinking down, clasped his little hands as if in supplication.

"Well, I get awfully worked up and excited, you know, and I hardly seem to know what I'm doing and suddenly, I can't seem to help myself and . . . Oh Andy, what will you say? I tear off all my clothes and so on and I go dashing about the place stark naked."

"What?" exclaimed Andrew, sitting bolt upright.

"There you are! I knew it would horrify you."

"Do you mean to say this is a regular habit of yours?"

"Yes, and that isn't all. It's getting steadily worse. That's what I meant about Jekyll and Hyde. Because I do it now without realizing, I mean, after a few drinks and so on. Last night Anguish and I had a bit of a party and this morning my clothes were found in a pile beside the lake. And I don't remember the first thing about it."

"This is a serious matter, Bertie," Andrew gravely told him.

"And where is it all going to end?" his lordship inquired.

"Where indeed? You took the words out of my mouth. Could you stop drinking for a while?"

"Well, not very easily, you know, till Anguish goes home. Reverend Mother has kindly promised to find him some maids, and then he'll be leaving. But while he's here I'm afraid it's a case of the flowing bowl and all that. You are horribly shocked, aren't you?" he concluded, wistfully.

"I'm solicitous," Andrew replied. "You see, I've . . . well, never mind. But it would be very unfortunate if the religious festivals here were marred by unseemly incidents, wouldn't it?"

"That's what terrifies me," Bertie eagerly assented. "I mean, all this beautiful simple piety and so on. I ought to be an example, instead of which I'm a whited sepulchre. I say, though, it is a relief to get it off my chest. One of the awful things was that nobody knew. I've never even confessed it, you know. It doesn't seem to fit into any of the categories. Oh, Andy, what shall I do?"

"It might be a good plan if you stained yourself with woad. At least you wouldn't be so visible."

"But where should I get the woad from? Oh, I see, you're joking, Ha ha, you are funny! Perhaps if we laugh at it, it'll blow over by itself."

"Perhaps," said Andrew, doubtfully.

"You don't hate me, do you?" asked the little lord.

"Of course not, silly. I'm just marvelling at the number and varied nature of the problems that beset us all in the Christian Oasis."

Andrew lay back in his chair with a sudden revival of uneasiness. Few people sink so low but what they cling on to some one principle at least, to anchor themselves to their self-respect. Thus the forger may be scrupulous in settling the accounts of his tradesmen, thus the drunkard may carefully feed his pet canary before setting out on a blind; and thus Andrew, now dead to shame in so many ways, still fully intended to keep his word with regard to the ghost. The thought of not being able to do so came first as a shock to his vestigial sense of honour; and in the next moment he began to wonder what his legal position would be. If one of the parties to a contract defaulted, surely the contract itself was void. He decided to have a word with Felim at the earliest opportunity; and this too weighed on his mind, as he had hoped to keep the arrangement dark from that keen observer.

The little lord, on the other hand, was much restored by the act of confession and was looking about him with the alert, refreshed air of a baby who has just been sick in somebody's lap.

Each busy with his own thoughts, they remained silent. Aloft in their elm, the rooks were still hard at it. First one, then another, would open his beak and caw portentously, to the accompaniment of a nodding of sleek black heads and the preening of feathers. Now and again a member of the council voiced an opinion unacceptable to the majority and was indignantly cawed down, while a little shower of leaves and twigs came fluttering to the ground. Then the oldest and fattest rook put in a soothing caw or so and the parliament resumed the study of the problems before it. The youngest and leanest rook, unable to get a caw in edgeways, flew off in a marked manner.

Presently there was a ringing cry of "Cooee!" and Anguish came bounding like an antelope through the

French windows of the library and down the path to where they sat.

"There you are! I've been hunting for you all over!"

The master of the house roused himself to say, "Anguish, you don't know Andy Butler, do you? Andy, this is Angus Ferguson."

Anguish acknowledged the introduction by a circular movement of the hips, as if he were about to perform a hula-hula.

"My dears! sorry to crash in! but I've been talking to that old sweetie, Mr. Wimbush," he cried. "Oh, he is in a state. You'll never guess what's happened."

"Let me get you a chair and you shall tell us about it," Bertie suggested.

"No, no!" said Anguish, waving him aside. He flung himself down on the grass on his tummy, cupped his chin in one hand and kicked up his heels behind, in the style of Peter Pan. "Do you know what all this to-do's about? The village idiot has seen the Virgin Mary. Isn't it too, too marvellous? And the Roman Catholic Canon has told the Bishop and the Bishop's gone roaring up to Dublin to see the Primate and ask if it's all right. And the village idiot is in bed, under a mound of flowers, like a corpse. And old Mrs. Craig has sent the servants home and has bolted and barred her doors. She's sitting in the front hall with a shot-gun across her knees. And Amanda! my dears, *Amanda!!* is trying to make out that King Billy appeared in her grounds last night, riding his white horse. Everyone, but everyone, in the place has gone stark, raving mad. Mr. Wimbush is going to see his own Bishop this evening. Now what do you say to that?"

His listeners received the news each in his own way. Bertie opened his eyes as wide as they would go and said, tremulously, "So that's it! O Anguish, how splendid! How beautiful and how splendid!" Andrew lay back and closed his eyes again. "Dear God!" he murmured, brokenly. "Dear God!"

"Now Andy, why do you say 'Dear God' in that skeptical way?" asked Bertie, in gentle reproach.

"It was that, or remain speechless altogether."

"You materialists lose an awful lot in life, if you don't mind my saying so," Bertie chided him, his eyes shining. "One has only to tell you something wonderful, and straight away you know all about it. If it was some mundane thing, you'd take time to make up your minds. Don't you believe there may be more things in heaven and earth than are dreamed of in your philosophy?"

"No," was the simple reply.

"But, dear Andy, if he saw it!"

"Who? The village idiot?"

"There isn't a village idiot," Bertie said. "Anguish, who saw the vision? You mustn't go touching things up in this naughty way. I'm sure all that about Amanda and Mrs. Craig is pure invention. And Mr. Wimbush is the last man alive to use the word 'idiot' of anyone."

" 'Not quite as other boys are' was how he put it," Anguish conceded. "But there was a wealth of meaning in his eye. It was someone called Malachy Lynch."

"There you are! Malachy is a dear good boy, but a little retarded."

"He was stealing your rabbits when he saw it!" crowed Anguish. "I haven't told you the best of it yet. I'm keeping it as a honey-last."

"I don't mind at all if he was, Anguish," Bertie said, almost sternly for him. "At least, I mean, I wish the people wouldn't because they know perfectly well they can come and get rabbits openly whenever they like. They do so love to do things in a roundabout way, you know. It's really rather odd of them. But Anguish!" he cried, as a new thought struck him, "do you mean to say that Our Lady appeared on my land?"

"That's where Malachy was, anyway," laughed Anguish. "And do you know whereabouts? In the Folly! What a venue!"

His high giggle broke out afresh, supported by a roar in the bass from Andrew.

"O Patrickstown! Patrickstown! *Ville Lumière!*" Anguish rattled on.

"I shall really be rather vexed with you two in a minute," said the little lord, mutinously. "Of course I can think of more appropriate places than the Folly, I mean, but it's not for us to say, is it? Our Lady is entitled to appear where She likes. It may be Her way of showing that the past is dead and forgiven. And I should have thought," he went on, while his eyes filled with tears and the corners of his mouth pulled down, "that friends of mine like both of you, that I'm so awfully fond of, wouldn't have tried to spoil my happiness in this wonderful . . . this tremendous . . ." He broke down completely now and buried his face in his hands.

"Bertie darling! sweetheart!" burst from Anguish.

"Bertie old fellow!" came from Andrew. Both were appalled.

"On my land!" he sobbed. "You don't realize, I mean."

"There, there, there," they said.

"After what I was telling you about myself, Andy! In spite of it all, I mean! And on the same evening! She deigned, She condescended . . ."

Even Anguish looked slightly ashamed of himself, and

Andrew could hardly bear it. At some future time, he knew, the mighty gusts of laughter now tearing his insides would have to be given full rein, if his system were not to be wrecked. But it must keep. The seismic effect on local events of one who sorrowfully believed himself to be no more than a dead leaf floating at the edge of the stream was something to treasure up and savour to the end of time. For the moment there was only the little human being to think of, in all his sweetness and sincerity.

"Of course it had to be on your land, Bertie," he said. "Didn't I tell you, you would justify Patrickstown one of these days? You wouldn't believe me."

As he thought how true this prediction had been, there was another terrible surging up of the demon mirth, which he fought down by an iron effort of will.

"Let us all go up to the house and have a little drinkie," Bertie wailed, mopping his eyes. "I'll pull myself together presently. I'm so ashamed. Breaking down and that sort of thing. What my poor father would have said! Of course, he wouldn't have cared for any of this. But it's so wonderful. And you have been so kind to me. And I was so nasty to you. . . ."

Incoherent, tearful and yet deeply happy, he was helped to the house by his abashed and humbled friends. There under the influence of a bottle he kept for great occasions he made a remarkable recovery and electrified them both —almost beyond astonishment as they were—by a gifted impersonation of the Madam of a brothel in Marseilles, discovering that someone had fobbed her off with a counter-feit note. Outside the evening quietly wore away. With a few last weighty observations, the rooks adjourned until the morrow. In every window in the village as the dusk deepened a candle was lighted, in case the Visitor should return and be doubtful as to Her way. The Canon, making an uneasy nocturnal prowl, noted this and shook his head.

"If they've any sense in them at all," he said to himself, "they'll allow Her."

SEVENTEEN

Next morning as Mrs. Mangan set about her household tasks, she was waylaid by Seumas, the white hope of the Catholic Press, who asked for a private word with her on a matter of importance. Mrs. Mangan looked at the spotty youth with aversion. He had in his coat both the badge of a Pioneer and the gold ring of an Irish-speaker: things which, in her view, worn separately were signs of an unquiet brain and taken together could mean no good at all. It was clear to her also that he was about to complain of something or someone, for he was fairly bursting with self-righteous malice. She laid down her duster with a sigh and motioned him into her parlour.

"Mrs. Mangan," he commenced, "we know of course that ever since Certain People were refused room at a Certain Inn, innkeepers have had to be careful."

Mrs. Mangan saw this as a reference to an English hotelier in the neighbourhood, who had once mistaken old Lord Tipperary for a tramp and threatened to set the dogs on him; and she waited patiently for him to continue.

"Their doors must be open to all and sundry, lest once

again a welcome Visitor be excluded," the horrid youth droned on. "But there is one guest in this house who ought not to be here."

"You'd be thinking of Mr. Butler, I suppose," said Mrs. Mangan, keenly. Seumas could hardly be referring to himself, and Andrew was the only other.

"Just so, Mrs. Mangan. Mr. Butler. Oh! I am not speaking now of the mischief he has made and the sorrow he has brought on a kind, good old Irish priest. It is, if anything, worse than that. I am sorry to tell you that Mr. Butler is a thief."

"Ah, get away with it!" Mrs. Mangan's tone was peremptory.

"I assure you, I caught him in the act," Seumas proceeded, with lugubrious enjoyment. "I opened my door this morning to take in my shoes, and wasn't he there in the act of carrying them off? And didn't he drop them at once and run like a hare when he saw me?"

"And is that right, Mr. Sherlock Holmes?" inquired the proprietress with heavy irony, placing her hands on her hips. "Well, now I'll let you into a secret. He was after cleaning them for you. Didn't you know he was the new Boots here?"

She opened the door of the parlour for him in a way there was no mistaking, and as he passed out fired a parting shot at his back.

"And did you really imagine he'd want those shoes of yours, half the size of his own, and with a hole in the toe a mouse would run through blindfold?"

When Seumas, somewhat rosy in the face, got back to his room he glanced out of the window and there, sure enough, Andrew sat in the yard, wearing one of Mrs. Mangan's aprons and scraping some vegetables. Seumas considered the matter thoughtfully and drew out his note-book. Materialist Writer Humbled, he wrote.

The uncomfortable feeling that his interview with the landlady left behind was soon forgotten, for just before luncheon he was called to the telephone to receive some joyful news.

"Is that yourself, Seumas?" said the editor's voice. "Well then, it's O.K. Go ahead with the story and give it all you've got."

"She appeared?" shrieked the reporter, almost beside himself.

"She did. It's a wonderful chance for you all right, being on the spot. We're clearing the front page for you. We want the story by three this afternoon. Just a sober factual account of what's happened so far, to begin with, and to-morrow you can start on the follow-ups and colour stuff."

"And suppose She were to appear again, Mr. Kavanagh? Would that be in order?"

"It would, of course. It's the green light, I'm telling you. The sky's the limit. Now jump to it, there's the great fellow."

And Seumas jumped. All thoughts of luncheon went out of his mind at once. His hand trembled so much that at times it could hardly guide the pen. He sat there fever-ishly covering one sheet of paper after another, tearing them all up again, mouthing the words aloud and twitch-ing all over like a rabbit. By half-past two he had his factual masterpiece ready and all that remained to do was to run through it once again, checking a point here and altering a word there. The article ran as follows:

When first I came to Patrickstown I found a little Christian community in mourning. It was mourning its good name, foully snatched from it by one of those itinerant journalists that England sends us in such large number. The fellow had hinted at odious practices in the local convent, whose worthy sisters belong to an Order famed for its piety through the long centuries of its illustrious establishment (? please look up which Order). Of their own grief, we shall say nothing: It is easier to imagine than to describe. Of the grief of the saintly old man who directs them in matters spiritual, we need say nothing: it has found practical expression in a way known to one and all. But what, ah what? of the simple Catholic souls of the town who had ever looked up to the Convent as literally a beacon of Catholic practice and Catholic virtue? It is no exaggeration to say they were brokenhearted.

Today how different is the picture! Help has come, and from a Quarter whence help always comes to those who simply and sincerely believe. The lie has been given, and by a source that brooks no question, to him who with filthy pen, sought to smear the radiance of the nuns' repute.

And let us, in all humility, consider the channels through which Grace has chosen to work. They might be described, without offence, as the highest and the lowest: thus proving that considerations of class do not enter the Divine reckoning. On the one hand we have Lord Patrickstown (earl? viscount? check, there's a good fellow) whose reconciliation with our Holy Mother Church in (date?) afforded such joy to the faithful throughout our beloved country. On his land it was, in a little rustic bower set up by one of his forbears, Protestant, true, but estimable, for quiet meditation: in this little haven of peace and tranquillity, I repeat, was vouchsafed the miracle that has changed the town overnight from a scene of woe to one of rejoicing.

And who, ah who, was thought worthy of the still greater honour and privilege of witnessing this miraculous intervention? "Another of the idle rich!" I seem to hear our parlour Communists cry. No, gentlemen, no: nor one of the spoilt darlings of our universities either, who use their little pitiful scraps of learning to pick holes in our sacred religion and cry down those who in fatherly love lead the pure in heart of Ireland towards their Eternal Home. No, and again, no! A simple youth, no more, a youth of the town: the only child of a widow looked up to by all for her unaffected piety: a boy of friendly ways and innocent pastimes: a poor boy, possessing neither wealth or influence, or even good looks.

YET UNTO HIM WAS IT GRANTED TO SEE OUR BLESSED LADY HERSELF THE NIGHT BEFORE LAST AT ABOUT TEN-TWENTY P.M.!!

Small wonder, then, if Patrickstown today looks bright and fresh and garnished, like one of the new housing estates outside Dublin. Small wonder if all day long the sweet bells chime, calling the faithful to new devotion and thanksgiving. And small wonder indeed if the Pastor of this happy little flock has today the air of a man, let us say it in all reverence, who has risen from Hell. Ah, what a load of care is lifted from those aged shoulders! As I watched him this morning, hurrying to and fro on his sacred errands, truly it seemed to me that a Light not of this earth was playing about his venerable brow.

On second thoughts, Seumas took this sentence out. It would fit better, he reasoned, into the moving description

of next Sunday's Mass that was already assembling itself
in his head.

One last word. What of the cause of the former
mischief, the profane meddler and busybody whose
vile insinuations plunged this quiet little place into
sorrow and shame? Where is he? Is he, surrounded
by his like, quaffing champagne in the lounge bars of
Fleet Street? Is he boasting of his achievement, what
time he cynically puffs at a cigar? He is not. It is
gratifying to know that even the corrupted press of
the pagans over the water has seen him for what he
is. Never again will he get a chance to spew his lies
in even the questionable columns of the *Daily Packet*.
In a short time he has sunk to the very bottom, where
he belongs: he is now employed as the Boots in Mrs.
Mangan's first-class hotel in Patrickstown, where his
duties are to clean the shoes and peel the potatoes,
both of which, needless to say, he performs very
badly.

But we must be charitable. The bestial assailant
of Maria Goretti lived to expiate his crime in humble
repentance as a gardener and to assist, with overflowing heart, at her canonization. Our Lord Himself
forgave His murderers. Let us, therefore, ignore and
forget Mr. Andrew Butler: let none jeer at the fallen.

More tomorrow.

These last two words, of course, were a service message
and not to be taken as part of the text. At three o'clock
when Dublin came through on the line Seumas squeaked
out this effusion to an impassive stenographer and then
set forth to cull new flowers for the morrow.

In the normal way Mrs. Mangan was not a reader of

the *Catholic Pillar*. The only newspaper she saw at all regularly was the *Maryville Clarion,* whose garbled accounts of local events minutely familiar to herself gave her a great deal of pleasure. But since the *Pillar* man was under her roof she had, with her usual courtesy and for the time being, ordered a copy. As she began to read Seumas's article on the following morning she was disposed, for the first time, not to regret this move, for he seemed to her to reach heights never attained by the *Clarion,* not even in the palmy days of the Doped Greyhound scandal. When she came to the passage concerning Andrew, however, she thought she was going to faint. It really did look to her as if most of the grief in the world came from the inky tribe to which Seumas belonged. Either, like him, they wrote lies and there was sure to be a crossness all round: or, like Andrew, they wrote the truth and then hell itself broke loose. Sure, she'd said that Andrew was the new Boots, but what of it? Tears came to her eyes at the thought. It was nice thanks all right for the hand he was giving her, till she got on her feet again and could afford proper help. The poor lady moved about the place like someone in a dream, stealing fearful glances at Andrew whenever they happened to meet, trying to gauge by the look on his face whether he had yet seen the defamatory print.

She had never had monkeys like Seumas in the house before. The clients of former years were decent, solid gentlemen whose only talk was of fish and weather. Once indeed there had been a solitary guest whom the others scornfully dubbed "The Intellectual" but that was merely because he took the temperature of the stream before choosing a fly. And now fresh tribulation was on the way. Her desperate prayers to Heaven for a full house again were about to be answered, but answered, as prayers often are, in a way quite different from what she intended. At eleven o'clock she received a telegram which said:"PLEASE RESERVE SINGLE ROOM TONIGHT UNTIL FURTHER NOTICE IRISH EXAMINER." This was closely followed by three more, from the *Irish Thinker,* the *Irish World* and the *Cork Plain-dealer.* After that was a lull and then two more arrived, one from the *Northern Observer* and one from the *Ulster Whig.* There was peace for a little and then, like a knell, came a telegram signed Esmé Pearl. The last one of all shattered her nerves completely. It said: "KINDLY RESERVE ONE ROOM WITH PRIVATE BATH PHONE GARAGE TO-NITE THRU COMING WEEK ALSO ARRANGE CABLE FACILITIES POSTOFFICEWISE RESERVING EXCULSIVELY THREE TO FOUR EACH AFTERNOON CORDIALLY TIME LIFE FORTUNE." Reading this, Mrs. Mangan thought she must lose her reason.

Felim telephoned in the course of the morning. "Hullo? Butler? Look here, what *is* going on in your place? I suppose you've engineered the whole thing?"

"It's spendid, is it not?" asked Andrew, complacently.

"Never in my whole life did I have a case like it," Felim complained. "I don't know if I'm on my head or my heels. One minute they're asking to serve the writ in England. The next, they want to withdraw the whole thing. I assumed you had fixed that up, so I didn't even bother to write and tell you. And now all this. I'm sure you're behind it: don't tell me you're not."

"As a matter of fact, I wanted to have a word with you about the withdrawing of the action. I'm a little worried," Andrew confessed. "You see, I agreed with Mr. La Trobe that he should stop all proceedings and I would remove the ghost."

"The what?"

"The ghost. G-h-o-s-t. There's a ghost here that gets on the Canon's nerves," Andrew said, patiently. "Now,

Plunkett, when I undertook to remove that ghost, I honestly believed I should be able to keep my word. But I am no longer quite so sure. So I was wondering if, when you come to draw up the agreement, you would put in a clause to cover me, say for example, 'the Defendant for his part *will make all reasonable* efforts to remove the ghost,' instead of the bald undertaking?"

"I don't know what you are talking about," said Felim, with deep emotion. "I can only say there'll be no ghosts in any document drawn up by me. More than my reputation is worth! As for what you've been up to, it clearly beggars description."

"Oh, I've negotiated trickier settlements than this in the Congo," said Andrew, airily.

"I daresay you have. I'm sorry, Butler," said Felim, gravely, "I doubt very much if I can continue to act for you. I simply am not accustomed to these English methods."

"Ah, g'wan out of dat!"

"Holy Fly! will you listen to him? It's uncanny," Felim breathed. "I think you'd better come on up here and see me."

"I'm sorry, I can't. There's a great invasion of the Press, and I must help to get about eight bedrooms ready."

"What's that you're saying? Was that part of it true?" came in startled tones. There were sounds of a throat being cleared, and Felim's embarrassed voice went on: "Er . . . Butler?"

"Well?"

"I haven't known you very long," Felim said throatily, and coughed several times: "but I mean, that is, if you were in any sort of difficulty . . . er . . . temporary difficulty, you know, I'd be only too glad to help."

"You sound more English every day," said Andrew gaily. "Of course I should be delighted. When will you come?"

"Er . . . wouldn't it do by post?"

"By post? A correspondence course? Naturally not."

"What are we talking about?" Felim wished to know.

"Aren't you coming to help make beds?"

"I was offering you a loan actually."

"A loan? It's very good of you, but why? I'm drawing a comfortable salary from the University."

"Will someone come to the rescue before I go mad?" Felim appealed. "Listen here." He snatched up the newspaper and read out the paragraph which described his client's new duties and his manner of carrying them out. Andrew was so angry he could hardly speak.

"How dare he? The little rat! There's no one peels a prettier potato than myself, and as for the shoes, you'd shave by the light of them," he cried, passionately. "Oh, I shan't let it go at that. You come on down here at once, Plunkett, I'm going to need a witness."

"There'll be no more litigation from you, Andrew Butler," Felim said, firmly. "Ireland can't stand the pace. But I'll come all right because I can't resist it. My clients will all lose their cases and my practice will go to hell. But it will be something to remember on my death-bed."

"That'll be nine beds, so," said Andrew and rang off, still muttering with fury.

Others beside the hotel proprietress and her staff were feeling the pressure of sudden and unexpected work. Telegrams of congratulation were beginning to pour in from every part of the country, addressed to Malachy, Lord Patrickstown and the Canon. In the normal way about five telegrams came to the village in a year, spaced out in a way that gave Mr. Lynch time to recover from each, for he was in dread of them. The very sound of the word would cause him to shake like a jelly. As for sending them off from his end, he required twelve full hours' notice before he would undertake it, to accustom himself to the idea; and, as a means of speedy communication, they had more or less been abandoned. Now he stood in his shirtsleeves, his collar ripped open, his eyes bloodshot, scribbling the messages down on any old paper bag within reach, for the forms were all used up, and sending those that came for the Hall down to the Canon and the other way round, in a delirium of revealed incompetence.

Many of the villagers industriously set to work on a number of little ploys. Having gained their religious point, they now turned to activities which, they reasoned, would also be appropriate. The price tickets on the goods in all the shop-windows vanished, to be replaced shortly by others of a kind more in keeping with the town's new dignity. Honora O'Toole laboured day and night confecting stocks of her celebrated coconut-ice, in the papal colours. Every man who could use a knife at all began to carve Mementoes of Patrickstown. Various idle good-for-nothings started busily rehearsing their role of Engaging Local Character. The thirty-five licensees of the town laid in heavy replenishments.

The Canon was here, there and everywhere at once. On several occasions in his brief career Seumas had chanced, in spite of himself, to write a few words of the truth, and this was one of them. A mighty load of care indeed had been lifted from those shoulders. No longer a national figure of fun, he instead was covered with glory, pure, unassailable and official. The note of warmth in the Bishop's voice as he apprised him of the decision and congratulated him on it was sign enough that a fresh page had been turned; and His Lordship's concluding remarks had filled his cup to overflowing.

"About that question of the English newspaper and the nuns, Canon," he had said. "I wonder, would you agree with me that it's best forgotten?"

"Oh, I would, my Lord," the Canon fervently responded. "We've all better things in our minds just now."

"Then fix it up, will you? unobstrusively? And if you've been put to expenses, why, we can talk it over. Old Mrs. Casey left me a sum for charitable work in the diocese. I can see no reason why you shouldn't have a bit out of that. After all, she died in your parish."

It was all most satisfactory. Yet Canon Peart had no time to savour his new happiness, for there were a thousand and one things to see to. To begin with, there was the Folly. The Bishop had promised to come and bless it in ten days' time and it was expected that the ceremony would be attended by pilgrims from far and wide. There was even a rumour that the Prime Minister himself would be present, and that of course would mean the Cabinet too, and, not to be outdone in piety, the leaders of the Opposition. Like a good general, the Canon went up to Patrickstown Hall to study the terrain and make his dispositions. He had never been to the Folly before and when he saw the marble figures he realized at once that steps would have to be taken. The idea of the Bishop and his retinue moving in solemn procession between those rows of lewd figures was not to be entertained for a moment. To begin with he determined to have them taken away, but then he found it would not be easily done in the short time that remained. They appeared to be standing lightly on the ground but in fact they were firmly attached to pedestals sunk in the earth.

He therefore went to the convent and gave the Mother

Superior his orders. The older girls were to be released from their studies and put immediately to sew garments of a kind that should blot out the statues' shame. They were to be made of coarse white calico, open down the back and tying with tapes behind, like the robes used in an operating-theatre: there were to be long Mother Hubbards for the females and brief skirts for the males; and he wanted them quickly.

Reverend Mother and her nuns went into action at once with their habitual obedience. The needlework class of seven bewildered little souls toiled away early and late, rubbing their weary eyes and cowering under the ringing slaps of their overseers. In under three days the job was completed and the Canon marched to the Folly again with the bundle under his arm.

He would entrust this duty to nobody else: it was work for a man in Holy Orders, he grimly reflected. Had he known of this wanton display, he'd have spoken to his lordship long since. A pretty sight for the eyes of innocent Christian lads, when they came poaching about the place! A terrible influence on them all right! The Canon judged of this from the powerful and unlooked for effect it had on himself. He got the skirts on the men easily enough and without the flicker of an eyelid. Clothing the girls was a more complicated operation altogether and one fraught with spiritual perils he had never foreseen. To begin with, he had to get the arms in the sleeves and, although it sounds simple enough, the Canon had never before dressed a female body, of marble or anything else. Furthermore, the smooth perfection of the maiden's contours set up a train of ideas that was greatly to be deplored. Muttering a prayer, he tried to do it with his eyes shut, only to find that his groping hands were now caressing her bosom and that the sensation was far from being unpleasant. Castigating himself mentally, he opened one eye a little way and succeeded at last in roughly forcing the sleeves on the arms. Then he darted round to the back, with a sigh of relief, to tie up the tapes. Here, he thought, it should really be safe to open his eyes again; but the first thing they fell on were two sweet little dimples, just above the haunches, one on each side. Do they really have dimples there? marvelled the captivated man, before he could stop himself; and then, in the next moment, he groaned aloud.

"Oh God, I'm a nice one!" he cried in agony, furiously tying the tapes as if his life depended on it.

By now he was shivering violently all over. Five of the nymphs still waited and he doubted he should ever be able for them. "You would!" he snarled at the Devil: "it's just like you!" Then he recollected where he was and what had happened and how once again help had been given from the source that never denied it; and walking up to the Folly he kneeled down and looked pleadingly at the door.

"Mother most Pure, Mother most Chaste, Mother Inviolate," he prayed, "honest to God, I'd not blame You at all if You never spoke to me again. You'd be entirely within Your rights, in my opinion. When I think of what You've done for us here, I could kick myself from this to Maryville, and that's the truth of it. Mother most Amiable, help me get the gowns on those girls without any more incidents. If You can't be bothered with me, and I would understand that, do it for my people, the way I won't be disgracing them now, in the happiest time of their lives. *Ave Maria, plena gratia . . .*"

Having finished his prayer he rose to his feet and, advancing on the nymphs with an air that boded little good for them should they try any more of their nonsense, he dressed them firmly one after the other, as if he had been doing it all his life. Then he took out a box of matches and a stick of wax and sealed all the knots in the tape, for he was a man who thought of everything. At last, with his mind entirely at ease, he turned back to the village.

This had been but one of the myriad administrative details that claimed his attention. He was so busy that he scarcely knew which way to look. He must see Lord Patrickstown and arrange with him for a car-park to be set up in the grounds of the Hall. Five hundred cars would there be, perhaps? and at five shillings a bonnet? Jasus, that'd be great gas all right! He would have to work out all the details of the procession and the ceremony, rehearse the Children of Mary in their part and see to it their mothers dressed them properly. The prominence to be given Malachy in the celebration was giving him food for earnest thought. He was assailed from all sides by requests for permission to set up refreshment tents and booths for the sale of local products, and each of these would have to be carefully considered and his own financial stake in the succesful ones defined. Ah, he'd pay off the old bathroom in no time at all! This thought no sooner entered his mind than he smote his forehead, amazed at his own forgetfulness. Hadn't the plumber sent in a receipted bill that very morning, with a prayer for further commands? His postbag was so full these days, and so gratifying in content, that he could hardly take it all in.

It was characteristic of our Canon that, once the Bishop had spoken, not the slightest misgiving about the miracle ever visited his head again: he simply threw himself heart and soul into the tasks of organization. It was equally characteristic of him that the weakness in himself, revealed in the encounter with the marble nymphs, led him on to think of similar weakness in others. Two terrible blots there were on the parish and both would have to be wiped out before the Folly was blessed: Bridget Mac-Carthy and Lizzie O'Rourke must be induced to leave the town before the ceremony took place. He was not yet sure how this could be achieved, but of one thing he was certain. At last he was in full control of the people again, and he would give them a burst at Mass on Sunday that would leave them in no doubt of it. Oh, and he wouldn't mince his words either! It would never surprise him if the two evil-doers didn't slink off on their own after it, without any further action by him.

On the following Sunday, then, he faced his crowded church with an expression on his face that the people knew all too well and for some time past had sorely missed. A shiver of gleeful anticipation went over them as it might over a crowd of children at the curtain-rise in a theatre of Grand Guignol. As so many strangers had come to the village he decided for all their sakes to mention no names but to confine himself to a general denunication. Those who were not in the know would put it down to a credit-able zeal, and those who were would get the flavour of it without any specifications.

Having alluded to the great mercy vouchsafed them, and paid a fulsome tribute to the Bishop, he proceeded to his argument.

"Do we really imagine, I wonder," he asked, "that we are worthy to receive the gift that has come our way? Because if we do, I can tell you all now we are living in a fool's Paradise. Why, there are things going on in Patricks-town today that would bring a blush to the cheeks of ancient Babylon. There are frantic lusts and heathenish practices that would have put those old Roman emperors in the shade entirely. Cleopatra herself would give up the

222

ghost, to see the competition she'd get here. That's all out of history, but we'd have to scour even the modern world, London and Palm Beach and that, to find the match of some of us. And I want to tell you something, my dear brethren. We can't make fools of God in the way we make fools of each other. He'll let us go on a bit and then He'll creep up on us. It wouldn't surprise me at all if He didn't settle a few accounts between this and Thursday. If one or two people I have in mind fell dead in their tracks, I'd tell you frankly I saw it coming. I'm not guaranteeing it, mind, but it's on the cards. And straight to everlasting torment they'd go, as well as missing the Bishop. I advise them to think it over. As for the rest of you, I'm doing the best I can while poor Father O'hOgain is convalescent, so don't anyone be letting me down. And just because Our Blessed Lady came among us, don't be getting above yourselves either. You're far from perfect, I don't mind telling you. Far from perfect: and that's one of me typical understatements."

With these carefully chosen words, he glowered round the church a last time and turned away to the altar.

His sermon pleased everyone except the parents of Bridget MacCarthy, who all but died of shame. Bridget was at home playing with her baby brother and Lizzie was sewing herself a new pink satin blouse, so that in one sense the Canon might have been said to be wasting his breath. But the people saw that he was his own dear self again. Little knots of them gathered outside the church afterwards to discuss his remarks one by one and point by point, and all agreed that it was an education as well as a treat to hear him. There was a roaring trade in illicit drink at the back doors of the pubs that morning, a sure sign always that the Canon had come up to scratch and

one that had not been known for many a week. Patrickstown felt at last that the days of hazardous innovation
were over and, deeply content, prepared to enter the
sweet familiar grooves of the established order.

EIGHTEEN

By wednesday all was in readiness and Patrickstown could take its ease in happy anticipation of the moment when the Bishop should place the crown of glory on its deserving head. The report that An Taoiseach was to attend the ceremony proved to have been unfounded; but one of the Directors of the Abbey Theatre was definitely coming and it was thought he would do nicely instead. A special train was to run from Dublin, and extra buses from many parts of the country. The only cause for alarm now was the weather, which was clearly preparing to break once and for all. While the air grew hotter and stiller, great clouds of an ominously vivid blue were massing themselves above the mountain peaks and forming the subject of anxious comment; although for the most part the people remained calm, in the assurance that the storm would think twice before it wetted a Bishop.

Somewhat to Bertie's private relief, Anguish decided to leave on the Wednesday afternoon. Too galling to miss the party, he said, but he had already stayed a fortnight longer in Ireland than he ought to have done; and since his employers' first telegrams of inquiry had all been delivered to the parish house by mistake, the one that finally reached him was expressed in forcible terms. Tearfully they packed his trunk together, each promising the other endless correspondence and eternal fidelity and reunions all over the globe; and Bertie forced a lovely pair of ruby cuff-links into Anguish's hand, which closed on them like a sprung trap while its owner repeated over and over that it was a shame to rob him and oh, he simply couldn't.

One of Bertie's endearing ways was to believe that his friends loved each other as much as he loved them himself. He thought that Andrew would not easily forgive him if he were not given the chance of saying good-bye to Anguish and he therefore determined to look in at the hotel on the way to the station. It was quite a little procession that drew up at the door. First came the governess-cart, containing Bertie and Anguish. Bertie had laid aside his cheerful clothing in honour of the great things afoot and was simply and neatly dressed in a suit of dove-grey shantung. On his head was a straw boater with, sole decorative touch today, a lilac foulard tied in a wide, floppy bow at the back. Anguish was arrayed from head to foot in white banin, hurriedly copied from Bertie's by the village tailor, and with his face more thickly powdered than ever looked very much like a strolling player on a beach. After the pair of them, came a pony-trap with two young women in it. Bringing up the rear was a hay-cart, bearing Anguish's luggage, immensely swollen by gifts from Bertie, and any number of brown paper parcels.

Mrs. Mangan, alert as ever, was the first to perceive that a visit was impending. She was in her front parlour, supervising the work of Andrew and Felim, who were both hard at it polishing her silver. It was above all the second vehicle that attracted her notice. The two girls in it were an oddly assorted pair and in fact they were paying no attention to each other at all. The younger of them sat with a downcast look on her sweet face, nervously playing with the clasp of her bag; remote from the company in which she found herself, withdrawn from the gaiety of the beflagged, beflowered scene, she waited, lost in the contemplation of some inward pain. The second, dressed up to the nines, gazed about her with an air of expectant vivacity and launched, with an eye on the gentlemen ahead, a bright remark from time to time, following it up with peals of theatrical laughter.

As Mrs. Mangan took them in, she gave a startled cry of "Oh Christians!" and stood with her hand pressed over her mouth, staring as if she herself were the privileged witness of a second vision.

"What is the matter now, Mrs. Mangan?" asked Andrew, looking up from the blackened tea-pot on his knee.

"What in the Name of God," Mrs. Mangan inquired, in the dire tones of one who has had as much of the miraculous as she can put up with, "is his lordship doing with Bridget MacCarthy and Lizzie O'Rourke?"

She was soon to be fully informed in the matter, as Bertie jumped lightly out of the cart and came running into the hotel.

"Good afternoon, Mrs. Mangan! Isn't that Mr. Felim Plunkett? Good afternoon. Hullo, Andy. Earning your keep? That's a good boy," he said. "Do come and say good-bye to dear Anguish. The poor fellow has to go, you know. His office got a bit shirty and so on. He's dying to see you!"

"All right," said Andrew, with reluctance. "Just let me get my apron off."

"You've passengers, my lord, I see," Mrs. Mangan said, curiosity getting the better of her manners.

"Aren't they sweet? They're going to Anguish's aunt, you know. In Tunbridge Wells. She's bed-ridden and all that. I do think it was wonderful of Reverend Mother to find them for him so quickly, and when she has so much else on her mind. And the Canon himself has written them each a stunning reference. Confess, Andy," his lordship prattled on, "he's not such a bad old boy after all. Fancy taking the trouble, I mean, at a time like this! And such kind things as he said! Could say from his own knowledge how pleasant and willing they were. Exemplary Catholic girls, you know. There's a bit of a catch in it, of course. I mean, if they do things for you they expect a return and so on. Well, fair enough. I'll tell you about it presently. Come on or we'll miss the train. . . ."

Andrew went out with him and politely wished Godspeed and a pleasant journey to Anguish.

"*Promise* to look me up in London!" cried Anguish, tenderly folding Andrew's hand in his.

"I will, of course," falsely replied Andrew, trying to recover this hand.

"Because you'll break my heart if you don't!" He shook a playful finger and the ruby links sparkled in the sun. Then he turned away with a final air, as one who closes a book, and informed Bertie they should lose the train if they didn't look sharp. The little cortege moved creakily on down the road under the bunting and the flowery arches, while Anguish fanned himself with his hat.

Mrs. Mangan in the meantime had thrown her wonted discretion to the winds and had shared with Felim the wonderful new joke. They were both savouring it when Andrew returned to his tasks.

"I've asked the poor little chap to come back here for tea," he told them, tying on his apron again. "He'll be lonely without that pet monkey of his. What are you laughing about? His hat, I suppose."

The Canon's subtle manœuvre amused him a great deal less than it did them; in fact, it brought everything English in him, submerged for so long, frothing angrily to the top.

"I suppose my sense of humour is deficient," he said, in the tone of one who supposes nothing of the kind. "I see nothing funny in playing a trick like that on a poor helpless old lady."

"Well, now, the Canon was looking to take the quiet way out of it," said Mrs. Mangan soothingly, as she wiped the tears of mirth from her eyes.

"You're as bad as Tom O'Sullivan, with your 'poor helpless old lady,' " Felim chided. "What do you know about her? A virago, very likely. And as for playing tricks —look who's talking!"

"That was different."

"Ah, to be sure. It always is."

"But it was, Plunkett. I did it in self-defence," Andrew said, recovering his good humour as he thought how clever he'd been. "And it's an old accepted principle of unarmed combat, you know, using the enemy's weakness to trip him."

"He's a Saxon after all," said Felim, gleefully. "Never short of a principle to back him up!"

"I come here," said Andrew, oracularly, "a poor sick broken man, looking for peace and quietness. I am plunged almost at once into a welter of insanity. I look about me. I observe. I note that if one says anything simple, obvious, sane and irrefutable the people are ready to tear one limb from limb. I find on the other hand that the assertion of something utterly wild and lunatic, if not indeed criminal, not only puts everything right again at once but earns one the warm respect of the community. Now wouldn't I be the great old silly, Mrs. Mangan," he said, in a beggar's cajoling whine, "if I didn't take the advantages of it?"

"I've no idea at all what you're talking about," Mrs. Mangan replied, "but it sounds good sense."

"You know very well what's he talking about. Don't be telling me!" said Felim, sternly.

"Oh, that!" said Mrs. Mangan, with a light laugh. "Sure, and wasn't he right?"

"I'm the only honest one in the place, that's perfectly clear," Felim sighed.

"I believe you are honest, as they come over here," Andrew agreed, looking at him with interest. "But what I can never make out is, where exactly do you stand?"

"Oh, on the periphery of chaos, like everyone else," Felim told him.

Mrs. Mangan now gently intimated that perhaps they were talking too much if the silver were to be finished before the end of day. As they obediently bent to their work again, she left them and went with swift intent steps to the kitchen. The everyday sweetness vanished from her face as the door shut behind her, and she took up a long rusty knife with a murderous gleam in her eye. As a final touch to her preparations, she was about to make an onslaught on the army of black beetles which for too long had regarded the place as their own. For the next hour she crept hither and thither, lunging, thrusting, slicing, and expelling her breath in an "Aaahhh!" of ecstasy over every corpse. Presently the floor was dark with mangled bodies, her face was red with triumph and her hair halfway down her back. But no matter how many she slew, fresh reinforcements were always coming up. From the dank recesses of the sink, the greasy wastes of the garbage pails, the grimy fastnesses of the range, they steadily poured, climbing over the remains of their comrades without concern, as if dedicated to a purpose too sublime for the fate of individuals to matter. At last, exhausted, she gave in and, wiping her assassin's blade on a dish-cloth, helplessly put on the kettle for tea.

"I'm afraid I shan't be very good company for you," Bertie dolefully warned the others on reappearing. Nothing depresses me like people going away. And I was just beginning to know Anguish and to appreciate him. Of course we should have had no end of trouble with him tomorrow, so it does cut both ways. But I think he is the cleverest person I ever met—except you, Andy—and with such a heart of gold."

They did their best to comfort him and turn his mind to other things.

"You mentioned a little *quid pro quo*, for getting Mr. Ferguson the maids," suggested Felim.

"Ah yes, to be sure," Bertie chuckled. He took a letter out of his pocket and studied it for a time, while his cheeks dimpled and his eyes shone with what seemed, as far as he was capable of it, to be malicious amusement. "Of course, no one has said anything to connect it with the maids," he went on, passing the communication to Felim, "and it was bound to happen sooner or later. And why not now? It's all I can do for them. And it's all they ever wanted from me."

"I can hardly believe my eyes," Felim stated, after an interval.

"Read it out," Andrew said, "and let's see if my ears are similarly undependable."

Felim took a breath and in a voice that quivered slightly from time to time began to read:

DEAR LORD PATRICKSTOWN,
 Patrickstown Demesne: Convent Lands
On this most happy occasion in the township's history, my Clients the parish trustees desire me to call

your attention to a matter which they believe you will consider with sympathy. Your Lordship will of course be aware that extensive lands now included in the Patrickstown demesne do not properly belong to it at all and in fact were filched from the Convent in the dark days gone by, and by methods it is not proposed at present to discuss. Historical proofs of this exist and may be seen at my office, if Your Lordship so desires. Up till now, as Your Lordship will agree, no steps whatever have been taken to right this wrong. The Reverend Mother has obtained the use of one small strip of unproductive land, but this she has done ostensibly by courtesy of yourself, and not as its true and rightful manageress. It is now felt, however, that the time is ripe for a new appraisal of the situation. The convent lands include the site on which the Folly is erected and in view of the recent Sublime Event it is surely arguable that they should return to those hands most suited to receive them. It is appreciated that this would affect the avenue leading from the main gates to the Hall, but my Clients hasten to assure Your Lordship they would raise no objection to your continuing use of same. Further, although in no way bound, they would be prepared to discuss a reasonable compensation for the demolition of the Folly, in place of which it is desired to build a chapel of ease. The marble figures will be either returned to you or disposed of, as you may think more suitable. We shall be glad if you will deal promptly with this application and naturally prefer at this stage not to dwell on the protracted and expensive processes that a refusal would entail."

When he had finished reading, there was a short, reverent silence.

"No, no: just as I thought," said Andrew, pulling at his ears in a concerned sort of way.

"And whose ineffable signature, do you suppose, is at the foot of it?"

"No, no, no!" bayed Andrew, throwing his head back.

"He is a naughty fellow, isn't he?" smiled his lordship. "I'm sure he thought of it the evening you were there in the wood together."

"Lord Patrickstown, can you be one of these land-grabbers?"

"Oh no, Mr. Plunkett, I'm afraid that part of it is all rather nonsense. I mean, we've had these lands over four hundred years, and the Convent was only put up in 1911. As a matter of fact, it is built on land that the Land Commission got from us, for a song. I'm curious to see their historical proofs and so on: I'm sure Mr. La Trobe's ingenuity is equal to a little job of that sort. But it doesn't make any difference. I mean, it sounds a cocky thing to say, but I'm not absolutely a fool. I've seen the writing on the wall ever since I was received."

"Bertie, you're not going to capitulate? I'll never speak to you again," shouted Andrew; but then, as his little friend's face clouded over, he hurried on, "Oh, don't mind me. But you can't, you can't! It's too utterly monstrous!"

"There's nothing for it," said his lordship, simply.

"Then I'll bring the ghost back: hang me if I don't," thundered Andrew.

"Surely, Andy, a clever chap like you doesn't believe in ghosts?" was the gentle reproof to this.

Andrew gave a hyena-like laugh and buried his face in his hands.

"What you don't realize is, that I don't mind," Bertie said. "There are no heirs to this place, not one. They'd get it at my death and they may as well have it now. They shall have the whole job and not only the piece of land. I've an income from my mother, you know. Her family was Trade, luckily, rosaries and statues, you know, staunch Protestants of course, but remarkably warm. I shall go and potter about in Kensington, as I've always dreamed of doing."

He folded his hands and leaned back in his chair with a happy little sigh.

"Now, dear Andy," he continued, on a note almost of authority, "you are not to start working yourself up all over again. I must say, if you don't mind, that the English people I know are rather given to fretting over trifles. They pretend to be very calm and sensible and so on, and the first little thing capsizes them altogether. Don't you feel yourself that it is true? Look at all the fuss you made, just because the poor old Canon tried to sue you! Anyone would have thought you were Latimer and Ridley rolled into one. And look how jolly everything is, now. You simply won't give things a chance to work themselves out."

"How true: how beautifully true, how splendidly put," said Felim, with the utmost gravity.

Andrew stared, wild-eyed, from one to the other.

"And here is Mrs. Mangan, with our tea," Bertie concluded, cheerfully. "Let us all have a cup and then I must go home and finish up the odds and ends for tomorrow. The Bishop is lunching with me, but you must both come and dine. I mean, if you'd care to. I've still got a bottle or two of champagne; and I don't think you've seen my take-off of La Dame aux Camélias yet."

NINETEEN

THE procession to the Folly and its blessing by the Bishop was agreed by all to be the most successful religious event of the year. The attendance went far beyond anything the Canon had dreamed of, and there was a good leavening of celebrities and notorieties. The press photographers were rushed off their feet: the arrangements worked with no more than reasonable hitches: the weather, although unbearably sultry, held until all was over; and throughout the proceedings, like incidental music, sounded the sweet chink of coin as trusted members of the community ran hither and thither among the pilgrims collecting for the new chapel, the altar society, St. Vincent de Paul, the African Missions and, last but not least, the Canon's own parish fund. Nor was the lay interest neglected. In one glorious day Patrickstown not only wiped out the stain on its reputation but recouped itself for the long weeks of drought.

From early in the morning the faithful came pouring into the village, in buses, motor-cars and on foot. The Sergeant of Guards took one look at the milling crowds and retired to the barracks to rest. He simply was not equipped to deal with movements on this scale and it seemed to him better to put his feet up and take it easy than to make a spectacle of himself. For a time, indeed, it seemed that confusion must prevail. Cars descending the main street three abreast met an equally solid phalanx coming up and, both sides being unwilling to give way, remained nose to nose, their owners glaring defiance through the windshields. On top of that Miss Amanda Browne had determined, by aggravating matters, to strike a blow for Protestantism. Mounted on her favourite white hunter and accompanied by the Patrickstown and Maryville hounds, she trotted to and fro, urging her steed on wherever the assembly seemed thickest. The hounds dashed here and there, now snatching a luncheon parcel, now caressing a terrified child, their pleasant deep voices vying with the canticles of the pilgrims, their tails flailing the air in an ecstasy of honest enjoyment. Only upon an urgent message from Mr. Wimbush did Amanda consent to withdraw; and she then set off at a canter down the Maryville Road to meet the serried ranks of people just debouched from the special train, scattering them as chaff in the wind and drawing the weaker brethren among them after her in the vague hope of seeing some sport.

With the collapse of the secular arm, there was nothing for it but to send for the spiritual; and soon the burly figure of the Canon was seen racing, megaphone in hand, to where the massed cars implacably waited.

"What the hell's going on, at all?" he bugled. "Back away down there, and turn up the avenue through the iron gates. Didn't I spend the whole of last evening plastering the country with notices? Can't you read, any of you? You've overshot the mark altogether."

Muttering, the drivers so addressed prepared to inch their vehicles back. One of them pulled his window down and, sticking his head through the aperture, treated the Canon to a long, meditative stare. It was Mr. Tom O'Sullivan the barrister, who had taken a sudden fancy to see his reverend client in the flesh and against his natural setting.

"Go on there, get moving. We haven't all day. You'll find the car park in the grounds. Tickets, five shillings. Don't be arguing the price of it, either. You, there!" he said violently to Mr. O'Sullivan, "what are you staring at? Don't you understand English?"

"I'm very pleased to make your acquaintance, Canon," said the barrister, amiably. "My name's O'Sullivan and I was pleading for you in that action of yours, you know."

"There never was one," said the Canon with finality. "So how could you plead in it? Don't be talking. And get that yoke out of it, will you? Before you mess us up altogether."

Mr. O'Sullivan obediently put his engine in reverse, and began creeping backwards down the slope to the gates of Patrickstown Hall. " 'My client is the best type of Irish Catholic priest, humble, zealous and charitable,' " he murmured dreamily. What a good thing it was, he reflected, that he so seldom knew anything about the cases he undertook.

Having tamed the motor-cars, the Canon turned his mind to the people on foot. "Come along! come along! Sure, you'll be sitting down in a minute. Be saying your prayers but keep moving," he vociferated. "And by the way: if any one of you should see Our Blessed Lady, let's have no panic. It's quite on the cards you will, so keep cool." Here he made a sudden dash into the crowd and, like a sheep-dog, hustled a scantily dressed young woman out to the side of the road. "I'm ashamed of you, woman! This isn't a Palais de Danse," he told her. "Find something to wear, or be off." The young woman broke into tears. The Canon's restless eye now fell on a young man with a cine-camera slung over his arm and he darted away in pursuit. "You haven't a permit for that thing there," he snapped. "I gave out all the permits myself. I'll have no unauthorised snoopers today. Up to the parish hall and give the fee to the Committee like a gentleman, or leave the camera outside. Hurry along!" he continued through the megaphone, "get in your places, we're going to start. Now remember what I'm after telling you. We're honouring Our Blessed Lady today, because she came to this parish. So if She comes again, and it would never surprise me, don't lose your heads. Just say a prayer and keep quiet. You'll all be better Christians for this day's work. There's millions would give their eyes to be here. You'll never see anything like it again, I can safely say that. Now then, up the avenue and away over the left to the Folly. I've written out markers, plain as daylight, you can't miss the way. Quick sharp, now. Sing if you like, but keep going."

At this moment a little boy ran up to say the Bishop had come and was robing in the vestry; also that the procession was due to move off in another ten minutes, two of the Children of Mary had been sick with excitement and the rest were showing signs of strain. Another messenger arrived on the heels of the first to complain of Cat's-Eye O'Keefe, who had sold no fewer than thirty-six authentic buttons from the jacket of Malachy Lynch at a charge of five shillings apiece. The Canon stared distractedly round and thrust the megaphone into the hand of the person nearest him.

"Make yourself useful, you," he was beginning, and saw too late that it was Andrew Butler. "Hadn't you the decency to stay away, then?" he demanded in a furious undertone.

"Isn't that rather ungrateful, Canon?" Andrew smiled at him. Raising the megaphone to his lips he bawled, "Please keep moving! We want you all in your places, so the procession can begin. Don't slacken now, ladies and gentlemen. There is a first-aid tent in the grounds, if any should be overcome. How was that?" he asked of the lowering priest at his side. "Wouldn't you say I was born to it?"

"God alone knows what you were born to," snorted the other.

"Onwards, onwards, pilgrims! There's a Bishop close behind you!" boomed Andrew.

"Let's have no sneering anyway," the Canon told him sternly. "And none of your monkey tricks, mind. I'll give you a chance to help us today, out of charity. So behave yourself, if you can." He dealt him a last threatening glance and hurried away to his other duties.

Megaphone in hand, Andrew climbed a grassy bank by the roadside and gave his attention to the crowd before him. There were bookies with purple cheeks and bushy brows, pale, spotty seminarists, pretty girls in high-heeled shoes and feathery hats, stout Catholic mothers of enormous families, country boys with big cheek-bones and shaggy mops of hair, enthusiasts with tight lips and bitter eyes, fat genial businessmen suffering from the heat, friars in coarse habits and sandals: all Ireland seemed to be streaming past with the dull vacant look of the shepherded on their faces. The stillness of the atmosphere, the peculiar leaden colouring cast over the scene by the thundery sky, somehow heightened the effect of unreality: once again Andrew had the sense of moving in a dream. He drew out the flask provided by Mrs. Mangan and took a pull at the whisky.

"Ladies and gentlemen, please make haste! The Bishop

is ready to leave in procession! We mustn't hold him up! Pass along as quickly as you can!"

Am I really doing this? he wondered. He wished that Felim would come along, that he might anchor himself to his cheerful sanity: the farce at which he was assisting was too enormous to be supported alone. A shrill outburst from the upper end of the village now intimated that the Children of Mary had launched into their opening hymn and soon the first little white-clad figures could be seen wending their way down the flower-bedecked street. Behind them came the acolytes bearing the cross and banners from the church: after that, in quiet dignity, paced the Canon, followed by the Bishop with mitre and crook, and the villagers of Patrickstown proudly bringing up the rear. Andrew took another hasty swallow from the flask.

"Hurry, please! Not a moment to lose! Do come along, I beg."

The people obediently stumbled forward, like beasts at the touch of a goad. Andrew watched the last of them pushing their way through the iron gates, the megaphone slackly in his hand, the whisky coursing through his bloodstream and inducing an agreeable sense of dissociation from the whole fantastic affair. Squeaking like mice, the little girls drew level with him, the sweet faces under the white veils bent to the ground, the tiny gloved hands pressed prayerfully together. The boys manfully held their banners aloft, their eyes raised heavenwards with a touching air of childish piety. The Canon strode past, now calm and official, a look of serene assurance on his great face, his rich baritone mingling from time to time with the piping trebles. The Bishop, his mitred head trembling slightly on his shoulders, was the pattern of fatherly wisdom and benevolence as he followed the Canon. Then, at a respectful distance, came Bertie in all the splendour of full morning dress, warbling away like a gay little sparrow: and after him Malachy, the smugness of whose countenance went beyond the power of words to describe, with his mother, Mr. Lynch and other notables of the village.

Not one of them so much as looked at Andrew, until recently the very hub of the village life. He felt as if he were at the closing scene of some bizarre musical comedy, where all the principal characters assemble on the stage for a final chorus. The brothers La Trobe went by, an outstanding trinity, their beautiful eyes rapt, their voices ringing out as sweet as a bell. Mrs. Mangan tripped along, in her best black and her pearls. Cat's-Eye O'Keefe, his pockets bulging with fraudulent spoils, almost rivalled the Bishop in the gravity and importance of his demeanour. With relief Andrew now caught sight of Felim's handsome features among the sea of mesmerised faces. Eagerly drawing himself up, he tried to attract his attention and exchange a glance of mutual comfort, a knowing wink as between two sound men in a host of lunatics. But Felim was singing away with the best of them. Andrew scrambled down the bank and stood, with a sudden awful premonition, where his friend, his guide, his life-line must pass within a foot or two. Slowly he drew nearer and nearer, until Andrew heard his voice easily riding above the rest.

"Oh Vir-hir-gin Ma-hary,
Wha-hat shall I do?"

sang Felim devoutly, and turned full upon Andrew a look in which there was not the faintest sign of recognition.

Andrew slowly climbed the bank again and sat down, resting his head against the stone wall. What he had just seen had bereft him of all power to think. The phrase that Felim had used about standing on the periphery of chaos flashed into his mind: he himself felt that he was safely embedded in its very core. He had been looking forward with intense pleasure to the moment when, having done chuckling with Felim over the events of the day, he should reveal to him the full richness and scope of the jest. Now he saw that the joke was far more complex and ramified than he had supposed, and that it was on him. Dully he stared after Felim's departing head, mechanically reached once more for the flask. Above the mountain the first deep mutter of the approaching storm was heard and it seemed to him the sky itself was giving way to huge, involuntary mirth. The very landscape wore to his anxious eye a mocking aspect, while the stream appeared to be laughing itself silly. Did you really think anything was to be depended on here? he thought it gurgled, as it hurried on its way to join the river. Andrew applied himself steadily and with growing insistence to the liquor, thankful for the sense of removal it brought him. Gradually the sound of chanting died away: above in his meadow MacCarthy's donkey replaced it with a furious burst of his own: from beyond the peak came another grumble of amusement. For half an hour or so he loitered in the grass, the events of the past weeks drifting confused in his memory, until the last drop of whisky had gone and he knew that he was drunk. Then he rose unsteadily to his feet and wagged an indignant finger at the moutain, glowering purple above the little village.

"I understand why Ireland lives by the bottle," he cried, loudly and passionately, and reeling a little, made for Mrs. Mangan's Hotel.

The storm that broke at a decent interval after the conclusion of the ceremonies was the most pleasurable incident in the Canon's crowded and pleasurable day. He took

it for a sign that Heaven itself was guaranteeing the return
to normality of the village and all that was in it. Hour
after hour the rain beat down upon the parched earth,
until the street and the paths and boreens were transformed into rivers of mud. As the afternoon wore on the
pace slackened and it turned instead to a gentle drizzle,
veiling the mountain from sight and imparting a melancholy air to the whole countryside. The land was weeping
once again: there were to be no more blue skies or strong
clear light, no warmth, gaiety, sunshine to lead to the dis-
turbance of order.

The Canon sat drinking in his study and passing affairs
in review, in a glow of contentment. Oh! his troubles were
over and he'd bested the lot of them! The pile of letters
on the table before him testified to his majesty and importance in the eyes of the country, and the money! it had
come pouring in all day, better than Niagara Falls. Idly
he picked up one of the letters, noted the English stamp
and opened it. It came from Packet Newspapers Ltd. and
had apparently crossed in the post with certain communications of his own:

DEAR SIR,—We have now had an opportunity of considering the letter written by Mr. James Patrick La Trobe,
your Solicitor, in respect of statements made in an article
written by Dr. Andrew Butler and published by us. Our
lawyers are replying to Mr. La Trobe today but we wish
meanwhile to write to you personally, offering our most
humble apology for the matters complained of and express-
ing our great concern that a man of your position and
standing should have been exposed to so unjustifiable
an attack. We agree that the article in question was wholly
without foundation and, while we published it in good
faith, trusting in the integrity of our correspondent, we

cannot but feel ourselves to have been at fault in doing so. We unreservedly withdraw the damaging and offensive allegations made therein, sincerely regret their publication in our newspaper and are pleased to accept the terms laid down by your solicitor for a settlement.

Yours faithfully,

For and on behalf of Packet Newspapers Ltd.,

PULVERMACHER.

The Canon gave a short bark of mirth.

"Bloody fools!" he grunted.

Next he opened a long envelope, of excellent quality paper and sealed with green wax which bore the impression of an imposing family crest. A look of surprise, following by one of indignation warming slowly to rage, came over his face as he read the contents, written in a fine Italian hand:

MR. JAMES PATRICK LA TROBE, SOLICITOR

In Account with the Very Reverend Ignatius Peart, P.P.

All-morning attendance on yourself to discuss measures to be taken in respect of article in *Daily Packet* newspaper.

Necessary correspondence arising out of this.

Attendance in High Court, Dublin, on four occasions.

Research, planning, and meditation on how best to bring action to successful outcome, including several sleepless nights.

Attendance on thirty-two witnesses who should appear on your behalf.

Reimbursement for gratifications necessarily offered to above.

Purchase of legal volumes needed to satisfy myself on certain points of law in connection with your case.

Petrol and other inevitable expenses, arising out of the need for mobility.

Medical attendance necessary, owing to condition brought about by worry and overwork in respect of your case.

Expenses of holiday for convalescence, prescribed in above . . . . 300 Guineas.

Canon Peart tore this document into very small pieces. It was Patsy La Trobe all over to rear his evil head on this happiest of days, like a serpent in a bank of flowers. Schemes for the suppression of the plague-spot flitted through the Canon's head, each more fanciful than the last and all, as he was secretly aware, foredoomed to failure. But the wretch could whistle for these monstrous fees of his. Let him sue! The Canon's face relaxed once more at the mere idea of it: at the thought that henceforward anyone, anywhere, should ever offer him a challenge of any kind whatever.

His good humour returning, he got up and walked over to the window: fondly his eyes rested on the grey saturated garden, the dripping trees, the rain coursing down the panes of glass, the pools collecting on the lawn, the flowers beaten flat to the earth, the dark, sullen sky promising unlimited dampness in the weeks ahead.

"A lovely soft evening, thank God," said the Canon aloud; and slowly, thankfully, reverently, he drew down the blinds.

ABOUT THE AUTHOR

HONOR TRACY first began to write after the war, when she was living in Dublin. There she was associated with an Irish literary review edited by Seán O'Faoláin. She also contributed short stories and articles to English and American periodicals. She has had three books published in England—non-fiction on Japan and on Ireland, and a short novel, *The Deserters.*

She wrote *The Straight and Narrow Path* in Italy in the fall of 1954, while recovering from a long illness. Recently she has been at work on a book about Spain, where she spent the summer of 1955.